Clare Curzon has several identities. She began her literary career in 1962 writing crime fiction under the pseudonym Rhona Petrie. Then in 1972, after her first ten novels were published, she wrote *Greenshards*, a paranormal psychology novel, and for this and four historical novels steeped in witchcraft she became Marie Buchanan. Finally, having gone straight' for eight years, she returned to her life of crime, this time as Clare Curzon. Most of her mysteries under this name have featured the highly successful Superintendent Mike Yeadings and his Thames Valley team.

Clare Curzon was born in St Leonards-on-Sea, Sussex, worked extensively in Europe before her marriage, and now lives in Amersham, Buckinghamshire.

GUILTY KNOWLEDGE

CLARE CURZON

A *Virago* Book

First published in Great Britain by Virago in 1999

Copyright © Clare Curzon 1999

The moral right of the author has been asserted.

A CIP catalogue record for this book
is available from the British Library.

ISBN 1 86049 686 5

Printed and bound in Great Britain by
Creative Print and Design (Wales), Ebbw Vale

Virago
A Division of
Little, Brown and Company (UK)
Brettenham House
Lancaster Place
London WC2E 7EN

This one is for Mrs Sue Healey,
Curator of the Thames Valley Police Museum at
Sulhamstead, with my warm thanks for her generous
assistance and for a delightful time spent in the
archives.

One

We had planned a quiet evening, a small family gathering for dinner after a day of lazing in punts with lunch al fresco in the shade of old willows. The swooning heat which had sent us down to the river hung on barely relieved and, trudging back through whipping meadow grass, with even the children lagging, we faced a wild light reflected in Stakerleys' many windows. But by the time we reached the house the sun had ceased to blaze, hidden behind low bars of black cloud. Only an angry yellow showed through cracks in their edges.

It was the last day of August and, although we did not know it then, the end of the heatwave. Yet our unease at a building storm was nothing to the fears I would shortly face.

Once indoors I ensured there was ample hot water for all, and that two menservants were available for carrying up the heavy cans before I took my own bath by our bedroom's open window, with Patsy pouring a delicious stream over my heat-prickling shoulders. Luxuriating too long, I was the last to join the gathering in the drawing-room.

The other ladies were clustered about the octagonal table where Geoffrey was exhibiting his butterflies; Mama tiny but stately in her hobble-skirted plum taffeta, Isabelle in rose, Mildred, my elder sister-in-law, in a limp confection of beige lace. I wore the kingfisher-blue silk Mama had brought me two days before, cut severely as she says becomes my style, but tremendously *à la mode*. As ever, her first act after lunch on arrival had been to examine my wardrobe and discard any garment whose drapes hung contrary to the latest fashion's dictates, or that failed to make a significant statement about bosom or *derrière*.

And as ever, I allowed the pillage, confident that she would make good use of the booty she finally bore away. Fine costumes are not of enormous importance in my life, but colours are, and I was secretly delighted with her gift. Because there is no jewel existing to complement that vibrant shade, I had put on the fine ivory necklace and carved earrings which Laurence brought back for me from China the summer we became engaged.

The little group broke up as Nanny, flushed and rather breathless, brought in the children to say goodnight. I guessed that the long day spent outdoors, together with the oppressive heat, had made them fractious. Lucy's pretty face had a sulky droop and she moved more awkwardly than was usual. I was thankful that her long flounced nightdress hid the ugly iron on her leg. Edwin's mouth was bravely puckered and he still blinked back unshed tears. Despite Nanny's presence the minx had been taunting her little brother again.

While they made their rounds, offering their hands to be shaken but getting the hugs and smothering kisses which privately they hate – especially from gentlemen with prickly moustaches – I went through to order the oil lamps extinguished in the dining-room and the tapered candles lit in their silver branches.

The softly gleaming table was faultless, place settings

2

precise with folded napkins stiffly erect on crisp, snowy linen, a scented crimson rose afloat in each crystal finger-bowl. The cutlery shone. There were glasses for claret and champagne. The gentlemen's port tray stood ready on a small side table. A single oil lamp shone over the credenza from which Laurence had banished all candles, laughingly protesting that they threatened to singe his eyebrows as he carved.

The heat was suddenly unbearable. I ordered the sashes on the curtains to be tightened and the long windows thrown open to the troubled sky. Then, as I stood in the doorway for a final admiring look, the first flash sliced the room with a hectic violet-white light. Thunder crashed almost straight upon it, making the net inner curtains billow towards me on a rush of torrid air. Candle flames streaked sideways, some went out, and the little Welsh maid gave a stifled scream. For a moment the room itself seemed to be lurching with the light, and I flung out a hand for support against the door jamb. My heart thudded so strongly in my throat that it seemed to be surging out. In that instant I knew it was more than an ordinary storm: an evil omen. That last safe moment was one that would be struck static in my mind for the remainder of my life.

I rejoined the others until old Hadrill called us in for dinner. We were all a little on edge after that first overhead crash, our voices unnaturally loud as the storm continued to roll about the hills for some ten minutes before the rain came lashing down in gusts that rattled the shutters on their iron hasps. Geoffrey, sniffing the air like some inquisitive rodent, said, 'Thank heaven for that. Now it should be cooler.'

In the dining-room Hadrill abandoned his wine bottles to help the footman close the windows. Laurence looked round at our faces and smiled. 'Let's leave the curtains open, shall we? To watch the distant lightning. It's really rather fine over the Chilterns.'

I was uneasy. It's all very well for the gentlemen to seem brave, but lightning is electricity, and I know that's dangerous. I sensed in it an almost personal threat to us.

Laurence, at the table's head, sat facing the outdoor world. The lightning continued behind my back, but I caught each flash in the huge gilt mirror on the opposite wall. Shouldn't it be covered with a cloth? I was sure I'd read somewhere that lightning could strike you dead through the glass.

'The children,' I mumbled and started to rise, but Laurence signalled disapproval with his eyebrows. 'Leave it, darling. Nanny will manage them quite well alone. Let's not suggest that they should be nervous.'

Gentle, but a rebuke nonetheless. I wasn't normally a coward and we both knew that. Yet tonight . . .

'Didn't think you were that jumpy, Eugenie,' Geoffrey needlessly commented. 'Storms don't scare Isabelle,' he boasted.

'D'you mind that positive tempest up in the Trossachs, m'dear? Caught us out in the wilds with no shelter but a lean-to cattle shed and a stone wall. Belle never said a word. Whipped out some playing cards from her reticule and kept us amused until help arrived hours later in the shape of a farm cart with a tarpaulin hood.'

Too scared to dare admit it, I guessed. My sister-in-law could brazen out situations when it suited her, but faced by physical threat she was as soft-centred as her pretty exterior implied. I watched her now, flushed and talking too rapidly, twisting in her seat and tapping her wine glass to bring Hadrill across for a refill.

I marvelled that once I'd been so in awe of her, so dazzled by the soft blond wisps escaping from her sweetly piled

4

curls, by her tiny hands and enormous blue eyes. Certainly too by the fact that her father was a viscount, her grand-father an earl. The Honourable Isabelle Delmayne, as she was then, and a fashionable bride of eleven months.

I'd been sufficiently instructed to know that hers wasn't the noblest of titles, but to my innocent ears then 'Hon-ourable' had an almost holy ring. I had fallen over myself in my haste to take it literally.

It was a relief that the days of her dominance over me were past and that my little family could no longer be endangered by her wilful passions. Even as I told myself this I caught my mother's slaty eyes upon me and knew she followed my thoughts. And it was at this moment that Hadrill took a message from the doorway and came swiftly across to whisper in my husband's ear.

Laurence frowned, bemused, not anxious. 'What can he want?'

It seemed that the butler was not in our uninvited visitor's confidence over this: Hadrill, normally so rigid in his observance of propriety.

'Well, if you will all excuse me I'd best find out.' And Laurence rose, screwing his napkin into a ball. He turned whimsically to his father, seated half-way down the table where he could be supported on either side. 'We can't after all keep the constabulary waiting, sir.' And chuckling at the impression this last made upon us all, my husband strode out.

Lord Sedgwick grunted, trying to voice his disquiet. Since his second stroke two months previously, his speech was badly affected, as were his right arm and leg, which was why he now sat where his elder daughter could assist his eating. He banged on the table with his good hand and mumbled.

I understood in the main what he strove to say. 'Struck,'

I made out, and then 'village'. Clearly he was distressed that that first flash of lightning could have damaged some tenant's home.

I jumped up and moved to the window. 'Geoffrey, see if there's any sign of a fire from the back, will you?' For myself, peering out, I could barely penetrate the sheeting rain to catch far-off flashes over the Chilterns. Dr Millson rose and came across to me, 'Eugenie, I may be needed.'

'Wait until Laurence comes back,' I decided. There was no knowing what disaster had brought the local constable cycling out here on such a night. Surely if someone's life was in danger he would have asked for the doctor at once.

Geoffrey returned with the comforting news that there was only the usual amount of light showing in the village's direction. He had dispatched a chambermaid to look out of all the third-floor windows in case some outlying farm had caught fire.

So we returned to the table and while we waited for Laurence to enlighten us we peeled peaches and ate our first early figs from the orangery.

'Nothing of real concern to us,' Laurence announced airily, loping in with his amiable, long-chinned smile. He signalled to Hadrill who joined him behind my chair and together they loosed the curtain sashes and let the heavy velvet drop over the windows. Before returning to his place he laid a hand gently on my right shoulder, then drew the back of his forefinger softly up my cheek in a familiar caress.

'Apparently there's an oak struck down in Gasson's Hollow, but it should burn itself out without anyone's interference.'

'Is that what the constable came to tell you?' It seemed hardly important enough.

6

Laurence threw up his coat tails and reseated himself, selected a fig and neatly quartered its wider end in the Egyptian fashion. Up the length of the table I watched the purple flesh fall back over his long fingers as if in a dream. Already nothing was quite real to me then.

'There was another matter,' my husband said, 'regarding some missing traveller.'

He chose to explain further. 'Apparently a foreigner has been staying at the White Hart. He went out walking yesterday and failed to return, leaving his luggage and money at the inn intact. There's been a search party out for him until the storm rained them off. I've arranged for them to take a look through our outbuildings.'

'Hardly pleasant weather for a prolonged country stroll,' said Geoffrey urbanely, 'but not, one would think, any matter for great concern. The man's probably called in on friends and stayed overnight.'

'It seems not,' Laurence disagreed. 'As I said, he's a foreigner and speaks almost no English. But he did manage to explain that he was hoping to trace a kinsman who once lived in this neighbourhood.'

'What kind of foreigner?' Isabelle demanded slowly, her voice husky and the words a trifle slurred.

'Mediterranean. Spanish or Italian, the landlord thought. He registered under the name of Martello.'

'Like the old coastal towers we built against Napoleon,' Geoffrey bleated, beaming at his own cleverness.

But my blood ran suddenly chill. In Italian, as I well knew, 'martello' meant 'hammer'. And with certain villages up in the Trentino heights a hammer was the symbol for revenge.

But it wasn't to northern Italy that my mind was suddenly transported then. Instead memory swung me back further to one fateful morning just before Easter eight years back, before ever I had left these shores. My very last morning at school: perhaps for me the end of innocence. Certainly it had been the occasion of receiving much unsolicited advice. Which I was shortly to follow in a way the well-wishers had never intended.

ii

Miss Constance, dear little fusspot bundle, was standing there with clasped hands and bright, brimming eyes, saying, 'Oh my dear, I do wish you every happiness, every success. Never forget what you have learned here, what you have already achieved. You are gifted for drama. Do have the courage to continue, to use fully your potential.'

What had she really meant, as I took my leave of her? Something special, I'd thought. Since then I have come to believe that, besotted with literature and the spoken word, she had been half in love with the youth Cesario I'd played as Viola in her production of *Twelfth Night*. She was so much the romantic, restrained under the schoolmistressy discipline of her older sister (secretly dubbed the Abbess: keys officiously clanking in a beaded chatelaine hanging from her waist like a nun's rosary).

Overall it had been a memorable day, with the humping of luggage into the conveyance sent by Skinners, then the arrival home by horse carriage – by the back way, of necessity – to encounter Papa leaning on the water butt, banished with his baccy from the house, and to be folded in his comfortable arms. His brown eyes teased me as the van man bore in my tin trunk.

'How does it feel to be really grown up?'

I'd laughed. 'Lightheaded. Light everything. Floating between two spinning worlds.'

With a smile that wrinkled the fine skin beside his eyes, his gaze shifted. He puffed and watched the aromatic smoke curl upwards. 'Well, before your feet touch ground again, take care that your shoes are perfectly clean.'

I saucily lifted my hems to show off my ankle boots, polished bright as fresh wet blackberries.

'Splendid.' Then, a little apprehensive under the banter, 'Have you no regrets for the life you've left behind?'

'None whatsoever, provided I can still keep my friends.'

Nodding, he advised me sombrely – a *non sequitur*, I'd thought then – 'You must live every moment of every day with your whole heart now, because no opportunity ever comes twice. Will you promise me that?'

How gloomy, I'd thought, easily promising what he'd asked. But then Papa was privately a disappointed man, although I hadn't thoroughly understood it at the time because he managed to draw sustenance from his few remaining freedoms.

'And now?' he challenged.

'Now I shall go and present myself to Mother.'

Liberated and rashly confident, I dared to go round to the front door, rang the bell like a client, and let myself into the hall. The opulence of its waxed mahogany and twin potted palms rewarded my assumed sophistication. I imagined for a moment that I belonged.

Ahead of me and half-way up the semicircular stairway a lady trailing a magnificent bustle gasped as a minia-ture dog escaped from under one arm and fled down towards me.

As it went to race by I scooped it up, warm and silky and eager, its tiny ham-pink tongue flicking wetly on my cheek. I looped up my skirts and ran up to return the little treasure.

And so I had my first sight of the woman whose life

was so inescapably, so fatally, to be bound up with my own.

She was the most beautiful person I had ever seen.

Complexion, features, colouring, figure, were perfection. Her hair, above a sweetly dimpled face, was a floss of spun gold, pinned up under a show-garden of a hat with a gauzy veil in pastel sweet-pea shades. She smelt of pink roses.

From the gallery Mother stared icily down. At once I saw my country-bumpkin gawkiness through her eyes, and was utterly confused. What folly, what presumption, to imagine that being no longer subject to a school code of conduct permitted me such familiarity.

And with no ordinary lady, as I was later to learn; but a distinguished one. An Honourable, no less. Social rank had been a subject touched on by the Misses Court-Withington, but not encountered in the flesh.

Mother's eyes had gone hard and black like currants; as they do when she is extremely vexed. The iris is palest grey, but this seems to disappear as the pupils enlarge with emotion. I knew even then the physiological explanation, but it did nothing to still my alarm.

Little more than five feet two inches in height, fine-boned, straight-backed as a Jacobean chair, she has an indomitable nature. Even her most distinguished clients seemed wary of her, despite the way she made a show of conceding place to them. It is probably the reason for her success, so that for the most part they feel honoured by her accepting them, rather than the reverse. And then she is certainly skilled, with an eye for fabric textures, line and colour: no common provincial dressmaker, but a creative tailoress with a strong sense of fashion. Which gives her a certain importance. In these days of changing values, social success can sometimes hang on the cut of one's jib.

I was as near the head of the staircase as the foot, but there was no choice for me then. I stumbled over my excuses and prepared to flee by the way I had come. But Mother forestalled me, soft and sweet as sugar-dredged marshmallow (but iron inside) commanding that I should take the dear little doggy down for a bowl of water. Meaning that I should remove the wretch before it could foul her good carpets.

The lady cooed her gratitude, waved pink-tipped fingers at me and continued up towards her fitting. It was the senior seamstress who came down afterwards to recover her pet.

The second time, some weeks later, the lady came unaccompanied. She specifically asked for me to attend her while the fitter adjusted the hem of her new tea gown. So, against Mother's previously expressed intent, I was allowed to penetrate her worldly palace of satins and chiffons and furs, with a plump velvet pincushion strapped to the back of my wrist.

Following in Mother's career was one of many things that were to be denied me. I had begun to wonder how I was meant to spend my life now that studies were assumed to be over. The hours were longer now that I spent so many alone, and I soon found it hard to pour all my heart into shopping for gloves or taking afternoon tea with older ladies approved by Mother. Reading – my favourite occupation – was socially frowned on as unhealthily exclusive.

Many of my school friends were 'finishing' abroad or travelling with their families for the summer months. I'd found few enough to make up a party for tennis or to go riding and I'd been obliged to decline invitations to two coming-of-age dances, having no one to chaperon me, Mother being exhausted at the rush of work they had occasioned and not trusting any other lady to take over the duty.

Nor was I allowed to enter Papa's workshop any more for fear of contact with his 'coarse young men'; even though Papa, as master printer, was most particular in the choice of apprentices, all from decent addresses and respectable backgrounds. Chapel people, every one.

Mother was Church, but we never attended. Her reason was that if we were seen to favour one place of worship above another it could offend important clients of the other persuasion. It amazes and amuses me now to recall how empty and narrow were the rules we lived by in St Leonards-on-Sea at the turn of the century.

'You have been raised as a gentlewoman,' Mother said coldly when I queried my new non-life as the empty weeks went by. 'There is no call for you to have an occupation.' And she swept from the room.

I supposed then that I must sit with my hands in my lap until some gentleman materialized and chose to propose marriage. I said as much to Papa once.

'Would that be so terrible, Eugenie?' he asked wistfully. 'What is it you most want of life?'

'Everything!' Meaning eternal sunshine; the sky's blueness; a sense of reaching forward, upward, aware of this new tingling tautness in my breasts. To *use* myself.

'Life itself, that is what I want. To control my own being.'

'Freedom. Ah, that old illusion.'

It had been then that Edith called urgently down the back staircase for me to bring fresh pins and join Madam at once in the salon.

'And she says to be certain sure you're tidy!'

I ran to the mirror, piled my dark hair in a 'cobra' coil above my ears and pinched my cheeks to bring colour to them. My sailor dress was fresh on that morning so should pass muster. This summons was so unusual as to be significant. There was surely only one client who would specifically have asked for me.

Only a fortnight after her last appearance the beautiful lady was making a third, unannounced, visit. It was to order an entire wardrobe. In unrelieved black.

At barely twenty years of age, the Honourable Isabelle Delmayne was suddenly and tragically a widow.

Two

i

It was some chance remark of Geoffrey's that returned me to the present. I smiled at him and nodded, having quite missed the sense of what he'd said. Fortunately it was time for us ladies to withdraw, so no one appeared to notice my abstraction as we rose and Laurence slipped into the vacated place beside his father. 'We shall be with you directly,' he promised.

The storm continued, circling twice before finally clearing eastwards, and we stayed together in the drawing-room, deserting the piano to play bezique and whist until it grew quiet and we felt sure our rest would be uninterrupted. The searchers had left after half an hour, having found no trace of the missing foreigner in our barns or stables.

My father-in-law had sunk into one of his trance-like states and Laurence had two footmen carry him upstairs in his chair. For myself I was too restless to welcome bed.

Part of my mind was out in the rain-drenched night where the relentless downpour would surely have raised the level of the river. I could see the rushing brown torrent tearing at muddy banks, carrying off all manner of debris to lodge at the base of the little red Japanese bridge. How would it withstand the rising flood? Surely it would be torn from its wooden piers and end as matchwood. When the men went down to repair it, they would clear the wreckage, and then perhaps . . .

The others had dispersed. Laurence stood by the open door, waiting. 'Eugenie, it's gone two o'clock. If your mama still intends to leave at nine, you'll need to be up early.'

He came over, stood behind and wrapped his arms around me. Never, I thought, had I needed so much the comfort only he could give. Yet I pushed him away. What made me do that? Nerves still aquiver from the electrical storm? Or resurgent guilt?

I felt him watching me, not rebuffed but thoughtful. Clever Laurence, don't understand too much. You must never guess the empty dread that possesses me, at the discovery that time past is not done away with but can come back to haunt.

He simply took my hand and led me from the room. 'You're tired. I'll not trouble you tonight,' he promised softly as we mounted the stairs together.

But when I was dressed for bed, sitting there with my hair loose and the silver-backed brush heavy in my hand, I felt the onrush of such passion that I cried out, 'No! Trouble me! Trouble me so that it wipes out all my other troubles ever!' And I ran to fling myself on him.

He whispered that I would crush my breasts against the handkerchief bundled in the pocket of his night-shirt. So obligingly removed the whole garment, and then my own.

We made love with such fervour that I fell asleep straight after. To dream that I had strangled him, pushing his lifeless body down into the surging river. His open eyes

15

stared blindly up at me as the brown flood-water closed over. And all sight of him was lost to me for ever under the churning of torn branches and tumbling rocks.

I turned to run and a dark figure rose up before me. Its hood fell back to reveal Isabelle's accusing face. Slowly she raised an arm and pointed at me. She wore black from head to toe, the widow Isabelle, as we'd dressed her those many years before.

I felt the bank crumble under me as I fell backwards, backwards, into the flood.

ii

Captain Hugo Delmayne's heroic death had been emblazoned in all the London papers. The *Hastings and St Leonards Observer* also carried a portrait with an obituary for him, because although he was from a Dorset family, his wife had made several recent visits to stay with friends in our town. Locally we cultivated celebrities, to bask in their reflected glory.

He had been a tall, handsome man, perhaps some seven or eight years older than Isabelle, and swarthy as she was fair. In the *Morning Post* there was also an imaginative artist's impression of his being welcomed by Lord Roberts when he took up his commission with the South African Expeditionary Force.

Until then we had not guessed from Isabelle's demeanour how concerned she must be for her husband fighting against the cruel Boers. Our reverses had been disastrous and it seemed ironic that now when news from the scattered fronts was occasionally more cheering, such a fine soldier should be lost.

Later Isabelle was to tell me he was 'a darling man'

but that the alliance had not pleased her family. In fact she had eloped with him and been brought back by her papa for a more seemly public wedding. On meeting her father and grandfather I sensed a coolness still towards her which, perversely she didn't intend her lonely state of mourning to dispel entirely.

After that first visit to Mother's salon Isabelle had never again brought the little silky dog. If I ever considered the reason for this, I suppose I imagined it was out of deference to my mother's distaste for allowing animals indoors. Papa's gun dog, the black retriever Rory, which accompanied him on his weekly shoots with friends at Brede, was otherwise confined to the back yard and the printing workshop. Mother regarded Isabelle's toy dog in the same light, although I doubt it ever knew mud on its dainty paws.

Ignorant of high society, I hadn't by then discovered the Honourable lady's habit of sudden passionate attachments to pets and her equally intemperate abandonment of them. Nor that I was soon to fall within the category of these hapless creatures myself.

She cultivated me with a pretence of relying on my practicality, while always carefully deferring to my mother's judgement in matters of *chic*. There were occasions when her taste for adornment had to be restrained, and she allowed herself to be guided into plainer styles more suited to a period of deep mourning.

Mother was adamant in requiring this, particularly because there was already great pressure on her workroom due to existing local orders for autumn wardrobes; and extra refinements meant longer hours for her women at sewing-machines and hand finishing.

She was too self-confident to question why a society lady should patronize a St Leonards tailoress, rather than approach some famous London house of fashion. I wondered if there might arise some difficulty with payment. Conversations overheard between the two Misses Court-Withington had warned me that good family and good fortune did not always come together. The fees for two unnamed pupils' tuition had been left unpaid for several years.

But I was glad I hadn't voiced my doubts when the Delmayne account was promptly settled by her father the Viscount through his city bank.

His second Viscountess had been killed by a fall on the hunting field when Isabelle was only nine and her brother sixteen. On that occasion it had been judged suitable to put the child in semi-mourning, and apparently she carried no sad memory of that time, for she had a fondness for all shades of purple and violet, often wearing them from choice since they complimented her colouring. Years later when I once asked her about her late mother she stared at me with incomprehension. 'I barely knew her,' she said. And that was all.

My own mother had no compunction about reversing her principles when driven by necessity. Still outwardly a young lady of leisure, I was privately drafted into her employ on items of Isabelle's wardrobe, putting into practice hand-stitching learned at her knee, embellishing the simpler panels of satin, lace and net with jet beads and bugles. I attended all of Isabelle's fittings, sometimes deputizing for my mother when the lady called without an appointment. On more than one occasion I dared to suggest an alternative swathing of the heavy rear drapes, and won her approval. I sometimes caught her watching me with a curiously intense stare as though weighing something in her mind.

She had the good sense not to approach me directly with

her project. The first I knew of it was when, after supper one evening, Papa unexpectedly poured me a small glass of port and announced that my mother had been asked for my help by an important client. It would involve my leaving home for a matter of weeks, possibly even the winter months, to travel with the lady as her companion to a warmer climate.

His carefully neutral gaze gave me no clue to the identity of this lady. I ran through my mind the list of grim invalids who were always interviewed at ground-floor level and who hobbled out on sticks to be hauled in their Bath chairs along the seaside promenade by even more wizened and bowed old men for a few shillings a week.

I remember saying – to Mother, because the decision would certainly be hers in the end – 'I am not altogether sure I could be companionable for such a length of time.'

'Even abroad?' she tempted. 'There are inducements that might encourage you to be a little more gracious than usual.'

So already she was for it. And Papa? His face was expressionless. Surely if the prospect was too awful he would have made some move to protect me against it? I believe now, in retrospect, that that modest man was almost as unworldly as me then, accepting 'superior' people at their own valuation.

'Who is the lady?' I asked with foreboding.

And being told, I was overwhelmed by my good fortune: to have been chosen by that gracious beauty. And the 'warmer climate' mentioned would include travel through France and Germany to the Mediterranean coast.

I closed my eyes to keep all the happiness in.

'It may not be very lively for you,' Papa cautioned, as ever sensing my mood. 'As you know, the lady is in mourning for her husband. She plans a season of quiet withdrawal

19

from the world. You will need to be part nurse for her, part confidante, because there will certainly be times when she is in low spirits. Do you think you could bear that?'

To comfort that lovely, sad creature, oh yes. I had no doubt I could – *would gladly* – fulfil all she required of me.

iii

My mother's eyes were boring into me. With a start I realized I had again been lost in past memories and had not heard a word she'd spoken. 'I wish you a safe and pleasant journey home,' I said quickly to cover my default. 'But you're most welcome to stay on, as you know, and wait for fairer conditions.'

'I know better than to outstay my welcome,' she said severely, tugging on her gloves. 'And in any case, you know I find the country tedious in rain. Now that the hot weather has broken it will probably continue like this for weeks.'

It certainly looked that way, the rain falling heavily and straight as brass stair rods. I didn't envy her the damp carriage ride to London and the change at Charing Cross for the two-hour train journey to Warrior Square station. Most of all I would have hated arrival back at the empty house echoing still with the bustling ghosts of her active younger life. And no one to greet her return. Dear Papa gone. I had little thought I'd never see him again, never again hear his droll, gentle voice, as I left with the Honourable Isabelle Delmayne for the adventure of a lifetime.

Mother touched dry lips to my cheek and I squeezed her arm.

I could spare some late sympathy now for the woman who had ruled us before, because of the present void of her existence. Once so totally in control, now alone (but for two elderly servants) in an oversized house which she felt obliged to keep on as befitting the mother of a peeress of the realm. With nothing to look forward to but the occasional glimpses she permitted herself of her growing grandchildren, brief dips into the high life she believed her restrictions had trained me up for, and the inevitable progress of her crippling rheumatism.

Perhaps, I thought, as my husband achieved her stiff transfer into the brougham, she is relieved to be going. The pretence of feeling well over a longer period is too demanding for even her indomitable spirit. At home she may permit herself to relax, apart from impressing her cronies with the rich blessings with which God has justly rewarded her.

She leaned from the carriage window with one final instruction. 'I'm surprised you don't get a motor car, like Geoffrey's,' she told Laurence severely.

'Indeed I might. Thank you for suggesting it, mother-in-law,' he replied, amiable as ever. We stood under umbrellas to wave to her as far as the curve in the drive, then we went back indoors.

And there unease possessed me again. There was enough in the present to distress me, without dwelling on past choices from which all my later pain and deception were to spring. And lasting guilt.

Little less than an hour after my mother's departure the village constable came again. This time he had with him a Sergeant Best from Wycombe who spoke privately at first with my husband and me. He informed us that the lost foreigner was found. Or, rather, his body was now in police care under the coroner's jurisdiction.

It had been discovered on Sedgwick property, face down in the river, wedged among tangled willows, along with debris from the little red Japanese bridge which had collapsed and been borne downstream by the storm waters.

I was appalled that those fears of mine were now realized.

Laurence, grim-faced, granted permission for the staff to be summoned for questioning. We all, family and servants, assembled in the hall and Sergeant Best took up a commanding position five steps up on the grand staircase, from which he glared fiercely. Beside him our local constable tried to cover his evident embarrassment at upstaging the gentry.

Shocked at the implied slur, Hadrill had chairs positioned for Mildred, Isabelle and myself. At this our menfolk took up their stations behind each of us, as if posing for some official family photograph. Only my father-in-law, the Earl, was absent, left undisturbed at his mid-morning rest.

Why, the sergeant demanded, should the stranger enter Sedgwick property? Had he some connection with a member of the household? Was someone present holding back information which might enable him to identify the unknown corpse? Had the dead man at any time visited the house, been allowed inside? Or had anyone happened to observe him in the surrounding grounds?

The ladies of the party stayed throughout the interviews, but were not addressed directly. Laurence, Geoffrey and Dr Millson took it on themselves to deny all knowledge of the man. Hadrill introduced the staff individually and remained to ensure they expressed themselves clearly when picked on. They were naturally disturbed, since Sergeant Best announced threateningly that before immersion the man had been beaten and robbed. Not only his money but also his identity papers had been taken. This was a case of brutal murder for gain.

'Which would seem to indicate some vagrant attacked him,' Geoffrey suggested. 'What do you think, Laurence?'

'We do get homeless people calling here from time to time,' my husband agreed. 'But once they've been fed, unless we have work to offer them, they're sent on their way.'

'It makes our task the harder,' Sergeant Best complained, 'that the innkeeper failed to record the man's particulars, as is required in the case of a furriner. I can only assume he had strayed on to Sedgwick land, so called in here for directions, or was on his way to do so. As might also be the case with whoever set upon him.'

So the brunt of the questioning fell on the servants, in case they had dared receive unknown callers in their quarters.

Cook admitted she had kept on a young lad for two days in the previous week to fix new shelves in the pantry, and he had slept overnight in the stable loft. He'd been reasonably clean and more of a journeyman than a gypsy, but Perkins had chased the lad off after catching him with a clay pipe and matches up in the hay.

Best dropped heavily on this chance of a suspect, only to discover that he'd left three days before the foreigner arrived at the inn. And no one working on the estate had found any trace of the travelling lad after he was seen departing along the ridge towards Bledlow.

The police would doubtless get after him, but I was relieved that he sounded so harmless. If they caught him he would have a few bad hours while they looked into his history, but in the end they would let him go.

Only half conscious of the continuing inquisition, I sat by the window staring out at fields sodden under the summer deluge, and I remembered powdered snow blowing in cart ruts on a misted Italian mountain, the sullen family crowded into a tiny evil-smelling room, the ailing old man on his sick-bed, my own terrible misgivings. And Belle's urgent resolve that I should do as she ordered, whatever the cost.

Yet then neither of us had any notion what that cost might run to. Or that the debt could last as long as this before being called in.

I glanced across at Isabelle. Her drooping head had kept her face concealed from the two policemen, but I saw the white knuckles of her hands tensely gripping the chair arms, and I prayed she would hold on until our unwelcome visitors had left.

With a final rumble of authority and underlying threat, Best cautioned that anyone who later remembered a fact that might help the inquiry was obliged to come forward and present it to the correct authority, i.e. himself. Then nodding to Hadrill, he allowed himself to be shown out.

At the policemen's departure the staff began to file out and the family's artificially unconcerned front was broken. Isabelle unclasped her hands and raised them shakily to her forehead. 'How very unpleasant,' she said in a high, barely controlled treble. Geoffrey was indignant, Laurence silent and thoughtful.

I was left wondering how frank the servants' answers would have been without Hadrill on principle warning them to total discretion. Would they talk among themselves now that all authority was removed, share confidences, begin to speculate?

Few of them had been here long enough to witness my first introduction to this house. Isabelle had had her way about replacing those I met then. And her grandfather was now long dead, her father – the subsequent Lord Sedgwick

24

– increasingly incapable of remembering the travelling companion Isabelle briefly brought to be inspected.

As I rose and turned to Laurence, there came a soft thud behind me and a distressed cry of 'Belle!' from Geoffrey. At once, between them the gentlemen lifted her and laid her on the hall couch. Laurence would have rung for her maid, but I warned him to discretion. 'I'll go myself for smelling salts. Just rub her hands and arms. Get her blood moving. She's sat still too long.'

But it wasn't immobility that made her faint. It was fear. Yet when she came to she had an excuse ready prepared before she allowed her eyes to flutter open: she might be mistaken but she truly believed that at last she could be *enceinte.*

Poor Geoffrey was amazed and delighted, tenderly holding both her hands, and vibrant with adoration.

Cynically I watched the little charade played out as she refused Dr Millson's attentions, putting on a brave-little-woman's face and proclaiming she was content to wait in patience until she could be perfectly sure herself.

When we were alone together I charged her with the lie, knowing that for her pregnancy was impossible. It was cruel to give poor Geoffrey such hope.

'Best be careful what you say,' she hissed viciously. 'You have more to lose than I. If all came out between us, Laurence would accept his little sister's failings, but he could never again trust a wife who had deceived him.'

Three

Arrangements had been so swiftly made for my Grand Tour as the Honourable Isabelle's companion that they almost took my breath away. Mother's main concern was that I should be decently and appropriately equipped. New shoes were ordered, showroom dresses were altered, the waists taken in and false-hem extensions added inside in case I should continue to shoot up. In the end these proved unnecessary but Mother was anxious because already, at seventeen, I topped her by six inches, and the Honourable Isabelle by three.

What most worried her was that my costumes might be too showy for my station and my employer's state of mourning. Basically she chose for me plain shades of silver grey, adding either frogging or braiding of black and violet, but could not resist adding two really splendid dresses 'for later on' and a travelling coat of olive wool velour trimmed with velvet. Never had she been so generous while claiming to have her eyes set on practicalities. 'You never can tell where this may lead,' she said portentously.

Financial arrangements were agreed through Mother, since at seventeen I was considered too young to be aware of the value of money. While travelling Isabelle would cover my expenses and provide some pocket money. A small emolument would be sent by her grandfather each month to my home and added to my childhood savings. In addition Papa privately passed to me four crisp, white five-pound notes 'against contingencies'.

My great concern was that there should be room in my luggage for some books. How terrible to be stranded abroad, with only my schoolroom acquisition of languages, and to have nothing to lose myself imaginatively inside. Even if my new world was all adventure and romance, there would still be that need. Papa, who understood, gave me his own copy of the New Testament and an anthology of English verse. I added only Hardy's *Mayor of Casterbridge*, determined to work at my French and German, then buy native books wherever I found myself.

Our first stay was to be in Deauville on the Normandy coast, but before then there was an obstacle to be cleared.

'I have to take my leave of the family,' Isabelle warned me. 'And you must come too, so that they can be sure you are a suitable person. Do you think you could possibly contrive to look quite a bit older?'

With such a warning I was prepared for criticism; but never for the vastness of the palace in Buckinghamshire which she called home, or the awesome authority of her grandfather, Earl Sedgwick. Never had I felt so insignificant and out of place. It needed all my play-acting skill to carry me through. Fortunately, petrified by such grandeur, I must have appeared severe and formal. My difficulty in finding speech passed as discretion. Later Isabelle was to tell me she'd had no second thoughts about claiming an extra ten years on my true age.

Even then her father, Viscount Crowthorne, complained it would have been better to choose a married lady for her companion. However, since we should be leading a secluded life outside society for some months, he preferred that I was not a fashionable hostess. It would be advisable to address me as *Mrs* Fellowes.

And so, grudgingly approved, I accompanied Isabelle on my first sea journey, crossing the Channel by steamer to France. The sea was boisterous, grey-green waves whipped into foaming peaks under a leaden sky. And I loved it, alone on deck, clinging to the rails and screeching back at the gulls that followed us out.

Accompanied by her personal maid, Isabelle had taken a berth below-decks, convinced she was no sailor. I went down twice to check on her. The first time she was groaning and pale; the second time asleep like a baby. I enquired of an officer the time we would be docking and woke her ten minutes before.

Deauville was not the social backwater I had expected. There were English people aplenty in the string of hotels that dominated the promenade; some delightful meals; good conversation; plenty of whist and bridge, with which Isabelle flirted but soon declared herself bored. After only three weeks we were packing our bags again and boarding a train for Paris.

Since her father had spoken of a social withdrawal I was not prepared for us to bowl through the splendid gates to the British Embassy, where Isabelle was embraced like a daughter.

'Darling child,' the ambassador's wife exclaimed, 'how wonderful that you should come just now!'

But I sensed some misgivings on her husband's part. He confined himself to kissing Isabelle's cheek and offering condolences on Hugo's tragic death.

'Ah yes,' said Lady Craven, abruptly reminded of the black veil on Isabelle's hat. 'My dear, our hearts go out to you.'

Their momentary awkwardness, which – diplomats that

they both were – they disguised heroically, arose from an imminent (and private) visit of Albert Edward, Prince of Wales, with a small retinue. Within three days all rooms at the Embassy would be taken. Much as they would wish . . . but in view of Isabelle's present widowed state . . .

Oh, the wretch!' she declared, unpinning her hat and dumping it on a *chaise-longue*. 'How very annoying of him. Such a wonderful opportunity to revel in his company again, and I'm to be prevented! I suppose he has Daisy Warwick still trailing on his arm and spouting this new socialism?'

Her host and hostess exchanged stiff glances. 'His guests are always welcome. As are you *always*, dear child, in normal circumstances. And for tonight, of course . . .' Lady Craven offered, making a sweeping gesture to offer all the facilities of the Embassy. She had made an art of the half-sentence, which struck me as useful for an ambassadress, leaving the hearer to please himself how it should end.

'And tomorrow,' her husband offered, 'we will find somewhere suitable where you may put up throughout the royal visit.'

Isabelle was in a sulk. Alone with her, I tried to draw her out, enquiring about previous occasions when she had attended the Prince and Princess Alexandra, either at the Palace or at Marlborough House, their London home. Quite soon she was happily shocking me with titbits of scandal about the great and good of court society. I ventured to question one of her extravagances concerning the Prince, and she snorted at me.

'You shall see for yourself. He doesn't trouble to conceal how his leanings are but it is all done with such elegance and insouciance. And it makes not one whit of difference to one's respect for him. You have only to go out in the street and see him passing by to know how much loved he is by all the people. That is, if the French can forget that they've been selling arms to the Boers and now look like supporting the losing side. Even though unofficial, this visit, like so many he makes, must be intended to win back some affection for our country through his personal charm.

'He's a great man and a good man. But also a real man who loves the company of lively women. So much fun to be anywhere near.

'And for two weeks I have been confined to pressing my nose against the window pane just to get a glimpse of him passing by in his carriage!'

She had much more to inform me on concerning the Prince of Wales. Frustrated in her desire to join his company, Isabelle could scarcely leave the subject alone. 'He should be made King, instead of the old Queen keeping him waiting in the wings. We never see her any more. It's like having no monarch at all. I've heard she's really past her duties, quite deaf, and her cataracts so bad now that she can't even read dispatches for herself. So she has servants do it for her when nobody from the government is there to help. But it should be Bertie standing alongside, instead of playing Master of Ceremonies to keep the people reminded that we do have some royal family.'

'Perhaps he would be less pleasant if he had to keep his nose to the grindstone of state matters.'

'I suppose you're right. Oh Genie, don't you feel sorry for men? I do. It must be quite awful to be one. I should really hate it.'

'Well, of course. We're women.' I smiled, my attention on the snarls in her hair. I often stood in for her maid at night-time now. It was when we had our most intimate discussions.

30

'But just imagine. Such responsibility. They're so bur-
dened with solemn matters; making decisions for other
people; making money; producing a family. Such stuffy
business. Small wonder they're always wanting to break
out and play the merry devil.'

My hands slowed as I remembered Papa, always so
dutiful and considerate. Much respected by his clients
and by the gentlemen he shared his shoot with, but made
little of at home, taken for granted by a self-centred wife;
even in money matters subservient, since he had sacrificed
the early profits of his printing works so that she might
equip her own salon in a superior neighbourhood. And
now she lorded it, everyone assuming she was the source
of any success he'd had.

But Isabelle was considering a quite different kind of
man. 'Do you believe they all wish to "break out and play
the merry devil"?' I questioned.

'Of course. And most need very little tempting to throw
over the traces. But some are too scared, little scuttling
mice.' Her fingers ran up the mirror and she peered out
teasingly at my reflection through a curtain of golden
curls.

I had to smile back. 'I agree I should detest being
obliged to shave every day,' I admitted, following her
original observation.

'Yes. Much more fun to watch,' she said with the familiarity of a one-time wife. 'But I think now I do really prefer
gentlemen with a neatly trimmed beard.'

She was surely thinking again of the Prince of Wales.
His naval-style beard had taken on, just like the new-style
knife-edge creases fore and aft in his trousers. Even Prince
George, his heir, had followed suit, and his bearded cousin
Tsar Nicholas now resembled him so closely that photo-
graphed together they looked like twin brothers. Seafaring

men. How much nobler our royals' faces looked than the fierce Prussians' with their waxed military moustaches. When invited to sail at Cowes, the young Kaiser Wilhelm's went most oddly, in photographs, with the uniform of an honorary admiral of our Royal Navy.

'We shall go on to Potsdam,' Isabelle suddenly decided, and I wondered if my fleeting thought of Victoria's German grandson had sprung silently from my mind to hers. Potsdam, I knew, was where he held court, close by Berlin.

Well, perhaps that was safer than Isabelle hanging about Paris in the hope of accidentally being discovered by the Prince of Wales. Particularly since it was now known that a new favourite, Alice Keppel, had replaced the political Lady Warwick, and was even looked on kindly by Princess Alexandra.

So I rose early the next morning, instructed the maid to start packing, and went myself to the station to see to booking our seats.

While travelling, Isabelle grumbled about the heat, the cushions, the food, the company. She showed little curiosity, no wish to know what lay behind the watchful foreign eyes cut off from us by barriers of language and custom. Her French was well pronounced but ungrammatical, as taught by a Breton governess, her German non-existent, her Italian confined to the same art and music terms which I had picked up at school.

This I found astonishing since she had travelled widely in Europe as a young child, with her late Mama and a governess. But then Isabelle was always content to be cocooned and her mother had probably moved in much the same company as in England, society transferring itself *en bloc* from place to place as the Season demanded.

Up until this point in our relations I was still under

her spell, accepting Isabelle as the centre of existence. If my admiration ever faltered I could find excuses for her mood. For her the moment was everything: she grasped it, and all in it that she saw as rightly hers. I could admire her for such energy and honesty, being myself too much the romantic, living in a past I tended to idealize and a dream future I hardly yet dared to believe in.

There had been some disappointments. Our travel was already proving an uncomfortable rush from place to place; and restlessness was no substitute for adventure. In the blur of foreign impressions, Europe was a magic-lantern screen of fast-changing images which I had no time to become familiar with.

Behind all this, and most disillusioning, I had gradually begun to suspect that Isabelle was not the sweet perfection I'd been so ready to believe her, and (although experienced in matters unguessed at by me) yet a strangely unformed person of sudden desires and rather shallow affection.

We were inconvenienced by the loss of her personal maid. Lizzie had moped during our weeks in Paris, far from her family and unable to converse with the French servants. In Germany she was constantly discovered weeping, became clumsy and was summarily dismissed, to travel back to England on her own. In sympathy I pressed on her one of the banknotes Papa had provided. She seemed grateful enough, but later I found that the other three had disappeared from my muff. I didn't dare to mention this disaster to Isabelle, nor my suspicions of the girl.

Until we found a German maid with a few words of English, I took on Lizzie's abandoned duties. It scarcely suited either Isabelle or me. On top of this, ever more frequently I felt myself less an equal companion than forced into the role of governess to an impulsive overgrown child.

Time and again I would have cautioned her, except that in my heart I knew her to be deeply unhappy. Soon I was to learn how near she was to desperation.

It showed in her new approach to fresh acquaintances. Almost anyone would do to entertain her, provided she already had no friends in common with them. Some were certainly persons she would not have looked at twice on home ground. Not that she was over-eager, but she practised a special sort of provocative aloofness that piqued others' curiosity about her. I suppose she was what the French mean by a 'coquette'. I was sure there were gentlemen – and some who were rather less – who were deceived into seeing personal advancement in associating with a wealthy and attractive young widow.

My fears for her should have made a dragon of me, but I was inexperienced in taking charge, and socially out of my depth. Instead I stayed with her, chaperoned her as best I could, endured the neighing laughter and inexplicable jokes, and firmly ignored the occasional hints that I should withdraw as unsuitable company hung on until the small hours.

There was one young-old man whose influence I particularly mistrusted. His weathered military face bore furrowed lines I could only think of as cruel, or at best sardonic. Certainly his glossy black hair was dyed. And he had an almost physical way of intruding on one while only standing indolently and fixing one with his gaze.

Isabelle seemed unaccountably taken with him. Perhaps as a rabbit is with a snake. We stayed four weeks at Potsdam, dining on the final evening at his hotel. He brought along a companion, a youngish Englishman whom he introduced as Sir Ralph Cruickshank, to be my partner while the Baron monopolized Isabelle.

I watched him fasten a corsage of gardenias to the black lace of her evening gown, and failed to make Isabelle's eyes meet mine. She must have known. How could she be insensitive to those lecherous fingers?

We were dined and wined and the conversation was lively enough, for Isabelle was in a kittenish mood, but I couldn't relax for fear that with too much champagne she would rashly permit some over-familiarity.

It was the first time I had tasted venison, which was served in a thick *compôte* of black cherries and I didn't care for the rich flavour. Perhaps I might have enjoyed it more if its aroma hadn't been overpowered by the pomade of the man beside me. It gleamed on his lank sandy hair, where the comb had streaked wide wet lanes so that his scalp showed through, shiny pink. His moustache, limper and longer than the Baron's fierce Prussian one, was almost ginger. He had little chin and even less conversation.

When Isabelle and I withdrew together she lit a cheroot – a habit she had recently taken up in private – and leaning against the cold hand-basin of the powder room, spoke with her eyes half closed. 'The *Almanach de Gotha*, Eugenie. Despite his claims I doubt we'll find the Baron features largely in it. The *Ligne Bavière*. Some minor Wittalsbach connection, because he held his commission with the First Regiment of Grand Cavalry. But I need to know everything. His family, his age, his home estate. And, of course, just how much in debt he is. You must research him for me.'

It shook me that she could suspect he was spurious and yet encourage the man. 'Isabelle, why trouble? We leave tomorrow for Heidelberg. There is no call ever to see him again.'

She laughed, like a little cough. 'Do you really think he will give me up so easily? No, he will follow us. Not immediately perhaps, but in a few days' time, he'll turn up, as if by accident, and go on playing his fish.'

'Then I sincerely trust you'll cease encouraging him.'

'Oh tosh, Genie. How indignant you get. Your face is quite flushed. Or is that at recall of some private compliment from the gallant Sir Ralph?'

'Isabelle, I beg you to consider how unwise you're being. Your reputation could be at risk. This man is—'

'Is what? Do instruct me, you with so much experience of the world.'

'I admit I'm ignorant in many ways, socially inept perhaps, but I'm not blind, Isabelle. Look at the people he calls his friends. All gamblers and drinkers. And the decent families to which you have entry regard you both most strangely when you come in on his arm.'

'So he sounds dangerous. I like a little risk in life.'

'Don't tease me, Isabelle. You have too much to lose to make mistakes now. Even widowed, you have everything else in life a woman could ask for. Why throw it all away?'

'Really, you make me sound like a common kitchenmaid lifting her skirts on her night out. What on earth "mistake" do you suppose I should permit the Baron to persuade me into? I am not easily to be seduced, whatever he may imagine. I simply wish to know whether I could stand the man as a husband.'

The silence after her words must have shaken even her, for she turned on me and said in a more friendly, comforting tone, 'Don't worry. I shall have decided for or against him by the end of the evening. And most probably against. I fear he's stingy. In the Highlands no one would offer me venison of such poor quality. So shall we go back to the gentlemen now?'

I gave in, confused and embarrassed by my own ignorance. I saw now clearly enough that I was in a false
position as Isabelle's chaperon. She required a strict matri-
arch, not an inexperienced girl to whom no one had
explained intimate matters beyond public behaviour in
polite company.

We rejoined the gentlemen for coffee and later agreed to
take a walk in the hotel garden. There were little coloured
lights strung out among the trees. In other circumstances I
should have enjoyed strolling there on this warm October
evening, with snatches of distant music reaching us from
the hotel's drawing-room, and the mosquitoes kept at
bay by the gentlemen's cigars. But somehow, while Sir
Ralph called my attention back to a fresh aspect of the
lighted terrace, I found that our two companions had
disappeared.

'I must stay with Isabelle,' I said sharply.

'Oh surely there's no need. You should allow yourself
a few minutes of freedom from waiting on her.'

'Hush,' I said, thinking I caught her laughter somewhere
ahead. 'Do you hear them?'

He cocked his head and appeared to be helpful. 'This
way, I think.'

Perhaps in daytime the path would have been clear
enough, but in the dark – and we were descending,
gradually leaving the lights behind – it seemed a maze.
We covered some rough ground, hurrying to catch up,
then found ourselves beyond all sound and sight of the
hotel. Here the tall bushes were denser and the grit path
had given way to hummocky grass. There was nothing to
be seen in the dark but the starry sky above and the dim
glow of Sir Ralph's white shirt-front beside me.

'There's no one this way,' I said impatiently. 'Let's
retrace our steps.'

'If we can find them.' He seemed to be laughing silently.

And I was suddenly afraid. Rightly, because he whipped an arm behind my waist and pulled me close, while the other hand tilted my chin and he forced his mouth on mine.

I fought to be free, twisted my face away from the odious mixed scent of hair oil and stale cigar breath.

'If that is what you like, we'll certainly play,' he offered, releasing me a moment and then diving after me as I moved back ready to run. I would have cried out but I was ashamed that Isabelle should hear me and realize the predicament I'd foolishly walked into.

He backed me against a tree and I felt the rough bark tearing at the silk of my dress, then his body pressed hard against mine while he held my two wrists helpless above my head. I could not believe that he would do this to me, this man I had taken for a chinless milksop. But a man for all that, one without scruples, and so a danger.

Now I would have screamed, but he stifled it with one hand. The force of it drove my head against the tree and I felt the teeth of the silver back-comb, lent me by Isabelle, bite through my coiled hair into my scalp.

I had a weapon! Everything began to happen so slowly at that point. Or else it was an illusion because my mind was needle sharp and active. As he leaned back to force my eyes to meet his, I raised my freed hand and tore the comb away, letting my hair fall about my shoulders.

'Ah,' he breathed. 'That's better, my girl.'

Then 'A-a-a-agh' again, that rose into a thin shriek as I tore at his cheeks, the sockets of his eyes, striking again and again in my frenzy, feeling his blood run warm on my fingers. Then he fell away, howling like a dog.

I ran, dodging between trees, hearing his sobbing and swearing die away behind. Maybe he's blinded, I told myself. I could even have killed him!

The lights of the terrace showed now, framed between the clipped columns of a yew walk, and I knew I couldn't run farther into the open in my present state. One sleeve was torn from its seam and flapped about me. My hair hung in tangles like a gypsy's. And then the man's blood – my hands were sticky with it and the front of my dress drenched. There was nowhere to go, no one to run to.

What would have become of me then I don't know, had not Isabelle come hurrying up by a side path, alone and looking most determined. She took in my disarray at a glance and grasped me by one wrist, holding me firmly away lest I soil her dress.

'Now there's a pretty kettle of fish,' she said drolly. 'And what's become of your escort, missy?'

'Oh, that terrible man! Isabelle you couldn't imagine . . .'

'Couldn't I?' Such a strange tone of voice, part cynical, part compassionate.

I poured out what I had done. The curved back-comb was still in my hand. She could barely prise it from me, folding it in her handkerchief. I could see now that the teeth were all bent and broken but the stones still glittered in its rim. Mock diamonds, Isabelle had assured me when she insisted I should borrow it.

'Now compose yourself,' she ordered. 'I shall fetch our cloaks myself and have the doorman call our carriage round. When I order the driver to stop at the first curve in the driveway, where it's suitably dark, can I trust you to get yourself there safely without assaulting anyone further? Good, you shouldn't have long to wait.'

And, totally mistress of the situation, even perhaps enjoying it in some perverse fashion, she floated back to the terrace, stopping a moment to converse with a lady at a table there among friends.

I waited a while, shivering and silent, then made my way to where she planned to have me picked up. There was no sound any more from the direction I had left the injured man in, and it was only then that I began to wonder what had become of the Baron with whom Isabelle had gone walking.

Back in our hired rooms Isabelle played at nurse, ordering the new German maid to prepare a hot bath for me. When I emerged as near sweet-smelling and decontaminated as I felt possible, she had champagne waiting in a cooler and a feast of crackers with smoked salmon.

She was at her social hostess best. 'It should really be brandy after your *mauvais quart d'heure*, but it might seem odd for two ladies to demand that at this hour of the morning. And we don't wish to attract attention, do we?'

She eased out the cork with one elegant thumb and directed the flow into both our glasses. 'Let us drink to the damnation of all the male sex. For, God knows, there's little enough to be said in favour of them.'

Four

I slept fitfully and awoke late next morning. Isabelle was already dressed for outdoors, having breakfasted downstairs. 'I have news for you,' she said with lively good humour.

'Yes?' I said fearfully.

'As ever the perfect guest, I sent my card with a little note of thanks to our host of last evening.'

'To the Baron?'

'At his hotel, yes. And would you believe it, he had already left. Without a word, *and* without settling his account. He together with his valet, a young Englishman who was lodged up in the attics.'

'You don't mean . . . ?'

'Yes, your gallant "Sir" Ralph Cruickshank, no less. At some time after our departure last night they made off. Like Longfellow's Arabs, they folded their tents and silently stole away.' She sounded delighted.

'The Baron? But, Isabelle, that was the man you considered marrying.'

'Not very seriously, Genie, I assure you. Anyway there is no need now for you to go researching his background with that in mind. I satisfied myself last night that it would have been a disaster. He is not ready for a warm-blooded woman. His taste is still quite set on his pretty young boys.'

41

'You already suspected that, and still you considered . . .'

'Oh pish, Genie. What's the difference? I needed a husband and he needs a wife to pass himself off as half-decent.'

'There's no comparison between the two of you! Nor your needs! You know you could have any of a dozen good men, and you surely will, once your year of mourning is up.'

'*Then?* What good would that be? Oh, leave it, leave it. I've had enough of the subject.' She was suddenly in a black humour again. At the door she turned. 'Let it suffice that whatever you did commit last night it was not bloody murder and there is no warrant out today for your arrest. Which is just as well since you would probably not relish a German prison, especially with them all so sour to the English now, since at last we seem to be trouncing the Boers in South Africa. I really have half a mind to cut out our visit to Heidelberg and go straight on to Italy. Not that we English will be much more popular there at present.'

I said nothing, pushing back the bedclothes and starting to rise. 'Isabelle, I am truly sorry. I could so nearly have brought scandal on you. It's the very last thing I wanted, and I can see now how foolish it was to venture out alone like that with the wretched man.'

She came back and shook me gently by the shoulders, her mood swinging again to good humour. There was even something like affection in her eyes. 'You innocent! You meant well. You couldn't know I intended to evade you. As for your assaulting your tormentor, it shows great spirit.'

'But Isabelle, your lovely silver comb! It's ruined. How can I apologize enough?'

'It was of little value: the stones imitation, just like the

Baron and his wretched companion. I freely forgive you, if only you'll forgive me too, for leaving you alone.'

Impulsively she put her arms round me, leaning close so that she tipped her hat askew and crushed my breasts against her shoulders. 'We're friends, Genie, aren't we? Do say we are to be *true* friends!'

'Friends? Yes . . . I suppose.' Her impetuosity embarrassed me. I was unsure that our relative stations permitted such closeness, yet I was loath to offend her by appearing cold.

She rushed on. 'And between friends there are *never* debts to be repaid. You must always remember that.'

She was so earnest, so pretty then in her enthusiasm, I felt again that it was I who was older, and she the child who was not to be denied.

I must have smiled back at her. 'No debts between us. Of course not, Isabelle.' I was so grateful, I would have forgiven her anything then.

She slid her hands down my arms and leaned back to gaze full in my face. 'Oh, Genie, what a sad pity you are not a man! I would so gladly spend the rest of my life with you.'

We did go to Heidelberg. My enjoyment of that fairy-tale city, its romantic, ruined Schloss and its links with our own Jacobean royals was only marred by the background fear of consequences from my earlier brush with the Baron's catamite.

'Rest assured,' Isabelle insisted, 'there will be no repercussions. He overplayed the hand he was meant to deal you. The Baron will instantly have understood the reason for his injuries. He will scarcely wish to drag around a little friend with facial disfigurements, and one who manifestly shows interest in a mere woman. He will most certainly have packed him off home to England in disgrace. And without a testimonial.'

She was probably right, for no one followed us, and this left me to wonder about how she had dealt with her rejected suitor.

Over the next few weeks she again grew low in spirits, pale and listless, and the mail we had found waiting for us at the Gasthof did nothing to enliven her. I assumed this was all a necessary part of the grieving process, and that her best hope lay in finding interests outside herself, to prove that there was still much to live for.

We bought stout boots to go for walks up the *Philosophenweg* from where, except for its gaping windows, the wonderful red stone castle still looked intact. To cross the Neckar and climb to the Schloss itself brought home its full poignancy. Beautiful as it was, there was less in this scenery to lift one's spirits than to encourage nostalgic regrets.

How sad that the ravages of war should still remain from centuries earlier. I felt something like the presence of ghosts there – of Elizabeth Stuart and her dark-eyed German husband, joyous young people promised all the riches of Europe, but cast down at their very peak, through accepting the throne of Bohemia.

I comforted myself that we in 1900 lived in an age of enlightenment, when the idea of European war was unthinkable. Imagining such sudden and total disaster made me shudder. *Hubris*, hadn't the Ancient Greeks called it? The cruel revenge of the gods on humans who presumed too far.

Had I some premonition then of my own future, the unimaginable rise, and how at the peak of my happiness I'd be faced with a full reckoning for earlier follies?

But at that time I was of no importance, and innocent

enough – unless I count that first small deceit of assuming the title of married woman.

Papa's letters to me, which I'd received in Paris, were correctly addressed, for he'd have nothing to do with falsity. But my mother found it quite proper to write 'Mrs' next to my name. She wrote only the once that year, a letter twice redirected to reach me at the Gasthof, and so already twelve days old. My hands trembled as I opened the terrible black-bordered envelope addressed in her firm hand, but twice crossed through and corrected as it followed our travels. How could it be anything but what I most dreaded: news that dear Papa was no more?

The funeral had already taken place when she wrote. There had been so much to arrange, and she had been quite distraught at the suddenness of it. Pneumonia had taken him, following a severe chill after a day-long drenching at his shoot. He had not wanted to take part, already feeling a little under the weather, but two of the group had dropped out and he wouldn't disappoint the others.

In the event there'd been little to show for his trouble; just two brace of hare and three of pheasant, which had been hung under the shed's roof in the garden and forgotten until they were past being eaten. There had been no more than fourteen back to the house for funeral meats, but the church had been crowded to the doors and everyone had been so full of praise for his character and standing in the town. It had been most consoling to her in her sad bereavement.

There was no suggestion that I should come home and comfort her. Nor that a child could grieve as deeply as a wife. She added a paragraph of small news items and a list of ladies she was currently involved in costuming.

As postscript she added that in his will Papa had mentioned that I should be offered his guns and his good oak

45

desk. 'The desk is worth keeping but I assume you will wish the guns sold and the money placed for safe keeping with the money Lord Sedgwick sends as your wage.'

I was too shattered to weep then. I was so angry. With everyone. With Mother for her cold efficiency, with Papa for neglecting himself and allowing death to overtake him. Had he given up caring for himself because I was no longer within reach to share his life and companionship? But most of all angry with myself, because if I had been there it just would not, could not, have happened.

I re-read the letter again and again, willing it to tell me more, to contain some special message that he had entrusted to her to give me.

His two guns. Yes, he had always said they should be mine when he gave up shooting. This because I had sometimes accompanied him to the shoot and although I wouldn't fire on any living creature, he had taught me to use the lighter rifle on targets. How dared my mother assume I would get rid of the guns, the gift he specifically made to me?

And what of Rory? Had Papa entrusted him to one of his friends as he felt himself grow weaker? Or had Mother sent the poor beast to be destroyed?

And what did she mean by the *church* being crowded to the doors? Which church? Surely he would have wanted a service held at the Baptist Chapel above Warrior Square? Could she have been so insensitive as to override his wishes – for social reasons? And she had made no mention of where his body had been laid to rest. It was as though he had no grave, no place that I could later go to and kneel a while to honour him.

I knew now that I should never have left home, but that since I had, with so horrific a result, there would be no going back. I burned with a new and alarming rancour.

Isabelle left me alone for a few hours to mourn, then came and gently took me in her arms. 'Greta tells me you have received sad news. She saw the envelope.'

'The worst. My father has died.' I spoke shortly.

'Then you shall go home immediately. I will have the hotel make all the arrangements for your travel.'

'There's no point. The funeral is over. I'm not needed. It's too late, and there's nothing I can do to reverse what has happened. The very idea of home is abhorrent.'

My sharpness warned her. She gave me a doubting look and said, 'Think about it. This is no moment to make big decisions. Is there anything I can do to help you?'

'Nothing, thank you. I have to write to my mother now.'

'To express your sympathy. Of course.'

'To safeguard my inheritance.' I had not known I could sound so bitter. Isabelle would have been left in no doubt about my feelings, or lack of them.

'I'll leave you to your writing, then. And Greta shall take your letter to the post when you've done.'

Isabelle too had received messages from home. Three days later she confided that we would not be travelling on to Italy.

'My sister Mildred's there – or rather, my older half-sister – grubbing about in ancient ruins. My father expects us to link up but I wouldn't inflict her on you. I must think of somewhere else to go, for certainly there's nobody here.'

Nobody? Some very hospitable German families, besides the chance to meet learned professors from the University. It seemed that Isabelle was not content with these. Also she had refused to visit Baden-Baden because some of her London acquaintances were likely to be taking the waters there. It seemed she both wanted and did not want company. At the time I felt much the same myself, needing only one person and he beyond reach for ever.

Then, as we walked above the castle barely two weeks after the letter's arrival, it began to snow; huge lazy flakes that fast covered the lanes through the pine forest and settled thickly on our clothes.

'There, you see!' Isabelle complained. 'Now winter's coming early. We shall have to move south again. But I won't go to Italy. I can't.'

We turned back downhill, deprived of the promised view from the *Königsstuhl* by a dense blanket of white that rolled up and whipped around us as if we were borne along on a cloud. At river level there lay only a ragged carpet of snow but Isabelle's mind was made up. It would soon be November. 'We shall winter in Egypt,' she decided. 'I detest the cold. And besides, I believe some of Hugo's regiment are garrisoned there as a relief from the war in South Africa. There may be some tolerable officers I have met through him.'

We took a steamer from Marseille and arrived in Alexandria on 31 October. I had been with Isabelle for little more than three months and already this was our third foreign country.

There can be nowhere like Egypt. I was at once aware of its rightness, and that we were the intruding foreigners full of alien assumptions about the way we did things and what we expected. Not that we were alone in being outsiders. There seemed to be every nation under the sun besides, in a glorious, multicoloured mêlée: Turks, Levantines, Indians, Greeks, Italians, German, French.

The people of the Delta, however modest, had a serene bearing, but were easily moved to smiles and laughter. Their graceful carriage and the cool ease of flowing *galabiyas* made me envious, constrained as I was to hour-glass severity. I wished I could talk with them, but had to content myself with whichever hotel servants had learned a little English. Only the beggars distressed me, with their terrible sores and missing limbs, until I realized that they almost cherished their way of life, and England in the Middle Ages must have been equally gruesome.

We immediately ran into someone Isabelle knew, an elderly lady resident in our hotel, the childless widow of a cavalry half-colonel, who claimed her health prevented her returning to her home country of Ireland. She was brown and wizened like a shelled walnut, and although she moved stiffly on two sticks, her mind was shrewd, her tongue sharp and her little black eyes missed nothing. At home, I thought, village children would claim she was a witch.

She explained much to me of the country's recent history and economic difficulties. There was a constant flow of company, both service and civilian, to visit her suite, and some famous names among her acquaintances. As we pored together over the *Morning Post*, which arrived late by sea, she avidly read the war reports from South Africa written by 'young Winston, Randolph's lad'. And a treasured possession was her autographed copy of his *River War*, the author's sprawled handwriting followed by a curious, strong squiggle like a large cedilla; or perhaps the start of a question mark, as though he might finally doubt what he was currently about. Yet he wrote with easy assurance, precisely and with vivid description.

Although she thought our unescorted visit defied convention, Mrs Trevelyan didn't dismiss Isabelle as a ninny. I had the impression she admired impetuosity in women and regarded it as a worthy counter-attack on men's assumed superiority. Her immediate reaction to our arrival was to

49

summon a subaltern who was recuperating from fever following a bullet wound in his left leg.

'It does him no good,' she declared, 'to hobble along at my pace. His injuries are sufficiently recovered for him to welcome the challenge of two lively young ladies like yourselves to ride with. He shall take you to Cairo, and there you'll see the real Egypt, not just these obliging servants who pander to us here.'

Each new sight and experience made me love the country more. Lieutenant Gilbert Fairfield had hired a carriage for the journey and planned a circuitous route so that we might glimpse the great canal in which Disraeli had bought shares for Britain along with the French. For a while we drove parallel, but distant, to it and saw the weird aspect of large ships' funnels and upper decks sailing along the horizon of sand dunes. There was so much expanse of empty desert, and so huge a sky, it seemed we had gone to another planet. We stopped at a simple half-way dwelling to take lemonade and stretch our legs, then on again for a further two hours of limitless sand dunes.

The farms before Cairo were single-storeyed buildings of stone or whitewashed mud huddled under tall palms. Great squares of water were banked off from the Nile on either side to grow rice or hold fish for the city. The people labouring there looked strong and healthy, the dark-eyed, half-bare children adorable, running out to wave as we went past.

Compared with the elegant villas, tended gardens and open squares of Alexandria, Cairo was noisy, bustling, the air charged with unfamiliar spicy scents and other less pleasant odours. Past the huge dome of the Citadel, we turned to cross to an island, then regained the further bank and drove out westward, I think, to the Pyramids. At Giza we changed to horseback to ride round the Pyramids and view the Sphinx. It was almost unbelievable to be here, a transient modern beside these silent winesses to a long-past civilization.

There were donkeys and camels all decked out with fancy saddle-cloths in brilliant colours, hung with fat woollen tassels and little bells, to tempt the visitors. Some were tired and had scars or bare patches on their flanks. Others were surely treasured by the men who showed them off. I tried the high saddle on a camel, which felt most insecure when the beast lurched off in a loping run, but Isabelle declined the offer, put off by the creatures' peculiar groans and vicious-looking teeth.

She complained of sudden faintness and did look alarmingly pale, so we drove back to the edge of the city and sought temporary shelter in a shop that sold papyrus and hand-worked curios. Lt Fairfield blamed himself for overtiring her, took complete charge and, mistrusting the nearer hotels, begged us to accept the hospitality of a friend, a wealthy Cairo government official whose wives would take the greatest care of us.

Whatever our misgivings, we were in no position to refuse. Isabelle had a fever for three days, and the kindness of the Egyptian family was unimaginable. They were Muslims of Turkish origin, and the great house, Qasr el Mastaba, south of the city, had a separate walled court for the women's quarters. Until we left, over a week later, we were not to meet our host the Bey, but Lt Fairfield enjoyed his hospitality beyond the harem gate.

There were two wives, with some ten years between their ages. The older, Zara, was treated with great respect by the younger, Tammam, whom she loved as a daughter. There were three little girls quite close in age and an older boy of about seven. Who was the mother of which I never knew, and it seemed to them immaterial. If one child fell and hurt itself it would run to either woman and get equally fond comfort. But the children were reserved in front of Isabelle or me, sensing we came from a different world and had alien habits.

For all that, I tried to communicate with them and found they had a few phrases of English, taught them by the younger wife who had been a doctor's daughter in the Khedive's household. She was concerned for Isabelle and insisted on sitting with her overnight while I took some rest.

I wanted to telegraph to Lord Sedgwick and advise him of his granddaughter's illness but Isabelle wouldn't hear of it. In fact she became wildly angry at the suggestion, and I feared she was delirious. 'Give in to her,' Tammam advised. 'She should be yielded to in that state.'

Mrs Trevelyan arrived in an Italian motor car from Alexandria to visit Isabelle, stoutly denying it inconvenienced her. She came in more stiffly than usual on her sticks and was made much of by the Bey's two wives, with both of whom she carried on a sprightly conversation in Arabic, once seated. Her bird-bright eyes took in Isabelle's malaise in an instant.

'Perhaps,' she said privately to me as I saw her again to her conveyance, 'your friend is suffering from an overdose of attention. Tell me, young woman, for how long are you engaged to accompany her?'

And when I explained that the agreement was left open to Isabelle's requirements, she hummed through closed lips, then pronounced severely, 'It's always advisable to set a term to such arrangements in advance.'

Gilbert Fairfield was most attentive, coming to the harem gate the first morning with a gift of fruit and flowers, but I convinced him how well off we were for every material luxury. He was concerned that as European ladies we might feel ourselves cut off from the outside world. When I assured him that Isabelle was well suited, and that all I missed was exercise, he happily offered to take me riding each day until Isabelle was strong enough to leave.

He did not fit my idea of a soldier. There was nothing aggressive in his nature, although his tall frame was well-built and strong enough. His being so tall gave him a slightly drooping appearance, for he was constantly bending to take in others' conversation, being more of a listener than a talker. His face was sunken, the cheekbones rising sharply from crescent-shaped troughs that bracketed a beaky nose and ran from the inner corners of deep-set dark eyes down to the bony jaw. And inside them were finer lines bracketing the mouth which was mainly hidden by a large, floppy moustache. His fine, pale hair was long for a soldier's and fell towards his eyes. Possibly, on leave, he had simply forgotten to have it trimmed. Not a handsome face, but an intelligent and sensitive one; perhaps even a little melancholic. He looked to me more like an artist, or a musician.

On the second night I found I had guessed correctly. After a sultry day it was pleasant to sit out in the cool courtyard reading by a rushlight one of the books Mrs Trevelyan had kindly brought to entertain us. And strange sounds reached me from the main house. Above a persistent drumming came the wail of some unfamiliar stringed instrument and then joined, I fancied, by a flute fluttering in cadences quite foreign to the European ear.

I thought I caught the sound of voices, men talking, quietly laughing, then some snatches of song. And after a few moments of silence the unmistakably deep rich tone of a cello playing an air I knew well but couldn't put a name to.

Zara came out through the beaded doorway and stood

beside me. 'Friend,' she said, pointing over the wall and then to me. 'Play music for husband of me.' It was the first time I had heard her try to speak English.

During our horseback outings together Gilbert Fairfield spoke of his family in Cheshire: his clergyman father, his half-blind mother and the three older sisters. The eldest had married a schoolmaster and they had a little boy of four. The second was recently engaged to marry, and it seemed that the youngest, to whom he felt closest, must stay at home to act as her mother's eyes.

He asked gently how long I had been widowed, assuming that this was the bond Isabelle and I shared. So I explained I had never had a husband to lose, but had assumed the title at Lord Sedgwick's persuasion, to make me a more suitable lady companion for his daughter.

If Gilbert disapproved of this deceit he gave no sign, turning his head away and remaining silent for some moments. When at last he spoke it was to point his whip to a falcon wheeling overhead and to tell me its name in Arabic.

I enjoyed his company, as I believed he did mine. We rode together each day, often out to Giza by the Route Josephine, which Napoleon had ordered to be built for his Empress. There we would leave our horses with a blue-robed dragoman and walk in the sand to admire the Sphinx.

He was in thrall to Egypt, and fascinated by the new-style archaeology which scorned the mere collection of ancient artefacts, concentrating instead on reconstructing the history of the periods they came from. He had met William Flinders Petrie, currently just returned from London to take over the dig at Abydos from the French. Now perhaps there would be better control of the valuable exhibits which had tended to find their way into private collections or be thrown out as rubbish by the Cairo Museum. Gilbert confessed his own ambition to become qualified to join him when released from the regiment.

I mentioned Isabelle's half-sister visiting Roman sites in Italy, and he said he had met her in Luxor almost a year back. She was very knowledgeable about pre-Christian religions, having written a monograph about engravings in the temple of Amun at Karnak.

It was as he enthused over the rebuilding taking place there that I felt a sudden urgent curiosity: as to how it would have been if he, and not the despicable Ralph Cruickshank, had been walking with me in the dark garden at Potsdam, him holding me helpless, backed against a tree.

'What is it, Eugenie?' he demanded, seeing me shiver. 'You haven't taken a chill? I'll never forgive myself if I've overtired you.'

And then there was curiosity no more, because he had taken me in his arms, and when he realized my eager submission he gently kissed my forehead, my cheek, and then found my mouth with his own.

So, in an instant, I was faced by the unbelievable: I was in love. And was loved in return. And the glory of it was like nothing I had ever imagined.

Five

For all that it was November the weather continued uncomfortably sultry, doing nothing to relieve the depressed state Isabelle had fallen into. She had no energy for anything and I feared causing offence to our new Egyptian friends by inflicting her uncertain temper on them longer.

'I really feel we must move on,' I told Mrs Trevelyan when next she came visiting.

She agreed, and suggested a journey upriver by passenger steamer, perhaps as far as Luxor. She would see to it, choose a vessel suited to Europeans and make bookings for four, including herself.

We had parted with Isabelle's maid Greta at Marseille, as her family needed her back in Berlin, and I was now responsible for her duties as well as my own. When I queried the numbers for our party, Mrs Trevelyan explained that she was including Lt Fairfield. He would soon be required back with his unit in the Sudan. She was sure he would take kindly to charming female company for part of the way.

I wondered if she could have guessed our secret, but I trusted his promise to say nothing until I had found a suitable moment to confide in Isabelle. While she was so taken up with her own misfortunes it seemed heartless to admit what happiness I felt. It took all my acting skill then to conceal the bubbling state of my heart. Gilbert treated us both with equal kindliness, and as the Nile's magic unfolded and the heat eased, Isabelle improved and even began to regain her teasing ways. She was quite taken by Gilbert, and I began to feel less uncertainty about confiding in her.

So much resting and rich foods of late had taken their toll of her dainty figure. I was kept busy with my needle letting out seams and adding small embroidered panels. She had grown accustomed to the looser robes her Muslim hostesses had recently provided, and in imitation of their flowing lines I converted a lilac wrapper into a quite passable lacy afternoon dress.

What did cause me some unease was the change in Isabelle's complexion as she again came into the open air. Despite her wide-brimmed hats and chiffon veils, there appeared strange blotches of brown pigment like outsize freckles, which required covering with calamine lotion before she would let herself be seen in public.

With all these distracting cares I had little enough time to talk privately with Gilbert about our future. He had explained there could be no announcement of our engagement until he had informed his colonel, and thereafter we must wait until I had completed my tour with Isabelle and she was returned to her family. I was impatient to begin our life together, but it seemed he must first fulfil his duties with the regiment and then look for some gainful occupation in civilian life.

He spoke no more of his ambition to study archaeology, and I took this to mean that once married he couldn't afford to become a student at Oxford. There would be no financial help towards this from his father because of existing family commitments. I had only a small savings account plus the undisclosed wage from Lord Sedgwick which waited for me in England, and

I doubted Mother would sanction any outlay on a penniless son-in-law. That had been no part of her plans for me.

It was frustrating to be held up by a mere matter of money. I even caught myself regretting that Papa had not thought to make some financial provision for me in his will, so that I might enjoy a modicum of independence. Perhaps he had meant to eventually, but put off the inevitable distressful conflict involved in accounting for it to my mother.

But as things had fallen out, I was not too dismayed. There might be some way in which Gilbert could follow his chosen work while learning from experts on site. And one surely ran up few personal expenses digging in a desert. For myself, riches were unimportant, and I would gladly starve myself to a scarecrow, just to be with my dear man.

With the future in mind I ventured to approach Isabelle, and quoted Mrs Trevelyan about agreeing a date to end our arrangement. I was in no way prepared for her histrionic reaction.

With a shriek like a gull's, she started from her chair, flushed, balled her fists and shook them at me. Then without a sound she fell to the carpet and all the colour drained from her face.

We had been in our quarters on the upper deck with the sliding door open on to the cool of a starry evening. Mrs Trevelyan, playing cards under the canopy aft, heard our commotion and instantly came hobbling in, barely beaten to it by a middle-aged commercial gentleman from Manchester. Between us we laid Isabelle on her bed. I loosened her clothing – she had forsworn stays for this journey – and waved smelling salts under her nose. The gentleman withdrew, embarrassed. Mrs Trevelyan, planted on the sole chair in our cabin, demanded how this collapse had come about and I told her.

If Isabelle's dismayed cry had sounded like a gull, the old lady's was the caw of a raven, full of something almost like malice. 'So now perhaps she must admit how badly she needs you.'

It struck me as a curiously heartless reaction to a young widow struck down by grief and loneliness. When I had made Isabelle's head more comfortable on her pillow, I turned back to ask quietly, 'Did you ever meet her late husband?'

'Hugo Delmayne? Indeed I did. A very pretty charmer, like herself. They were a pair, each competing to be more bewitching than the other. With the inevitable consequences.'

Before I could enquire what she meant, Isabelle's eyelashes fluttered and I bent close to catch her whispered words.

She clung on to my hand. 'Stay. Don't leave me, Genie. Promise you'll not go until I'm really fit and well.'

Behind me Mrs Trevelyan snorted, struggled to her feet and started to stomp out. 'I'm off to my cards,' she called back. 'I'd not trust a northern businessman not to peek at my hand!'

'Disagreeable old crone,' Isabelle muttered, struggling to sit up. 'She gets worse all the time. I really think her mind is going. She gets so confused when she can't remember things straight.'

She herself seemed to have forgotten that I'd made no answer to her plea, and I was thankful I had not mentioned my relationship with Gilbert. But retiring the next night as we lay moored off the jetty at Khmunu, she returned to the question of my service as companion. 'You're right. We should have drawn up some contract, Genie. It was

59

remiss of me. So let us do it now. Or when we reach Luxor I'll hunt out a lawyer with good English and we'll have it down in black and white.'

'That's hardly needed, Isabelle. At first we weren't to know whether we would get on well together,' I excused her. 'It could have proved awkward to make too binding an agreement straight off.'

'One could always have one written to include a clause that allows some escape,' she said airily. 'Not that we shall need anything of the sort now. You are so thoroughly satisfactory, and a dear friend besides. But let us settle on a date if you're feeling too permanently bound. I suggest we contract to stay together until Quarter Day in March. How does that suit you? If you agree, I will add one hundred pounds to whatever my grandfather is paying you.'

So much? But so long a time. And yet it would give Gilbert an opportunity to make all the necessary changes in his career. And how welcome the extra money would be to us. I was nearly tempted then to share our wonderful news with her.

'What do you say, Genie? Shall it be March? And by then I'll surely be quite my old self again.'

'March, if you wish. Yes.'

'Now I want your solemn promise, Genie,' she teased. 'It's too important a matter for us to be wishy-washy.'

I smiled, enchanted by her return to puckish spirits. 'You have my solemn promise. I'll not leave you before Quarter Day next March.'

'Good. And now will you cream all this horrid stuff off my face. After it's been on an hour it starts to crack and little specks rub off, to show the ugly brown spots underneath.'

'They're not ugly,' I lied. 'And besides, they're growing

less each day. I'm sure they'll disappear once you return to the English climate.'

The little steamer chugged and clattered and hooted its way south up the Nile in a slow, hazy dream of rich farmlands and poor peasant villages. We stopped often to unload goods or take on fresh provisions and there was ample time for forays into the hinterland to visit ancient ruins, camel markets or the occasional sugar plantation. This was my principal time spent with Gilbert, although other Europeans accompanied us from the steamer, so we were never left actually alone. I ached for more, as I knew he did, and every night I fell asleep imagining my head cradled on his shoulder.

Left on board, Isabelle and Mrs Trevelyan rested, played cards under the rear canopy, listened to the gramophone, and became increasingly irritated with each other.

Arrived at last at Luxor, and having settled us ladies in at our hotel, Gilbert continued by train to contact part of his unit camped outside Aswan. Two days later he was back with an invitation to take us there to see the gardens on Kitchener's island. He looked strange, with hair and moustache severely trimmed, his uniform immaculate, all suggestion of droop disappeared. Only his deep-set dark eyes reassured me, holding my own with a special intensity.

This extra journey of some hundred and thirty miles upriver was one which Isabelle declined, preferring to lie on the shaded balcony, drink chilled sherbet and eat innumerable confections of marzipan and dates. I offered to stay with her but she was in a strange self-punishing mood and wouldn't have it. I didn't press her, the last few hours with Gilbert being so precious.

Mrs Trevelyan was made of sterner stuff, endured the rat-tling train without complaint and, when we toured Aswan by horse-drawn gharry, regally waved to acquaintances, real or imagined, from under her lime-green parasol.

In the evening, while she rested at the Cataract Hotel, Gilbert took me by felucca to Philae where we walked along avenues of towering red granite walls and columns topped with lotus designs. As the sun sank into the west the stones seemed turned to blood, then chilled through blue-grey to black, as though all life had drained from a corpse. Tomorrow at first light, Gilbert told me, the rich colour would steal back, warm grey, rose, then peach, as though a body started to breathe again.

'This,' he said, 'is the temple of Isis, the greatest female deity revered by the Ancient Egyptians. She personified the Nile itself and regeneration: the Mother of Egypt.'

We had supper with Mrs Trevelyan at the hotel, where we were given excellent rooms facing on the river. Next day we all sailed across by felucca to Lord Kitchener's island for a picnic luncheon among the exotic blooms – but none more so than a great tree covered in white blossom which in an instant took to the air and flew off with strange hooting cries. Later we enticed some of these lovely birds to come close and I was told they were white egrets.

We returned early next morning by train to Luxor. Isabelle was still torpid, unwilling to make any effort to go out. On our last afternoon while she and Mrs Trevelyan slept we stole away to visit Karnak, the immense temple Gilbert had spoken of with such knowledge when in Cairo. He was in lecturing mood again and I listened more to his dear voice against the clopping hooves of the gharry horse than to the actual words he said, but I gathered his message.

When we entered the columned halls the engraved figures said it all. This great ruin of Amun, more like a city than a series of temples, was dedicated to fertility, just as Egypt owed its life to the fertility of the Nile. 'Before Christianity,' my lover said, 'nothing was thought immodest in illustrating the physical function of man and woman. It was recognized as compelling and good and natural, the pure source of all life. In its deepest mysteries this religion was a celebration of sex.'

As we stood alone among these towering columns he bent and put his arms tenderly about me, his voice no more than a whisper. 'I must be sure your eyes are open, Eugenie, when you come to me. One hears such abominable stories of ignorant young women panicked by the realities of their wedding night, and their husbands left impotent by the experience. Then what happy love there's been flies out the window.'

He took my right hand and laid it on the extended phallus of the god carved in profile on the wall beside us. And I left it there, my heart beating so hard in my throat that I could barely speak.

In that rare moment I understood so much that had been mystery before. At last I told him fervently, 'I am ready, my dearest. I shall be most willing when I come to you.'

We walked back hand in hand through the monstrous hypostyle hall in silence, and I knew then that I wanted to bear his children, and stay long years with him to watch them grow and have children of their own. My mind was in turmoil at the newness of it all, but I never thought it strange that I was inspired to passion by the graven image of a pagan god.

That evening after dining in our hotel, we were all to take a last carriage ride together along the moonlit river bank before Gilbert left for good. Isabelle had suddenly recovered her spirits and was at her most delightful. But in rising from the table, she managed to catch the lace hem of her dress under a chair leg, and since she needed it for the next morning's visit to a local fortune-teller, I was obliged to stay behind and mend the tear. Unhappily I watched Gilbert hand the two ladies into the carriage and swing up beside them, saluting me as I stood alone on the balcony.

I told myself to be patient. On Quarter Day in March I would be freed from all obligations. Our time would come when we should drive off, the two of us together, and no one would ever take my place again. And yet as I sewed I felt a sort of dread, hardly able to see my own stitches for the moisture in my eyes.

Alone at breakfast next morning, I was offered a small basket covered by a cloth. I thought it might contain fruit and I reached in my pocket for some small change to give the boy. But he shook his head. 'Lady, the effendi gives. Yesterday.'

Inside the basket was a tiny Egyptian kitten, and a note from Gilbert to say *au revoir*. He would write a little to me each day, but was not sure where he would be posted, nor how often the mail would go out from beyond Khartoum. If he learned we had already left Luxor he would arrange that it should be sent on to Alexandria, care of Mrs Trevelyan.

So, even although I was deprived of a last spoken good-bye, he had already written this and left it to cheer me on the first barren day after his departure.

The following morning Mrs Trevelyan announced she would return to the Delta. Although for some reason they were not on perfect terms, Isabelle was upset at this. 'You're all abandoning me,' she accused. 'Nobody cares what will become of me.'

I accompanied the elderly lady to the steamer that was ready to cast off its moorings, and saw her luggage safely installed in her cabin. 'Rest assured, Isabelle's malaise will cure itself,' she told me firmly as we said goodbye.

'Just a few days, I know, and she will be quite over this. She has simply not taken to the climate and is feeling sorry for herself. I would advise you both not to delay your return to Europe, although there's nothing really wrong with her, and little chance that she will lose the baby.'

I must have stared like a ninny, but luckily she was busy with her luggage dockets, so may not have noticed my shock.

She looked forlorn, standing apart from the others on the stern deck, and slowly growing smaller with distance. I waved until the little steamer grew indistinct, just a silver smudge on the Nile's shimmer, under a dark smoke smear against the perfect sky. Then I made all speed back to confront Isabelle.

'I was waiting to tell you.' She sounded petulant, as if Mrs Trevelyan should have kept the information from me.

But such stupendous news! Coming upon my own delight at the prospect of marriage and children, I could only be happy for her to have at least that living memory of the man she had loved. I said as much and she covered her own emotion well.

'Yes, well, there is that, of course.'

'But, Isabelle, Mrs Trevelyan is right. You shouldn't be risking your health out here. We must get back to . . .' I had almost said 'civilization', but stopped myself in time. '. . . to hospitals and midwives as soon as we can manage.'

'Yes, I suppose.' She spoke flatly. 'I had rather hoped . . . but there was little enough time for that. If only I had

65

not been so indisposed in Cairo, things might have fallen out more to my advantage.'

I let her ramble on, taking little notice, my mind full now of plans for her extra safety and comfort. But when I spoke of them she snapped at me. 'Oh, do be quiet, Genie. You simply don't understand anything.'

Short tempers and tears were, I knew, all part of the long uncomfortable months of waiting, and as a young widow Isabelle had so much more than that to distress her. There were a dozen questions I wanted answered: particularly how soon the baby would arrive; whether she had been able to give her husband the good news before his departure to South Africa; whether her family had known of her condition before she set out on this prolonged tour without a medical attendant. But clearly my concern was distasteful to her just then. For a while I must be patient for us both, because my first tentative questions were met with snapping anger.

Suddenly she burst out, 'Do you think I could *want* this wretched baby? I would have had it seen to in England before we left, but I was too frightened. I won't have them cut me about. I couldn't stand the pain. And besides, they could have killed us both!'

Unreason was another symptom, as I understood the condition. I must not look shocked, but calmly take in all she said, however appalling. To distract her I brought the kitten from my room and explained it was a gift from Gilbert.

She looked at it with disdain. 'What good is a kitten?' Then a little warmth came back into her eyes. 'But surely there was some note with it?'

'Yes. But it was private.'

'Then may I have it? Really, Eugenie, I don't understand you holding it back.'

'Private to me, Isabelle.'

'To *you?*'

She was affronted, but this time I instantly saw the reason. She had imagined some special relationship growing between herself and Gilbert, or at least had hoped for it.

He would never willingly have given her that impression, his behaviour towards her always being sympathetic and brotherly, as was proper for the recent widow of a fellow officer.

And besides they had spent so little time alone together. Except, of course, for that last evening when I had been left behind. Mrs Trevelyan had mentioned that she stayed with Mahmoud in the carriage while the younger pair went for a stroll. But it was impossible that Gilbert could have forgotten his feelings for me, however charming and superior he found Isabelle then.

Disturbed but not threatened, I went across to draw the blinds against the sun, checked that there was lemon water in the carafe by her bed, gathered up the kitten and quietly withdrew. All the time her huge, indignant eyes followed my every movement. It wasn't perhaps acceptable that a lady companion should attract someone her employer was drawn to, but I had no quarrel with it, and in my happiness could not foresee any damage.

Later, when we met before afternoon tea, I tried again to put my doubts to her about her health.

'The truth is, Isabelle, that I feel myself quite useless. I know so little about what is required to nurse a mother and baby. The whole business is a total mystery to me. I have to confess I even have no idea of how a child comes into the world. I mean physically, just what part of one it comes out of.'

She turned to look full at me. Her blue eyes seemed

to have become coldly opaque, as if a shutter cut off the person behind.

'I hadn't imagined even you could be so ignorant. But then you appear to have spent your life so far among the middle-aged and elderly.'

She stalked to the mirror and watched me in it as she dabbed her face with powder. 'Babies come out by the way they get in, of course. And for God's sake don't tell me I have to instruct you on that too. Even if you're not a country girl, you must have seen dogs performing in the streets.'

Her scorn was like a sharp slap on my cheek. So much for the fertile gods of Egypt; for my own desire for Gilbert.

No, I assured her: she would not need to explain that.

Dogs in the street, yes. It was to Papa that I owed that much understanding. When as a child I had pointed, amazed, at a frantically coupling pair, he had gently explained: 'They are making puppies. That is the way it's done. But for them it's a private matter, so we look the other way and walk on, child.'

Over the years I had worked out the human side for myself, checking my guesses with a discreet but knowledgeable friend at school, and it had seemed to me then that my parents must very much have wanted to have me, for them to have attempted anything so extraordinary and uncomfortable. Later I was to see the act as marital duty, but couldn't imagine how I'd ever comply with what was required. How far off that seemed now.

Isabelle was biting at her lip, clearly put out. I was ashamed of having vexed her in her frail condition.

'I'll find a book on the matter,' I promised. 'I believe there are such things to be had. But Isabelle, are you sure you should stay abroad? It would be so much safer for you in England with doctors and nurses whom you know and who speak the same language.' I was distressed for her, babies being so alarmingly big when you considered the tiny space they had to get through – if Isabelle was right about that, and I supposed she must be, for lack of an alternative. If only Mother or my teachers had thought to instruct me properly.

Now she was gnawing at the inside of her cheek, near to tears. 'I cannot go back! Especially where I'm known. Such scandal! No, I shall hide away in secret, whatever I decide to do about it in the end. It is just a question of finding the right people and paying them enough.'

To do what? It frightened me then. She had said 'whatever I decide to do about it'. 'It' surely being the unborn child – a helpless little human creature. And after her declared horror of being 'cut about', surely she could never contemplate having it destroyed before birth, as I once heard our washerwoman had done at St Leonards?

And then again, what scandal? Why must there be secrecy at all?

'You still don't see, do you?' And she actually stamped, her hands balled into fists as if she would like to strike at me.

But suddenly – at last – I did see. Or guessed. 'When,' I faltered, 'did your husband leave for South Africa?'

'Last November,' she said coldly.

Already a year ago. And she needed me with her until this coming March, by when she should be fully recovered.

A baby took nine months, I knew. So there would indeed be scandal. I had picked up enough court gossip while in Isabelle's company to know that there were many illicit liaisons among the married rich and powerful of the land. Husbands were sometimes deceived and – after they already had an heir – kept silent any doubts about

Six

i

We remained upriver another week at the hotel in Luxor, a time of uneasy waiting: for Isabelle the dreary endurance of gestation, and for me the frustrating absence of any message from the Sudan.

Bitterly disillusioned, I understood at last what Isabelle had been about in her desperate attempts to attract unattached men, as though in so short a time she could deceive one into marriage before the child's presence became evident. She had failed her family once by eloping, now she would do anything to prevent greater shame.

While I grieved for her dilemma I was beset by anxiety on my own behalf. It was as though Gilbert had been swallowed up by some dark presence lurking beyond the cataract at Aswan.

I hated the war machine that had sucked him in, even as I pitied the men who were obliged by their sense of duty to surrender their God-given right to free choice, submitting to the orders of senior officers possibly of less experience or judgement than themselves. By now I was familiar enough with the accounts of earlier campaigns to share Mrs Trevelyan's doubts about both the British and Egyptian higher command. Even more about the

71

politicians safe at home who governed their supplies and reinforcements. Their memories were short for wars they considered over. Even in South Africa now they ignored the endless local skirmishing simply because a peace with the Boers had been concluded on paper. And all the time lives were being lost, good men wasted, families bereaved, while in London governments fell and were replaced by parties of opposite interests.

I was too aware that Gilbert was no soldier by nature. He might not be of the stuff to survive an arduous campaign. I would have given anything then to be sure he would return fit and well to Cairo, to his friends and his violoncello, even if by then I might not be there to share him with them.

Although his return to duty was at a time when all appeared under control, nothing could guarantee that a second mad Mahdi might not rise up and fire the dervishes to fresh atrocities. The same passion must still be burning in secret among those savage mixed races united under Islam.

The Arabs in Sudan still controlled the wealthy slave trade, and there was equally fierce opposition to it. Money and principles were causes over which men went passionately to war. And such hideous accidents happened besides. I feared another steamer disaster at the cataract, as when so many servicemen on board had been drowned.

I began to see even in Egypt itself a dangerous mixture of peoples, like an experiment with chemicals which could suddenly ignite and explode. I needed to get Isabelle away. We were too near a source of trouble and she became daily more vulnerable. Yet I could hardly bear to distance myself from the place where Gilbert would be brought out if he were hurt in an engagement with the enemy.

At Luxor I went down every morning for the mail, which

Isabelle had arranged to have kept at the reception desk and sealed in a package under her name. Most times there was nothing. Mrs Trevelyan sent two notes from the Delta. There was a communication from the Cairo branch of Isabelle's bank. For me no more than an invitation from a school-friend to her wedding to a Hastings doctor: a voice from a lost lifetime. The envelope could barely have held another word, so many crossings-out had traced our journey from Deauville. Esther's wedding had taken place three weeks before the invitation's arrival.

With typical abruptness Isabelle decided on a return to the Delta. We shouldn't be travelling alone because Monsieur Tichard, a French archaeologist at our hotel, would be taking the same steamer in two days' time and would see to our comfort on the way. As if by now I wasn't competent enough to arrange everything myself. However, the decision was taken and at last we would be on the move. Once in Alexandria again, I felt sure I could persuade Isabelle to cross to Europe and make sensible plans for the birth.

On the morning that she made up her mind there had been a budget of letters, and I had such hopes that there would be one in it for me, but I was sent to the souk for rose-water while she read it all through, so I had to hold my eagerness in check. And on my return there was nothing from the Sudan.

I knew in my heart that Gilbert would do as he'd promised, writing some lines each day. Surely by now he could have contrived to get a message to me?

'I thought,' Isabelle wondered aloud, 'that we might have heard from our friend the Lieutenant before we left. But it seems he's like all the others; accepts one's hospitality and soon forgets. I fear we were made use of by him. It had struck me he was sadly ignorant of etiquette.

A disorganized young man. The cavalry will have its work cut out to trim him into shape.'

'I found his manners admirable,' I retorted hotly. 'And he's not ungrateful. In fact it should be the other way about. We'd much to thank him for. Perhaps he assumes we've gone back with Mrs Trevelyan, and his letters will be waiting for us there.'

'You've much to learn about men, Genie.' Isabelle stretched out in her *chaise-longue* and assumed a voice of jaded experience. 'There's little they require of a woman that can be provided at arm's length, let alone with miles between. No, if you'd any expectations there, let me assure you, he has galloped off into the sands and we shall hear no more of him.'

I might have been angry with her but for the faith I had in Gilbert's true affection. It overrode all else. But I marvelled at her angelic mouth uttering such coarse cynicism.

Monsieur Tichard fussed over marshalling our luggage, to the extent that I could have snapped at him. He made it seem so complicated, and himself so deserving of exaggerated praise. He was a political person, forever considering what benefit he could gain from his next move. He spent much of his free time in Isabelle's company, even persuading her to walk with him in the hotel garden where he paraded with my kitten, which he'd presumed to name Minou, sprawled across one shoulder like half an astrakhan collar. The little creature was terrified by such a height and clung on fiercely with its claws. When he finally decided to dislodge it, and one wild paw slashed at his exposed cheek, he pulled the kitten away and threw it to the ground.

On board he arranged for our three cabins to be adjacent, bullied the waiters to serve us in advance of other travellers and was generally over-attentive. When he pressed us to taste the range of French wines he had brought aboard (because the Muslim menu offered no alcohol) it was mainly to indulge his own considerable thirst for them, and the end of the first evening found him unsteady on his feet as he escorted us to retire for the night.

Whether or not his mistake was due to his being befuddled, I found his presence in my cabin at two the next morning, seated across the foot of my cot, more distasteful than alarming. His fingers touched my bare shoulder as he pulled back the sheet, and his eyes burned darkly above the pointed beard.

'You?' he exclaimed thickly, when moonlight struck my face as I roused. He recoiled, then leaned close again. 'But why not?'

My reaction was rapid enough. With both hands against his hard chest I pushed him backwards. Then I was out on the floor and through the door before he had recovered himself. The watchman came running when I called, and I coldly explained that M. Tichard had mistaken my cabin for his own.

Whatever he thought, the big Egyptian was impassive, bowed the effendi to his own quarters, then came back to examine my door chain. It was loose so that, with the door left a fraction ajar for air, there was room to insert a finger from outside and lift it off. This time, despite the oppressive heat, I locked myself in and listened while the watchman padded quietly away.

Monsieur Tichard had obviously not expected to find *me*, but Isabelle. I was thankful for his mistake. Such a fright in her condition was unthinkable. Now that the watchman was alerted he would make sure there was no repetition.

The Frenchman left our steamer next evening when we tied up at Esna. He had advised neither of us of his intention to do so, but it was clearly planned because there were three Europeans waiting on the jetty for him, one a youngish woman who threw her arms round his neck and kissed him passionately.

'His wife, one assumes,' Isabelle remarked drily. 'Well, I should have guessed.'

She retired to her cabin early and I remained sewing on deck by the light of an oil lamp. There were three dresses to alter, as she had grown another two inches round the waist.

Soon work was made impossible by flying insects constantly dashing themselves against the lamp. I took the dresses to Isabelle, meaning to collect Minou for her evening meal. But the kitten wasn't to be found.

Unusually, the cabin was in darkness. 'She's probably gone off with the Frenchman,' Isabelle mumbled from her cot. 'Well, there's less to trouble with.'

I searched all our part of the steamer, and had one of the crewmen look below in their quarters, but we never found the kitten.

In the morning Isabelle took me to task for negligence, claiming I'd left something sharp in the seam of one dress after adding a pin-tucked panel down the front. She had torn her cheek and one wrist when trying it on.

I apologized, but scantily, knowing I'd used no pins before basting the material into place. Isabelle must have caused the scratches herself on a badly fastened brooch, and I thought no more about it at the time.

There was considerable delay that morning in taking on some wooden crates, because the lading lists were incomplete, and a deal of arguing went on well towards midday. I took the opportunity to go ashore and walked downstream to where some camels were being watered. Nearby a small donkey was plodding in circles to turn a water-wheel. Above the creaks of straining wood and camel-leather thongs came the shrill sound of children's voices as they played on the bank farther down.

They were burnt almost prune-black by the sun and wore little enough, their slippery bodies gleaming with water. They tumbled about together in innocent glee like puppies, breaking off to try who could throw a stone farthest towards a target bobbing in the river. I walked in their direction, my fingers sorting out small coins in my baksheesh pocket.

When they noticed me, some puffed out their little chests to show off and redoubled their throwing efforts. The rest came rushing towards me for what they could get. I laughed and tossed the money in the air and they scrambled for it. Then I went across to see who was the best marksman.

The floating thing they aimed at was no goatskin bag but a dead kitten, already bloated by bodily gases in the hot sunshine.

I turned blindly away. I felt sudden terror for Gilbert, who'd given me the little creature. Dear God, let it not be an omen. For anything of his to be destroyed seemed the worst kind of augury for him.

I suppose I should have made the boys give me the little body so that it could be properly buried, but just then the steamer gave a single hoot. A puff of black smoke announced that at last the arguments were over and the goods for Cairo stowed. Unless I wished to be left behind I must make my way back and get on board.

I said nothing to Isabelle of what I'd seen. Perhaps as she had suggested, the kitten had followed the Frenchman on to dry land last night. Then it could have strayed and fallen in the river. I tried hard not to remember how callously he'd treated it before. But surely he had not deliberately killed it? I couldn't believe that my action in calling the watchman could have driven Monsieur Tichard to take such unspeakable revenge.

ii

'Darling,' Laurence said and touched the arm I was leaning on. My head had dropped forward and now my swimming eyes took in the marquetry surface of my walnut writing-desk. The image of the tiny, bloated carcass dispersed. The boys' voices, as they played on the Nile's banks, were replaced by my own children's, quarrelling in the next room.

'What is it, Eugenie?' Laurence demanded. 'You were in another world.'

'Nothing, my dear. I think I almost fell asleep.'

'You should have stayed longer in bed. It was a strenuous night,' he reminded me, smiling.

'A wonderful night.' I tried to sound roguish. 'Darling, do you think the children are actually killing each other?'

'No more than usual. This time I believe it's over some quite earth-shattering matter, such as who bent a lead soldier's sword.'

'I wish they hadn't to play at battles, Laurence.'

'You need never worry that Edwin will want a commission in the army. Lucy's the militant. Given time she'll make a fine suffragette, unless the fashion for it is over by then.'

'The cause won, I hope you mean.'

'As you wish, though Grandfather would turn in his ermined grave. Can you see your daughter in the Lower House at Westminster, an elected member? Because that's what they'll want next, once they're given the vote.'

A piercing scream brought me to my feet, and there was no more putting off sorting the children out. We took one each by the elbow and pulled them apart. 'Gentlemen do not attack ladies,' Laurence reminded his son firmly.

'Only cowards pick on someone smaller than themselves,' I admonished my daughter.

'He won't let me play with his soldiers,' Lucy wailed. 'And he never uses them himself.'

'Have you thought of offering him something in exchange?'

'He can have my old dolls!'

Laurence forestalled the next indignant outburst by suggesting that they should put on their rubber boots and wrap up for a walk in the rain. We would all go down to the river and see what damage the storm had done.

He had already been there with his steward and reported back to the Earl on levels of flooding in the water meadows. My father-in-law would have been distressed about the destruction of the Japanese bridge, which had been an anniversary gift from him to his second wife, mother of Laurence and Isabelle. Unlike the previous Earl who'd travelled widely and spent considerable time in London, he had never shown great interest beyond his own inherited estate and tenants. For him they had been a full-time occupation, and he'd devoted much thought to improving and beautifying house and lands.

In earlier days, when he could still speak easily, I'd heard him quote some lines of Alexander Pope which summed him up well: 'Happy the man, whose wish and care/ A few paternal acres bound/ Content to breathe his native air/ In his own ground.'

He had attended the House of Lords off and on, as a duty to monarch and country rather than to socialize with others of equal rank, and the only time I heard him enthuse about matters there was after mention had been made of Laurence's work in India for the Colonial Office. I was fond of the dear old man who had always shown great kindliness towards me.

'We should have had the bridge photographed,' Laurence said regretfully as we stood on the bank surveying its smashed base, the brave red paint all chipped and muddied. But, thank God, with no evidence of the drowned foreigner, as I'd dreaded.

'Your mother's so right, Eugenie. We're lagging behind in this age of wonderful inventions. It's up to us to encourage others to make use of them. We'll have not just a motor car, but a camera of our own, and we'll hire experts to teach us how to use them.'

'Can I learn, Papa?' Edwin begged. 'I should so love to drive a motor.'

Laurence laughed, lifting him in the air. 'All in good time, my lad. But Mama shall learn first and then you shall be her first passenger.'

'I'm to learn first?' I queried. 'To be your chauffeuse then?'

'Oh, I drive already. I frequently do in London. You see, there's plenty you still don't know about your husband. It's just that in the country I much prefer my horses. Now, which way shall we walk from here?'

'Down to the mill!'

'Upstream!'

The children shouted out together, and Laurence avoided further squabbling by awarding the choice to Lucy, since Edwin was promised the first motoring treat with me. So we turned and made our way down the river path, I with the greatest trepidation at what we might find at the junction with the mill-race.

Before we reached it, we came on a scene of disaster.

The police and helpers had finished there, leaving the mud churned up by their heavy boots, and deeper ridges where a gate or hurdle had been dragged up the steep bank as a makeshift stretcher.

So the body had not been carried so very far by the rushing current, because at this bend the willows, leaning to the raised surface of the water, must have tangled in his clothes and held him fast, face downwards in the flood. And still caught in their leafless wands were matchwood splinters of the little red bridge.

Laurence was aghast at realization of what we stood looking at. 'This must be where – Eugenie, I think we should make our way back now.'

The children were puzzled as much by our reaction as at the unusual appearance of the ground. 'What happened here?' Lucy demanded, astute as ever.

'Sadly, someone fell in,' Laurence answered, always believing we should tell the truth to our children. 'He was a stranger. Nobody we knew. Mama will take you back and ask Cook to make you hot chocolate. For myself, I've a fancy to walk a few minutes more, then I'll follow you indoors.'

I forced my mind to stay free of what had happened a hundred yards upstream no more than a few days back. Grateful for the sudden redoubling of the downpour, I drew the drenched hem of my skirts over one arm and raced with the children back to the shelter of the house and Nanny's care.

On his return Laurence found me trembling and sick in the first-floor bathroom. He ran water on a towel and wiped my forehead and the spittle from my mouth. 'Isn't it time you checked with John Millson?' he asked, holding me close.

'Perhaps.'

'Or some doctor in London, if you prefer. I would be so happy to know for sure that it is as we suspect.'

'I think it's no more than shock. At seeing where he – where the man – was pulled out.'

'Whatever it is, you need rest. I'm more sorry than I can say for taking you in that direction. It was a most disagreeable sight.' He threw the soiled towel in the bath, lifted me like a baby and carried me to our bed. Then he lowered the blinds so that the room was in half-darkness.

'I'll have Patsy come up with hot milk and brandy. Then promise me you'll sleep.'

I didn't deserve such consideration. How delicate and innocent he imagined me, and I let him continue without suspecting what far worse scenes I'd had to stomach and keep silent on.

I squeezed the hand that he laid on my shoulder, and he quietly left the room. Left me alone, to close my eyes and face the return of my persistent nightmare. On the back of my eyelids to see dark water swirling, a body endlessly falling; then back through time to other churned mud, with half-naked children throwing stones into the Nile. And bobbing on the water the hideous, bloated bag of fur. But this time, daring to outstare the kitten's empty, fish-nibbled eye sockets, I was quite sure. It really did have what I'd refused to believe on the actual occasion: a muddied mauve ribbon drawn tight about the strangled neck. The same kind of ribbon as in the little sewing-box Isabelle and I had shared on our journeys.

More ghastly still, as I seemed to watch, the body sank below the surface. And what rose in its place was the hideous drowned face of the man who had followed me, years later, all the way from Italy seeking blood money.

Seven

During our second stay at the hotel in Alexandria I thought often of Gilbert and longed for someone I could talk with about him. But I knew better than to mention him to Isabelle. Anything she might say would surely run counter to my trust in him.

When we had been together there were times when I seemed to be seeing with his eyes, from inside his mind, and feeling what he must feel. Gilbert too had somehow known in advance how I would act or speak. I saw then that that is what love is: an extension outside oneself, a projection into another's experience, so that we hardly know where we end and the other begins.

That was true enough of the little time we'd shared together, but now, separated by a thousand miles and in utterly different surroundings, how was such intimacy to continue? I warned myself that believing we shared a horror of warfare was a baseless assumption, because the Gilbert I had said goodbye to, spruce and soldierly, appeared almost a stranger. There must certainly be a part of him I had not met and might not comprehend.

But imagining beyond war and separation, I found myself living our future together, perhaps with Gilbert as a student assisting Flinders Petrie, working at the Abydos excavations for pocket money. It would be wonderful if he would include me in the dig. I was sure there were ways in which I could make myself useful, listing the finds and sketching them. I was quite handy with pencil and pen, even if I hadn't the knowledge and experience of the Professor's wife or of the impressive Misses Murray or Eckenstein.

Until I came to Egypt I had thought archaeology purely an occupation for hearty, horny-handed men, and although women had been equally fired by the fashionable interest, I had assumed their enjoyment went little beyond reading the illustrated books the presses were busily turning out for the general public. Then, learning from Isabelle that her half-sister had actually assisted at the recovery of Roman sites in Europe, I was sure I could do equally well because, not then having met Mildred, I assumed that the family had only a single mould for its female line. How unlikely that social butterflies could do better under demanding conditions than my down-to-earth self! So I rejoiced that even the field-work was proving possible for women.

Not that the professional men who spent their winters in Egypt, delving and labelling and fighting the bureaucratic bumbling of corrupt petty officials, were physically herculean. I understood that the Professor himself was far from robust, but driven by an insatiable thirst for knowledge. He would surely recognize the same fire in Gilbert and offer him a place at London University when he returned to England at the end of the digging season.

Then perhaps I would travel up to Cheshire and spend some months with my husband's family, the clergyman father and the half-blind mother, with frequent visits to the married sisters nearby who by then would both have children. And there would be babies of my own, Gilbert's and mine. Three perhaps, or maybe four. Two of them at least would be musical. I wasn't sure what gifts I could hand on. One might have my black hair and dark eyes, but what else? Gilbert had spoken of my serenity, which had drawn him from the first. But he hadn't guessed then at the tumult hidden inside.

Uncertain, I dared to ask Isabelle what she thought my special talents were. She looked at me for a long moment, head tilted, then said, 'Deception, Genie. You're certainly gifted at that.'

It was shameful. And by now quite true. I had to turn away so that she shouldn't see the effect of her words on me.

If I had never met her I would have stayed a more honest person. But then I would never have known Gilbert, nor perhaps the wonderful obsession of young love.

There were other British junior officers on leave in the Delta. Out of sympathy I tried to see something of Gilbert in them, but they appeared so trivial, in love with their uniforms, or their wit or their own slim, boyish figures. Possibly as deceptive as I was, they disguised any finer selves as easily as whatever hideous experiences they had endured. I looked in vain for sad, smouldering eyes with little drooping folds. Instead these others stared back with either smirking or bold invitation, making me want to escape from their presence.

These young men seldom came across Isabelle. She had by now given up her pathetic attempts at salvation through a hasty marriage, becoming a total hermit, shunning Mrs Trevelyan and hiding now even from strangers. She cowered in her suite, often in bed all day. Lack of exercise made her listless, her body heavy and her complexion blotched. I was becoming anxious for the growing baby's health. It was essential she seek medical advice, but she stubbornly ruled that she wasn't ready. It was during this torpid state that she received an unexpected telegram brought up by the hotel's bellboy.

For me the sight of that official-looking envelope could only mean disaster. I felt a strange tightening of the chest and my ears were full of the sort of sea sounds that you hear from a conch. This message had to be news that Gilbert was wounded, or even worse. He would not otherwise have had me contacted through Isabelle. It seemed likely that he had chosen her to be the one to break it to me gently.

I started mechanically to pay the boy at the door.

'Reply?' he demanded.

'You'd better wait.' He bowed and I took the hateful envelope through to Isabelle's boudoir. She was lying on a couch by the long window, unbathed and with her blond hair tousled. She stared at the envelope as if I'd brought her the means to kill herself.

'The boy's waiting for an answer,' I said flatly.

'It's pre-paid?'

'I assume so. Unless he's been instructed to wait in every case.'

With febrile fingers she tore at the flimsy paper, rapidly scanned the words inside, groaned, read again, turned the sheet to see if anything was written on the blank reverse, then whispered, 'Dear God! Dear God, what shall I do?'

Shamefully a wild hope sprang to life inside me. Some disaster personal to her? Not concerning Gilbert at all?

'My brother,' she managed to get out. 'He's on his way here. Oh, what shall I do? Where can I go? Genie, you'll have to stop him. He'd guess at once.'

'How can I stop him? Be reasonable, Isabelle.'

A new panic seized her: 'You can't betray me. Genie, swear you'll never betray me!' She buried her face in her hands and rocked from side to side in near dementia.

I scorned to answer any accusation so demeaning and

86

pathetic, took the telegram from her clenched fingers and read out the printed heading.

'The office of origin is Suez. It was handed in this morning at eight.'

Isabelle peered out through her fingers. 'That would be when his ship put in there from India.'

'Or he left this with the signals officer on board, to send after his departure. He could be here by road at any moment.'

'Does it make any difference *when*? He's *coming*. That's disaster enough. Now he'll guess what's happened to me. He'll feel compelled to tell Grandfather. Who'll cut me off. And I've hardly *any* money of my own.'

Avarice was a poor means of persuasion. She must have seen my expression stiffen, for she sat straight then, screwing up her face like a baby about to howl. She beat against the windowsill with a balled fist. 'Genie, you *have* to help me. I need you to get me through this! For God's sake, think of something! Can't you get me away before he catches up with us?'

Not knowing her brother's likely hour of arrival, I doubted it was possible. And rough travel could be dangerous in her condition, even if I appealed to the Egyptian Bey in whose Cairo house, Qasr el Mastaba, we'd taken refuge before. No, that was unthinkable, because his wives would see she was expecting a child and enquire why her own family was not protecting her.

'Isabelle, it's not practicable, in your condition. You haven't set foot outdoors for days. And if you rush off the very moment this telegram arrives it will look suspicious. There will be speculation. When he arrived to find you flown, someone in the hotel would be bound to talk. That would be worse than staying to face him.'

'I can't, I can't! Genie, you don't understand. To him

87

I'm the innocent little sister. I can't bear him knowing. Imagine the look in his eyes!'

That pained cry had more influence on me than her fear of being cut off from her life of luxury. A threat to reputation has some persuasive power, but affection even more. I put my arms around her and a little of my rectitude began to thaw. Isabelle was at last showing feeling for someone beyond herself, as I thought.

Compassion was to bind me further and drive me into fresh deception. It seemed that my fated path now was one of increasing dishonesty. There was little choice left me.

I read the telegram through. 'It says here, "visit you briefly". That sounds as if he doesn't intend to stay overnight. It could be that he has only an hour or two while his ship steams through the canal and takes on fresh passengers at the port here. And travel overland will have eaten into even that. Over such a short time perhaps you can contrive to conceal your condition. If indeed you feel you must. But eventually your family will have to know.'

'I'm not ready for exposure.'

So we were forced to dissemble. It would be impossible for Isabelle to remain hidden, lie low and avoid discovery, because everyone in the hotel knew where she was to be found.

But how had *he* got to know her whereabouts?

'Isabelle, did you write to him? Did you send him your address?'

'Of course not. You know how careful I've been to cover my tracks.'

She frowned. 'Yes, it is strange he's discovered where I am. Could it be through the Foreign Office? How frightening! Do they have information on every British person abroad?'

'There would hardly be paper enough to keep records

like that. Nor spies enough.' Then a suspicion struck me. 'Isabelle, what was your brother doing in India?'

'He went out to stay with the Viceroy. Then he was to go to the North-West frontier.'

'Is he a soldier, then?'

'No. He's a government official. What was it they called him? A Something-or-other Extraordinary.'

'Plenipotentiary?'

'That's right. We were all amused when he told us. Grandfather said he should be sure to have that engraved on his tombstone. It was so gloriously pompous.'

He worked for the Colonial Office. So he might have heard of her through one of his colleagues. But how much had he heard? 'Isabelle, doubtless he'll explain when you see him.'

'I won't see him. It's out of the question.'

'Isabelle, listen. You must receive him, but we can arrange that he doesn't notice your condition,' I said with more confidence than I felt.

'He's not blind. And he's not a fool. I'm twice the size of the sister he knew before.'

'On your feet and moving about, it might be evident, but in bed? Or on your couch here, with the blinds half drawn? We could say you had injured your foot. I could bandage your ankle to look like a sprain. Then with some shawls thrown over, we could disguise your outline. If you find the interview drags, you can always plead fatigue, being ordered by the doctor to rest.'

She ran her tongue over dry lips. 'You think it will work?'

'It's worth trying. So let's get ready. First, you must take a shower, then I'll make you look pretty in your best lace wrapper. If there's a chance before your brother arrives, I'll let it be known to other guests that you've fallen and had a slight accident. Then if he chances across any of them they'll tell the same story.'

All this time of discussion I had quite forgotten the bellboy. As I left Isabelle's suite I found him patiently waiting, seated cross-legged beside the outer door; a charming lad rigged out like a pet monkey, in voluminous purple Turkish trousers, white shirt, black bolero jacket and red, tasselled fez. I paid him well for the delay and scribbled a rapid note: 'Delighted at prospect of seeing you – Isabelle', for him to take back to the telegraph office.

The message must only have reached the ship after her brother had left, because he was with us within an hour and a half of his telegram's delivery.

I caught a glimpse of him as I slipped back into my own room by the private door from Isabelle's boudoir. Because she was small and fine-boned, I had expected that he too would be short. I should have remembered his long-limbed, autocratic grandfather, white-haired and white-browed, but pink and prominent-eyed as a boiled prawn. The father also was tall but a little stooping like someone accustomed to sit for long hours at a desk. This son was the tallest of the three, perhaps a couple of inches over six feet, and broad-shouldered with it. He had smooth, light brown hair, of much the same shade as his face, and a white-toothed, welcoming smile wide as a slice of melon. That was all that I took in of him as I quickly lowered my gaze and slipped away.

I was proud of the way I'd stage-managed Isabelle's big scene. With a little delicate touching up of her features she would pass muster in filtered light from the half-drawn blinds. Her couch was prettily arranged with a careless-seeming scatter of shawls, and the monstrously bandaged ankle in view at the end. Her smoothed cushions were dabbed with cologne. There were fresh flowers on a little table at her side, together with an opened book, a small brass and copper handbell and a straw box of Rahat Lakoum.

Despite all these precautions I was nervous, my hands trembling. I leaned my head against the door panel and unashamedly strained to hear their conversation, ready to run in and cause a diversion if anything went badly wrong.

In fear of discovery, Isabelle spoke rapidly, her voice high-pitched and a little breathless, but it would be easy to take this for excitement at reunion with a much-loved brother. His voice was deep and warm with a little lift sometimes at the end of a phrase, as though he smiled often. The interview was going well. I dared to go down and order lemonade and honey cakes to be sent up for them.

He stayed for precisely half an hour, as though deliberately measuring it; whether to accommodate the invalid or his own need to rejoin his ship, I couldn't say. I watched from the window as he stepped up into the waiting gharry, a lean figure in a pale tan linen suit. He was trotted away without giving a backward glance.

I bounded into Isabelle's presence. 'We did it!' she almost shouted. Then she frowned. 'At least, I think we did. It's not always easy to read Lolly's mind. But surely if he'd had any suspicions . . . Still, whatever he thought, he said nothing.'

'He took his time saying nothing. I heard a continuous buzz of voices and quite a lot of laughter.'

'He was telling me about his work in India, and some of the interesting people he meets. Oh, and see on that chair, what a beautiful sari he's brought me. I shall be able to wrap myself in that like a bundle of washing, right up until the confinement!'

The length of fabric was of fine, matt silk, saffron yellow

91

with embroidery in gold thread, turquoise and jade green. Isabelle slid from her couch and swathed it about her. It was a joy to see her so animated again.

'Did you discover how he came to know you were here?'

'Yes. It was in a roundabout way. Apparently Mrs Trevelyan corresponds with a military aide on the Viceroy's staff, and she mentioned me in a letter. This gentleman knew of the family relationship and spoke of it *en passant* to Lolly. Lord, how people will gossip.'

'It's as well that Mrs Trevelyan is discreet. I assume she never hinted at your condition.'

'She wouldn't have known of it,' Isabelle claimed confidently, and I didn't remind her of how I'd come to know.

'But I think we should be very wary of that lady in future. I forbid you to have any but the briefest encounters with her, Genie, from now on.'

I said nothing, taking the sari from her and folding it carefully over a chair-back. Isabelle subsided again on the couch, then immediately sat upright, her eyes dancing. 'And guess what news: our half-sister Mildred is even now travelling by train to Calais. They both intend a family reunion for Christmas at Stakerleys.'

'Doesn't your brother expect you to do the same?'

'Not exactly expect. He enquired if I had that in mind. So I told him I'd other plans. We were bound for Turkey, and couldn't reach England before February.'

'Why Turkey, Isabelle? There are safer places than Constantinople for you to have the baby.'

'We shan't *really* be going there. I just said wherever came first into my mind. And there's always digging going on in Turkey, isn't there? If Mildred can get involved in this present archaeology craze, so can I. The family should take my interests as seriously as hers. More so, in fact, since I am a married lady.'

'Or you *were*,' I reminded her gently.

'Don't be stuffy, Genie. Anyway, once we're in Italy – since we're free to go there now that there's no risk of running into Mildred – I shall straightway contact a suitable gentleman to accompany us. A retired doctor, no less; which should set your mind at rest. I shall write to him today and arrange for him to meet us on our ship's arrival at Genoa.'

So she had had this final phase planned for some considerable time; perhaps even when she spoke to my mother of travelling to 'warmer climes' for the winter. Certainly she had mentioned France, Germany and farther south. But she had kept quiet the notion of Italy then, for a reason. It explained both her vexation at learning that her sister was in the country, and her restless inability to settle elsewhere.

'Will he recommend a hospital for your care?' I asked.

'We'll decide on that when we come to it.' Her voice bit me off like a thread of sewing silk. Clearly, I could be trusted so far but no further. After all these months together, she still dared not be totally open with me.

'How soon do we leave?' I persisted.

'As soon as I have a reply from Signor Gabrieli and have collected sufficient funds in advance from England. You'd better check through our luggage and get rid of any outgrown or summery dresses. We shall need to lay in warmer clothes for Italy. I rather fancy going shopping in Milan.

'And another thing you can do is see that all our acquaintances here know the same story I have given Lolly: that as soon as I am about again on my bad ankle we shall be leaving for Turkey.'

Her plans disturbed me. Despite the reassuring thought of a medical friend to accompany us, it struck me as headstrong to leave no clue behind as to where we'd gone. 'Italy' was too vague an address to give. I determined to take one friend into my confidence, explain Isabelle's real intention, as far as I knew it, and trust this friend not to disabuse anyone else of their belief that we were with a group of archaeologists in Turkey. Despite Isabelle's instructions, that one friend should be Mrs Trevelyan, whom time had proved to be open-minded and discreet. And besides, when any mail came through for me she would have some place to send it on to. I would tell her I could be reached *poste restante* at Milan's main post office.

Two days after I told her, Mrs Trevelyan suffered a fall and dislocated her hip. It was from the reception clerk that I learned she had been taken away in considerable pain. I set out at once to visit her, loaded with such newspapers and books as I could lay hands on.

She was being well looked after in the University Hospital, but pain and the reminder of ageing depressed her normal high spirits. Whenever I visited after that I thought it wiser to keep to local gossip and equally frivolous matters.

On the day before Isabelle and I were to leave for Genoa I recognized it was likely to be the final farewell. Mrs Trevelyan seemed shrunken and much older, more openly abrasive. It appeared that doctors had now found more than dislocation. There was an abnormality of the bone formation. The dreaded disease was not named, but it was evident she knew the worst and refused to pity herself.

We sat for some time in silence, and she seemed content

to have it that way. Then at last, turning away to stare from the window, she said in a low voice, 'I am disappointed in you, Eugenie. I had not thought you so cold-hearted and neglectful.'

Her words pierced me. I couldn't believe she meant them. I had truly suffered for her, with her. Now, on top of that, I must feel guilt for having offended her at the end. I left Egypt with that extra misery and puzzlement, still yearning for news of Gilbert, lost to me in the deserts of Sudan.

Eight

We left Alexandria on a leaden day. The water within the harbour slowly tilted and heaved, an unpleasant gunmetal grey under a slaty sky. It did nothing to relieve my sense of gloom, but for Isabelle's sake I put on a cheerful manner and was promptly scolded by her for my 'damned insensitivity'.

Once she was installed in our shared cabin I went on deck to watch the final loading by giant cranes, silently addressing her *in absentia*. 'Despite everything, I still respect you, Isabelle, and I expect to receive equal courtesy in return.'

So straight-backed schoolmistressy, it was worthy of the elder Miss Court-Withington herself and I laughed out loud. Ignoring the curious gaze of a dark-skinned crewman, I unpinned and removed my travel hat. As yet there was no real wind so I resisted the temptation to let down my hair. Even in mid-sea I denied myself that pleasure, leaving it tightly swathed. I was so much older now than the *ingénue* schoolgirl who had crossed the Channel, screaming back at the gulls, less than five months before. Older and far less carefree.

Perhaps it was the knowledge that we travelled northwards that eventually persuaded me to go below for warmth. Certainly the brilliantly lit saloon was more welcoming than the high, dim smudge of sun no brighter than a sooty gas globe. I ordered Isabelle's meals to be served in her cabin and myself took luncheon in the first-class dining-room. The menu was still Egyptian, and I relished the length of crossing that should allow me to adapt my mind from Africa back to Europe.

I knew little of Italy beyond the geography skimpily touched on at school. But newspapers that reached us earlier from London had been full of the assassination of King Umberto, now succeeded by his son Victor Emmanuel III.

What was the idea that obsessed these murderous anarchists? Could anyone truly prefer chaos to order? Or was it only an intermediate stage they required before imposing an alternative cruel autocracy? Otherwise it must be a form of madness; perhaps in reaction to the rigid discipline of the priesthood in a Catholic country? But that could be ingrained Protestant prejudice on my part: bigotry was an unattractive vice and too widespread already. I should need to be open-minded to take in all the wonders of this new country, staying curious about how ordinary people lived, between such opposite forces and with a formidable pre-Christian heritage.

In Britain, it seemed to me, we were more fortunate, being a healthy mixture of races, religions and politics. One heard of anarchists certainly, and they had made bloodcurdling threats against the monarchy, but nothing was likely to dislodge our own dear Queen. We had no real zealots. Unless one counted the feminist suffragettes and the minority following of eccentric socialists like Mr Keir Hardie.

I abandoned such serious matters and gladly went back on deck.

A stiff breeze blew up when we were a few miles out and

continued for the rest of the crossing. It whipped up huge waves topped by scummy white bubbles like the foam on a glass of porter. Next morning I staggered along creaking corridors to reach the open deck, passing myself from handgrip to handgrip to the port side where it blew less. And I found the wind had opened up the sky with great patches of cobalt blue. So when at length we reached Genoa it seemed the world was reversed, because Europe was in bright December sunshine while we'd left Africa heavily overcast.

There was a deal of fuss over our luggage before I could deliver Isabelle by cab to the hotel she mentioned. But we were not to put up there. I was instructed to remain in the cab, parked with our bags at the kerbside, while Isabelle looked in the lounge for the physician who was to take care of her.

She returned within five minutes followed by a short, slight man whom she introduced as Signor Gabrieli and addressed gushingly as 'Dottore'. He took the seat beside her, so, sitting opposite, I was able to study his appearance.

He would have been in his mid-forties, swarthy with near-black hair and a matching pointed beard which showed streaks of grey. His face was lined, hard-set like a head carved in a tough wood such as teak. It seemed strange that with so little mobility his features should carry such deep tracks of past – of past what? – emotion of some kind: suffering, perhaps.

All this time he had kept his head lowered, listening to Isabelle's chatter, so I hadn't met his eyes. When eventually he looked up, at some reference of Isabelle's to me, I was shocked by them. They were a shiny black like anthracite, but shifty. And I knew the set face was a mask, with some quite different person hidden behind it.

98

The fugitive eyes slid away. He made some humming acquiescence to whatever Isabelle had been saying and left me to continue my survey. His dark frock-coat was old-fashioned and well worn, the shiny edges of its cuffs frayed and badly mended. Below them his fingers were nervously cramped, the nails split and not quite clean.

My heart sank. I was overwhelmed by the certainty of coming disaster. I recognized now the look I had caught in his eyes. *Il dottore* was a failure, and he knew it himself.

'Where are we bound for?' I demanded abruptly, cutting into Isabelle's flow.

She gave me the familiar little chin-tilted smile that meant she was at last confiding what had been a cleverly withheld secret. 'We go directly to Milan, by train. There are places reserved for us in the dining-car.'

More upheaval and transfer of luggage, more swarming porters attracted this time by the doctor's lavish use of the title *Contessa*. Isabelle shrugged it off. 'English titles are so difficult for foreigners to grasp.'

I installed her in relative comfort and paid the men off from Isabelle's purse. I had guessed Signor Gabrieli would be low in funds, and he'd ensured high expectations among the porters with his silly show of snobbery.

Isabelle had exhausted herself with the brief burst of vivacity. She seemed not to notice the state of the doctor's hands when he took her pulse, but lay back flaccidly in the rail carriage with one wrist posed theatrically against her brow and wished she was at journey's end.

Our suite at the Milan hotel was magnificent, high-ceilinged and cold as a Norfolk barn. I dismissed Signor Gabrieli to whatever accommodation he had arranged for himself, ordered a fire lit in Isabelle's bedroom and quickly had her tucked up with three stone hot-water bottles and a Shetland shawl for her shoulders.

She demanded brandy to wash down the tablets the doctor had given her, but she was asleep before I brought it. So I thankfully sipped it myself and put the tablets away in the pocket of my chinchilla muff. I told myself they might be of use at some later time, but already I was doubting the man's ability to prescribe wisely.

Next day Isabelle rose just before noon, took a light meal of soup and fish, then immediately insisted on going shopping. I was not required to accompany her. She went out on Signor Gabrieli's arm, her pale face heavily veiled. They were away just over an hour and my misgivings were increased when their return was not followed by a shower of purchases.

I believed Isabelle's pregnancy was too far advanced by now for her to risk an abortion, but my knowledge of such things was very limited, and I feared that in Italy the same precautions were not observed as would be at home. It was still Signor Gabrieli's shabby appearance that filled me with distrust. He seemed to fit too well my imagining of a back-street charlatan.

Isabelle, however, seemed no worse in health, staying in her room for several days and entertaining Signor Gabrieli for dinner with us there each evening. I had dared to remark to her privately on his shabby turnout and she had promptly handed me a bundle of Italian treasury notes with instructions to send him to a tailor. This foiled my intention of alerting her to doubt his professional standing. However, when passing on her message and the money I added a rider of my own: that he should also visit a manicurist. In this way I felt I contributed some safeguard towards any intimate exploration which Isabelle's condition should call for.

On the Thursday of the week following our arrival I was aware of some new excitement in the air. Signor Gabrieli had been absent for several days, 'making arrangements for the birth'. Isabelle had risen before ten and was impatient to receive an unnamed visitor.

I was dispatched to the foyer to listen for anyone asking for the 'English Contessa', and after a half-hour of hovering near the reception desk was rewarded by the arrival of a plump, neatly dressed middle-aged woman carrying a hatbox.

'Signora,' she addressed me, with the passion of a diva from La Scala, 'I 'ave comma myselfa.' We ascended to Isabelle together in the gilt rococo lift.

It was not millinery that she produced with balletic exuberance from the boldly striped hatbox, but a head of hair that seemed identical with Isabelle's. It caught me totally unprepared. I had not noticed any thinness as I brushed and combed for Isabelle each day. It seemed to me then that she must be suffering from anxiety, or a form of self-delusion which was perhaps a symptom of the later stages of carrying a child.

'Perfect,' she declared, clasping her hands in delight, but she made no move to put the wig on. 'Oh, do try it, Genie. Let me see how it becomes you.'

'I do eeta,' the little saleswoman insisted. She waved me to a chair and attacked me from behind, accompanying her firm actions with a rapid stream of unintelligible instructions in Italian on how it should be fitted.

It was farcical, but I permitted it since it seemed what Isabelle wanted. She even ran to bring a mirror so that I should see myself transformed.

The reflection hardly looked to be me any more. The rich blonde curls framed my face, softening the angle of my cheeks. I lacked the angelic curves of Isabelle's nose and chin, but for a moment I looked quite like her.

'Of course the eyes are altogether wrong,' she said

critically. 'But under a veil who's to know they're not dark blue?'

'Thissa is the signora oo—?' the Italian woman began.

'Exactly,' Isabelle said shortly. 'Can you do that?'

In answer the woman carefully removed the wig, balled it out with tissue paper and returned it with elaborate care to the hatbox. Then she regarded me critically, walked all round to get a view from every angle and declared, 'Issa more easy. *La signora ha capelli scuri come un' Italiana.*' And reaching up she began to take out all my pins, so that my hair cascaded over my shoulders, almost to my waist.

That was too much. I removed myself to my own room and wound it all back securely on top. Then I returned, determined to permit no further indignities.

At that point I was dismissed to order tea, and when I returned Signora Santucci was taking her leave. 'Seven days then,' Isabelle said, seeming well satisfied.

I let the woman see herself downstairs and followed Isabelle into her bedroom. 'Belle,' I said, all sympathy, 'there really is no need to worry. Your hair is as lovely as ever it was. You mustn't imagine it's likely to start falling out. Truly I would have mentioned it if I'd noticed your brush was doing any damage.'

She looked at me puckishly. 'Don't take on so, Genie,' she said. 'Let me indulge my little fancies.'

So we said no more about it. The pretty blonde wig remained in its box for a further seven days, until the Italian wigmaker's next visit. When she did arrive and produced her second work of art I was convinced that Isabelle had some mild form of dementia.

'What on earth would *I* need with a wig?' I demanded. It seemed her fear of baldness was taking on universal dimensions.

'Ah,' she said mysteriously and bowed her own head for

the Signora to brush the golden curls upwards and fasten them in a topknot. Then the dark wig, the replica of my own coiffure, was fitted over her head and adjusted. '*Ecco!*' said the wigmaker proudly.

The false hair had been dressed high in the style I had worn at the time of the woman's earlier visit, severely elegant. On Isabelle it looked quite out of place.

I waited until the wigmaker had been paid and departed before I questioned what Isabelle was up to. 'Do you seriously mean to wear it yourself?' I asked, incredulous.

She was purring with contentment. 'Of course. This is to be my disguise. From now on I am the English companion, Mrs Fellowes. And that leaves you, my dear Genie, to play the "Contessa". That should be a challenge for your performing skills!'

I stared at her. 'You are suggesting we exchange identities? Isabelle, that is utterly preposterous.'

She fluttered a hand. 'I would call it versatile. Oh, perhaps a trifle shady, at most. It is rather like a Gentlemen's Agreement. This will be an Arrangement between Ladies. Quite discreet. And essentially secret.

'You see, Genie, even out here it would be so talked of, a titled English lady seen to be *enceinte* and too long widowed. The news would certainly leak out and reach the ears of people who are no friends of my family. But quite different in your case.'

There was a long silence in which I expected her to realize the enormity of what she asked.

'Because you have a title, and I am nobody?'

'Exactly.' She spoke lightly and turned away, satisfied that I had capitulated, so she did not see my anger. Nobody, I swore inside, should be made to see themselves as nobody. And thinking those words, I saw the ridiculous illogic of the negatives and felt a momentary blockage of the bitterness which had threatened to burst out.

'You hardly flatter me,' I said sardonically.

'Oh, Genie, you know what I mean.' Her recovery was swift. She came towards me, arms outstretched, ready tears in the beautiful blue eyes. She reached up for my shoulders, to nuzzle my cheek, but I gripped her firmly by the elbows and held her away.

'Remember the child,' I warned. 'That must be our foremost consideration now.'

She took no notice, ploughing on implacably. 'Genie dearest, it would ruin me if this became known. But in your case it doesn't matter. And no one *will* ever know. You shan't regret it, I swear.'

Her eyes were starry with imagined success.

Because, as she had actually put into words, I was nobody. I, who had so proudly claimed I'd be my own woman. I could almost hear again my father's sad voice as we stood together in the garden on the day I left school and boasted the world was mine: 'Freedom,' he'd murmured. 'That old illusion.'

He, if anyone, had known that with every action taken we make our future options fewer. Now, already under an obligation through a carelessly given promise, was I to enter into a devil's contract, with all its terms undefined? To suit Isabelle must I be saddled, however temporarily, with a shame I hadn't earned?

I refused outright. And of course there were tears, accusations, pleading. 'Genie, I need your protection. I can't go on without it. I'll kill myself otherwise.'

'Nonsense,' I told her. 'You aren't that brave. Besides, it's wicked.' Not that any moral arguments were likely to dissuade her.

I steeled myself to leave her weeping, went for my hat

104

and the olive travel coat and set out in blustery sunshine to walk my bad humour off. But not my rebellion, as I hoped.

I must have walked for an hour or more. Clouds had built up and now a slow snowfall began, in drifts on the wind, the flakes clinging like dredged sugar on my dark clothes, reminding me of plum puddings and mince pies, and that Christmas was almost upon us. An early dusk caused the sreet lamps to be lit and the scene took on a new magic.

I found myself in a wide road full of traffic with brightly illuminated stores to either side. Their windows, crowded with fashionable clothes and glittering household goods, drew me. Well-dressed crowds were pouring in and out of their doors, some carrying brightly wrapped packages, others throwing money to street musicians at the kerb, shouting for cabs, crowding on to horse-drawn buses. They were lively, eager, voluble, belonging; and I wanted to belong somewhere too.

It might have been Oxford Street in London, but not sedater Knightsbridge. And yet not even Oxford Street really, for there were galleries of a kind I had never seen there, displaying paintings, tiles and glassware, heavy un-English furniture and bold ceramics.

I wondered what my mother would have said about the ready-made clothes on plaster models behind the glass. Nothing complimentary, I was sure; but for me their lines had movement, the colours were pleasingly vibrant.

It was unusual that my mother should have come into my mind. Since Papa's death I had hardened myself against the memory of her. Just briefly I felt that that had been unjust.

Then I saw that I had paused outside a grand stone building which declared itself a post office, and I remembered telling Mrs Trevelyan that I could be reached *poste restante* here in Milan. I rehearsed the Italian words I would need and went in to ask for any mail.

There was a single package addressed in a firm but unfamiliar hand. I produced my identity papers and signed for it. In near-euphoria I recognized the Egyptian stamps. The franking mark was smudged but could have been Alexandria's.

Now I couldn't reach the hotel soon enough, and the seclusion of my own room. I looked time and again at my name and the address as I strode purposefully in the direction I believed I should go. There had been only one occasion before for me to see Gilbert's writing: on the note with the kitten. This could be his hand, for they certainly weren't Mrs Trevelyan's spiky characters. No doubt he had written to her and she had passed the information to him that I could receive mail in Milan.

The streets were darker now, narrow and full of tall windowless buildings like warehouses. The hurrying figures, in twos and threes, were all male, seemingly workers returning home. One man approached and addressed me roughly; alarmed, I hurried on. Unreasonably perhaps, but I was in a strange land and spoke little of the language. Then at the next street corner I saw brighter lights ahead, turned towards them, reached an open square and managed eventually to summon a cab. At least the driver knew the hotel's name. Within ten minutes I was back indoors.

Isabelle was sulking. She had put herself to bed, and when I glanced in I saw only the hump of the eiderdown over the curve of her back. Which was just as well; it guaranteed me a little privacy to investigate the package.

There was a second packet inside. I scanned the end of the letter wrapping it, and my hopes sank. The signature was a stranger's: Ibrahim Albagouri, Doctor of Medicine.

I put off opening further. The letter could mean only one thing: Mrs Trevelyan had succumbed to the cancer. That wonderful, intelligent, bracingly acerbic mind was no more. That *dear friend,* because I had truly come to love her, whatever heartlessness she accused me of at our last meeting.

And she had made some provision that I should be advised of her death. So it seemed she had spared a thought for me at the end. I should be grateful for that much change of opinion. But I put off reading the letter for almost half an hour more.

Finally I faced it and found little enough to comfort me. Dr Albagouri wrote that she had died calmly and bravely, leaving the enclosed package with instructions that it should be posted to me in Milan. He regretted sending news of such sad import and assured me he was . . . et cetera.

The enclosure was wrapped in brown paper, tied with string and sealed with red wax, which made it look official and not a little frightening. But this was nothing to the horror of its contents.

I stared unbelieving at the worn booklet with its limp, stained cardboard covers bearing Gilbert's name. Inside was the record of his army service. My own name was written there too, replacing another that was erased.

Recorded as his next of kin.

I could not take this second blow, this much more awful death. I must have fainted away, for I came to, cold and stiff-limbed, on the hotel carpet some time later.

I dragged myself to bed and swallowed Isabelle's tablets with the last of the brandy.

Next day I looked at the little book again and learned that Gilbert had died of typhus at base camp three weeks before.

Nine

There was no question of telling Isabelle. I could not utter his name to anyone but myself, and this I did continuously, hunched alone in my room, rocking and weeping and trying to suppress the low animal noises that forced themselves from my throat. *Gilbert, Gilbert, Gilbert!*

I slept, exhausted, on that first evening. Next morning the feather-bed showed I had never moved; I remembered no dreams. It was as though I had been beaten unconscious.

There was suddenly no future. I had lived and now that was over. It hardly mattered any more what went on in the world outside my corpse.

Limply I let Isabelle have her way and make her plans. If Gilbert had still been alive I would never have accepted the charade. I would have kept my own positive identity and insisted on the freedom already promised for Quarter Day in March. I would have walked away from her without once looking back, and made my own self-centred demands on life.

But for the moment I was stricken. I hadn't the courage to refuse her anything. It took all my determination to conceal the devastation of my own world then.

However determined I was to cover my grief in public, Isabelle did notice a physical difference. 'You'd better use some rouge, Eugenie. You're looking peaky. It was that evening walk you took when you flounced out on me. It really does serve you right. I expect you've taken a chill because of it.'

And then, almost instantly, sugary with insincerity, she repeated her demand that we should exchange roles. 'You can't let me down, Genie. It will only be for such a little while. And what fun it could be for you, to be the Honourable Isabelle Delmayne. Such kindly charity, people will think, that she takes on the care of her piteous companion widowed in the last stages of child-bearing.

'Such an opportunity for a public performance for you. There are actresses in London who'd give their eye-teeth for the part. Genie, don't be provoking. I do believe you enjoy vexing me. And you know I can't possibly go on without your help.'

Hopelessly I gave in. It began with my dressing for the part and, black-veiled, leaving the hotel to find us hired rooms with attendance. In this I was obliged to use Signor Gabrieli as intermediary. He also attended my interviewing of staff when I had found a suitable apartment. The choice was difficult for me because Isabelle was adamant that the cook and maid should understand no English. My own Italian was still inadequate, so the doctor's presence was constantly needed to enable the household to run, not smoothly, but tolerably well.

When he returned to Milan after an absence of two days he was changed. The new clothes had almost made a dandy of him. He primped. He was more forward in manner, offering his opinion uninvited on matters that scarcely concerned him. When I enquired how he was able to abandon his medical practice for weeks at a time, he replied airily that he was semi-retired, a gentleman of leisure called in on occasion as a consultant. Conveniently he overlooked the poor state he had been in on our first meeting. It was clear that Isabelle was making him a generous allowance.

On our transferring to the new lodgings in a fashionable quarter of Milan he had become part of the household. I was now expected to address him as Vincenzo.

At that point my public performances became more frequent. I paraded my slim waist and the veiled head of blonde curls wherever and whenever Isabelle directed. More often than not my dark-haired dumpy little 'companion' came with me on a shopping expedition, indicating what finery I should buy.

We made purchases of china, curtains, furniture and statuary for the apartment, but mainly we were amassing new wardrobes of ready-tailored dresses which I was later employed in altering. We avoided the well-known fashion houses where Isabelle might encounter an English acquaintance who could penetrate our disguises, and made use of the stores where racks of almost identical costumes could be seen in more than one colour and several sizes. These I was well able to alter to make them distinctive.

The variety of textiles was impressive, and Isabelle loved to wander through millinery departments where long galleries were filled with spinneys of tall canes with fantastic confections poised on top of them. I found them rather distasteful, the hats reminding me of pictures from a more savage age when decapitated heads were displayed on pikes at London Bridge.

My main problem on these outings was to make my height less obvious. 'Isn't that what one first notices about a new acquaintance?' I challenged Isabelle. ' "A tall lady," doesn't one say? – then go on to describe hair and complexion?'

But Isabelle disagreed. Her pretty face and curls were the parts of herself she most admired (and by now she could hardly bear to catch sight of her swollen body in a mirror). I was instructed to take the greatest care to tint my pallor and display some animation.

Isabelle, for her part, did her best but made a feckless employee. She had found a vulgar little pair of high-heeled boots which, despite her condition, she wore under full-length skirts when we appeared together. Then with a hat more suited to the hunting field perched on the piled dark wig, she felt our relative heights were corrected.

Despite the agonizing grief that overwhelmed me from one moment to another in a sudden tide, I began to find a perverse kind of solace in my performances. It seemed that when I was playing Isabelle I was untouched by any pressure other than the need to project my borrowed charm and beauty.

In all these months spent in her close company I'd had opportunity enough to observe her little mannerisms, and I reproduced them now: her *moue* of displeasure; darting the bright, upward-tilted glance to reveal the dainty neck and dimpled chin; gestures with parasol or gloves; petu-lant shrugs; round-eyed flattery; a whole language with the eyebrows; cold hauteur when displeased. As I fell into the part, it amused me that she found it harder to dispense with these tricks herself when playing the colourless companion.

In the apartment, with the servants dismissed, she re-sumed her authority and would occasionally scold me for some 'caricature portrayal' which had presented 'the Honourable Isabelle Delmayne' in an unflattering light.

'But you do do that, Isabelle,' I told her once. 'You quite frequently do.'

Her mouth had tightened with anger. And I smiled back,

experiencing a bitter kind of pleasure at her annoyance. Beneath my disguise, when the actress became herself again, my heart bled for my lost love, and I saw no reason why she should not suffer just a little too.

I began to ask myself whether I didn't really dislike her. With new disenchantment, some of the respect had certainly gone and I knew my behaviour towards her must at times reveal this. And yet in a way I was fond of the pretty little noodle. I still found it acceptable at that time to dance a few steps to her tune, since I saw no other way to go.

There was obviously some danger in the impersonation I took on. Constantly I was on my guard against an encounter with groups of English visitors to Italy. And since high society was so fluid now throughout Europe I could unwittingly have encountered acquaintances from other nationalities who were familiar with the original I faked. Fortunately the weather had turned bleak and there were more fashionable venues than Milan to be found over Christmas.

We took little note of the festival itself, the few gifts we gave being beautifully wrapped by the shops on our behalf. From my meagre pocket money I bought Isabelle a fine woollen bed shawl, and for Gabrieli a cigar-cutter. Isabelle's gift to me was a pair of gold and amethyst earrings, and for the doctor a silk cravat.

For some reason Isabelle refused to dress a tree or to order special meals. On her insistence, however, we dared to take a box one evening at La Scala, sitting back from the lights and the inquisitive opera-glasses of spectators opposite and in the stalls. I had been informed that we were to hear *Pagliacci*, and expected to sit like marble, fighting the tears inside from overture to curtain fall.

But in fact it was *Lucia di Lammermoor* and, ignorant

112

of what to expect, I was unprepared for the music and overwhelmed by its convulsive emotion. The grandeur of the huge arena and the crowded auditorium vanished. There was only myself beset by all the unbearable pain of the anguished woman, and I left the theatre convinced of my own final madness.

Two days later a delighted Isabelle showed me a page from the *Corriere* which Signor Gabrieli had brought in. A short paragraph observed with pleasure that the charming and beautiful 'Lady' Isabelle Delmayne had emerged from half-mourning to attend a performance at La Scala.

'Aren't you afraid that the London papers might happen on this and reveal your whereabouts?' I asked her. 'Suppose it appears on the society pages there and you get a flood of visitors?'

Our exchange of identities had lulled her into a false sense of security. Now she was really alarmed and there was nothing for it but to lie low for a few days, both of us, with an assumed fever while *il dottore* was dispatched to complete secret arrangements elsewhere for her final reception and the birth. I had still not been informed of where this was to be or of how much travel it would entail.

There had been some doubt about the expected date of the baby's arrival. 'Somewhere, I suppose, between the middle of January and the first week of February,' Isabelle had first told me offhandedly. But since then Signor Gabrieli had calculated it more precisely, for 29 January. He was, or had been, a doctor, so I was obliged to accept this date, however much I doubted his competence.

The nearer the event approached the more terrified Isabelle became, and so the more dependent. I had the greatest misgivings as to the outcome, partly through ignorance of the final arrangements which she and *il dottore* kept from me, and also through fear that he would prove clumsy or inadequate in any crisis. It was unthinkable that serious injury, or worse, should occur to Isabelle after such prolonged subterfuge.

My own responsibility in this deception worried me, increasingly certain as I was that her family ought to be notified and some skilled surgeon or midwife sent out to attend her. Also it occurred to me at that late stage that the coming child had a father, about whose identity Isabelle had kept unusually silent. He surely had some right to be kept informed, because if the child survived while Isabelle (God forbid!) did not, who was to take on the little creature's welfare?

Even if all went smoothly, what plans were made for its future? I could not see Isabelle brazening it out as a *fait accompli* before the stern eyes of her family. She had no mother to soften the news to them, just a widowed father and a quite ferocious grandfather whose quoted speeches in the House of Lords witnessed his irreversible High Tory principles of family duty and strict propriety.

I remembered the occasion on which I had been presented to him at Stakerleys. Ruddy-faced, with bristling white brows and hair above small, fierce eyes, he had resembled a dangerous wild boar. One could well imagine tusks jutting from his cheeks as he prepared to charge the unwary trespasser.

He would condemn Isabelle's predicament as the just outcome of wanton conduct. He was, I'd thought then, a thoroughly patriarchal figure: something more than an Old Testament prophet thundering doom. Perhaps a *locum tenens* for Jehovah himself. I felt sure that, secure within his own unquestioned status, Lord Sedgwick could never envisage any purely female dilemma.

Thoughts of her family did not trouble Isabelle by now.

She had worries of a more personal nature. Not only her abdomen was swollen, but her face, neck, arms and legs too appeared heavy with fluid. She was no longer able to fit her feet into shoes, nor to walk far, although I encouraged her to take what exercise she could within the house. Her temper was short and her complaining long.

On Gabrieli's return after a further two days' absence, even he seemed disconcerted by her appearance. He re-examined her, took fresh measurements, asked more questions about the time of conception and declared that the likely birth date should be advanced by two weeks.

We were to move on at once. I was instructed to visit a local bank and arrange future wages for the cook and housemaid to be paid through its agency during our absence. For this purpose I found I was obliged to sign an authorization in Isabelle's name, and this appalled me, for I knew that forgery was a serious criminal offence.

It seemed there was no limit to what I must sink to in her service. I questioned what was left of my high principles and realized with shame that I felt more anxiety now over being found out than over the illegal act itself.

With the accouchement so imminent it seemed to me folly that we should be changing our venue yet again. But apparently Milan did not offer sufficient privacy, and Gabrieli had rented for us part of a *palazzo* in Venice, where no visiting English were likely to be staying at that miserable time of year. The *primo piano nobile* he called it, and I found this had nothing to do with music or rank, but simply meant 'the first floor up'.

It was not until we were installed there that I discovered by chance that, although empty and sadly neglected, this once fine waterside house with its arched Gothic windows and small stone balconies belonged to a distant branch of his family. So I assumed that they would

115

not be left out of pocket by the convenient arrangement.

To get to Venice we travelled again by train, a wretched journey in blizzard conditions with no heating in our carriage. I would have taken flasks of hot soup for Isabelle's sustenance, but Gabrieli assured me the guard would willingly supply all our needs. Which he failed to do, disappearing whenever the train stopped and leaving us short of the platform, so that alighting was impossible.

Towards our journey's end I was alarmed by the endless dreary marshland we passed over and the thought that we would be lodged on an equally precarious base. The idea of stone houses perched on wooden piles above a sandbank horrified me.

Finally the railroad ran by a long causeway from the mainland, across the north side of the lagoon, so we were not obliged to travel by water until we were already at the Stazione Santa Lucia on the main island. Then it was a short journey by two canals in a black-painted gondola, with porters following in another to bring up our luggage.

The old house was cold and damp with a pervading smell of mould. Some of the facing stone was badly flaking and the balconies needed repairing, for the stone arabesques were almost eaten away in places. My heart sank as I made a quick tour of the high-ceilinged rooms with their cold marble floors and walls, selecting two square ones at the front for Isabelle's own. Each had a wide, ornate fireplace of orange-veined marble and I trusted them to provide the cheerfulness and warmth which the great barn otherwise failed to offer.

Tired out by the journey, Isabelle was soon glad to sink into a bed warmed with cobbles heated in the kitchen's wood-burning stove. Two women were already in attendance, a slovenly cook-housekeeper with prominent, red cheeks which bunched like crab apples as she spoke, and a stern-looking nurse in her mid-fifties who would supervise the birth and look after Isabelle's baby when it arrived. I wrote that night in my new diary, 'Outside the Venetians are loudly celebrating the arrival of 1901. I cannot imagine a more sorry place to start the year in.'

But Venice was not always veiled in mist so that sea and sky seemed merged in suspension beyond its ancient stones. There were bright, crisp days when everything glittered, the gondolas danced on champagne waves and, viewed from the outer islands, the *Serenissima* city floated in pastel lustre on a turquoise sea. On such a morning washed with brightness I could sometimes persuade Isabelle to take the air, although she would lie behind drawn curtains in the little cab of our hired gondola.

Whatever other outings I suggested, she turned down out of hand. Venice was not new to her, she told me languidly. She had come here with Hugo on their honeymoon, so she had seen all there was to be seen on that occasion. And that for her was quite enough.

Ten

It rained almost continuously for days on end. The narrow streets and alleys had boards laid on them but the water came through to soak one's shoes and skirt hems. Everywhere there were liquid sounds that were quite Italian to my ears. Our small garden, within black iron gates behind the *palazzo*, sheltered a single bedraggled robin in its dripping evergreens, who perpetually complained, '*Non mi piace quest'acqua.*' Even the overfilled gutters seemed to gurgle incessantly in Italian, '*E vero, è vero, è vero.*'

Within the great house all surfaces were misted with a sad grey patina which returned however much they were polished. Everything we touched kept the marks of our fingers. I lived for a rare sight of the sun, when the houses of the Grand Canal were briefly gilded, washing a flush of cream and warm rose over their soft brick and ancient stucco. I began to understand why even great artists like Tiepolo and Veronese painted clouds like grubby, uncooked dough, solid enough for a pack of saints or angels to sail on.

On one of my brief sorties to art galleries I gathered up some English-language newspapers and magazines from the previous autumn, but even the women's pages failed to raise Isabelle's spirits. She often slept badly at nights and required my presence during the hours of wakefulness to play bezique or simply listen to her fretful complaints. I tried reading aloud news items to divert her, and so came across the report of an earlier speech by her grandfather in the House of Lords.

A staunch Tory, he had made a remarkable attack on his own party's foreign trading policy. There was even a surmise that he might cross the floor of the Lords and become a Liberal. I scanned the paragraphs ahead. 'It seems he admits British responsibility for provoking the *I Ho Ch 'üan* Rising in China.'

'Was that those awful Boxers? But the atrocities are over now. We've won, and everything's been settled, surely.'

'Lord Sedgwick begs to differ.'

'Grandfather never *begged* in his life. He simply revels in being perverse. Still, you may read it through. Let's see what he's ranting about this time.'

'He began by reviewing the past seventy years of Chinese history—'

'As if English history isn't tedious enough.'

'—and what he calls "the Imperialist Nations' irresponsible behaviour" towards that country.'

'He must totally have lost his senses. Everyone knows that the Chinese are backward savages who owe everything to us Europeans.'

Isabelle's 'everyone' excepted me. The elder Miss Court-Withington had been born in the Yangtse Valley and spoke often of what her missionary parents had learned there. The native Chinese had certainly been oppressed by the Manchu invaders from the north, but their culture went back thousands of years. They had produced rare works of art while we in Britain were still in the dark ages.

However, if those elderly missionaries were still alive, the recent massacres of Christians must have damped even their admiration.

I read on. 'He blames the British East India Company in particular for the earlier Opium Wars because, to have sufficient silver to buy all the tea for Europe's needs, they flooded the country with illegal drugs from India. More than half their exports to China were opium, which brought greater misery and squalor to people already brutally ruled.'

'Is that so? Well, Grandfather may remember all that; he's an old, old man. But it's all water under the bridge by now, and it's time he allowed us to enjoy the present.'

'Don't you think that he may be a little ahead of his time? To dare to criticize a government he's a part of?'

I looked at Isabelle propped up against her pillows. At last she was showing some slight animation, but I guessed her anger against Lord Sedgwick was less on account of his politics than for some other, more personal reason.

Yet the old gentleman was financing her high style of living abroad. It struck me then that perhaps he so thoroughly disapproved of his granddaughter that he happily paid to keep her out of his sight, like a disgraced remittance man banished by his family to Australia or Canada. Could it be that His Lordship had somehow guessed at her present embarrassment and had callously dismissed her to whatever fate should overtake her?

'Genie, do go on. What else does the old dinosaur say?'

I resumed reading silently, preparing a summary for her. 'Our more recent trading has been almost as reprehensible, and we are joined now by the French, Germans, Russians, Japanese and Americans. China has become so flooded with cheap manufactured goods that local handmade products can't sell any more; which further increases unemployment and poverty. Then, while China was defenceless after invasions from Japan, we Western predators also began annexing whole areas of the country. It is not surprising, he says, that resentment against all "Foreign Devils" pushed these desperate people to form secret societies and rise against us.'

'But what good did it do the Boxers, with all that slaughter and burning and torture, if they gained nothing in the end?'

'What is ever the point of war, Isabelle? I suppose it's the only choice that remains when you've tried everything else.' And I thought of Gilbert, by nature so unmilitary, tied to blindly following orders, involved in a career of killing or being killed. Gallant maybe in protection of a principle, but such heart-rending waste. And I pictured his case multiplied by millions; white men, black men, yellow men, all over the face of the earth, fighting to the death for what they thought was right.

'Don't be so depressing, Genie. Can't you find something more pleasant in the papers?'

I read on. 'There's something here about reparations.'

'What are they?'

'Money to be paid by China as compensation for the lives and foreign property destroyed during the Rising. It seems it's finally to be fixed at three hundred and thirty seven million dollars.'

'For them to pay us? That's splendid.'

'But the Americans think it's excessive. They want it cut to two hundred million.'

'How peculiar of them. But then they're already rolling in money and don't need more. Think of all those American heiresses who've been marrying into the best English families.'

'Your grandfather objects even to the smaller amount, since parts of China are devastated and the Dowager Empress's corrupt government has returned. He warns

121

that she will insist on harsher demands from the peasants, rather than dip into the bulging Manchu coffers.'

Isabelle frowned. 'He's against the Empress? That doesn't sound like Grandfather. He's always been loyal to his kind. His ideas must have changed, to take the people's part against authority.'

'You really can't admit that he has a soft heart under the gruff exterior?'

'It's a softening of the brain, more likely. And, to be fair to him, that *would* be something new. All the same, I can't imagine him crossing to the Opposition.' She yawned behind a languid hand.

Sedgwick the Tory making a Liberal speech. Yet every party must have some charitable feelings. For some reason then I remembered the journalist Churchill, whose book *River War* had so impressed me – the ex-soldier whom Mrs Trevelyan had fondly spoken of as 'Randolph's lad'. Having endured war in India, Sudan and South Africa, he knew how helpless the soldier was, fighting abroad, when politicians failed him. At that time he had slated Gladstone's Liberal government for delaying reinforcements to relieve the sieges of Ladysmith and Mafeking. Now he was in the Commons as a Conservative member, seeking greater power among the legislators who could send the soldier to his death.

Pragmatism, wasn't that what it was called, when experience made one change one's position? It seemed too that no single party was enough for all occasions. One side was more merciful in peace, and the other more reliable in dire crisis.

How would politics work if we did away with this division into parties, and every man voted according to his conscience? Surely this was the question which should most exercise us nowadays, rather than the side issue of female suffrage? Unless, of course, the women's vote could break the party-pack rule which men had imposed. And make war impossible? Or leave England disorganized, and therefore defenceless against other countries less advanced in their thinking?

I stared across at Isabelle and could only smile at the irony of it. The political theme had had the desired effect. She was now peacefully asleep.

For every eager suffragette, how many hundreds of thousands of women were there, like her, who found politics utterly boring?

Isabelle's falling asleep was convenient. My watch showed it was ten minutes short of dinner-time. It could allow me to take my meal without interruption and then serve hers later in her bedroom. Accordingly I went to the library to advise Gabrieli that we should be prompt to table.

The room was in semi-darkness. I made out the darker outline of his figure in a leather armchair. He was inelegantly sprawled on his back, mouth open, and breathing heavily. I thought at first he had helped himself too liberally to the brandy, which had become his habit of late, but I was wrong. There lingered a faint but distinctive odour in the room, and the flaccid hand laid across his paunch still limply held the ether pad.

He barely responded to the shaking I gave him, but the upturned vase from which I whipped the arrangement of hothouse lilies brought him choking back to half-life.

'How dare you do this when Isabelle might need your skills at any moment?' I shouted at him.

He looked dully back, curled his body into an ammonite shape, let his heavy lids droop and was again deep under, seemingly unaware of the drenched condition of his clothes.

I went in to dinner alone, vowing that before the evening

was out I would make Gabrieli give a good account of himself.

Whether he heeded our angry exchange or not I never knew, but at least if he pursued his habit he did so out of my sight. Yet it remained a further hazard Isabelle was exposed to, and I redoubled my study of the nursing manual I'd had sent out from Blackwell's while I was still in Milan.

Beyond relying on that, the severe nurse Margherita and the unimpressive *dottore*, there was only prayer left open to me. For some days I had been visiting the many churches I had come across when exploring the canals and piazzas.

As a result, my opinion of Catholicism had undergone a change. The devout attitude of the congregations had more than overridden my earlier prejudices against empty rituals, which I now saw to have some spiritual basis. I still found the Latin liturgy difficult to follow but could appreciate that even to ignorant peasants the constant repetition and the familiarity of the actions must make their significance clear enough.

Some mornings I managed to attend High Mass at San Marco Cathedral, or take a boat across for the later Gregorian service at San Giorgio. To maintain secrecy I felt obliged to avoid any English church, but, as a gesture of openmindedness, once slipped into the synagogue in the Ghetto Vecchio and discovered there an incomprehensible beauty.

Although I do not regard myself as a particularly religious person, it seemed to me that if God was to take pity on Isabelle's wretched state He should be approached from as many angles as possible.

It was when I returned in drenching rain from an early service at San Marco, ready to wake Isabelle and take up her breakfast tray, that the nurse met me at the head of the elaborate staircase. 'It moves,' she said.

There was no doubt what she meant. I heard Isabelle call to me from her room. 'Genie, I'm frightened! Come in and hold my hand.'

But not yet really in pain, Margherita assured me grimly: there was a long way to go yet.

I stayed with Isabelle until about two in the afternoon, when she fell into an exhausted sleep. The nurse had twice been in to examine her progress and left shaking her head silently at me. Gabrieli had not come near, but I knew he was in the house because fresh cigar smoke hung on the air. After her second visit I followed Margherita out and demanded just what she meant by the negative gesture.

'It will be a long time,' she said. 'Sometimes it goes on for days, nights. She must rest while she can.'

All that day Isabelle lay in terror, groaning briefly as the pains returned, then falling silent for a few minutes, while gusts of rain hurled themselves at the long windows so that the ancient house shuddered. I began to think it would be torn from whatever rotten foundations held it below the surface of the canal, and we should all be swept out into the open lagoon.

At midnight I insisted Gabrieli should attend her, and I slipped out to snatch a *frittata* in the kitchen. When I relieved the doctor he agreed with me that Isabelle was visibly weakening. She would close her eyes for only a few minutes, then wake again, begging me for some relief. And I could do nothing.

It was some time after five o'clock had chimed from the nearby campanile and a hint of dawn showed along the edge of the lagoon, that I started awake from a doze to hear Isabelle growling deep in her throat. Suddenly she caught at my hand, her nails cutting into my flesh.

'Genie! Genie, it's getting worse.' Her voice rose to a shrill scream. 'I can't stand any more. It keeps on getting worse and worse!'

I groaned silently with her. Margherita had assured me the process had barely begun. And that it *would* get much worse. As everything in our interlocked lives had been doing since that first day when I saw her on the staircase to my mother's showroom.

Life had seemed so simple and unspoilt then. Now we were caught up in sheer nightmare, incapable of controlling events or of breaking out. Trapped as her body was, in childbirth.

And yet even then she tried to get free, throwing off her covers and scrabbling to put her feet to the floor. 'No-o-o! I've had enough!'

I hung on to her. 'You have no choice. There is nowhere to run to.'

She screamed at me and and tore at my dress, then the pains took over again and she was begging me to make it stop. Margherita and Gabrieli had come into the room. He stank of brandy.

We laid her back on the bed. How long could it go on like this? She would reach the end of her strength, and then what? If the child didn't come, must we trust to knives in the odious Gabrieli's hand?

'She must relax,' he hissed at me. 'Tell her to relax, or she will do herself a damage.'

'Can't you give her something?'

'It could kill the baby.'

The truth is, I thought, he hasn't anything to use. No ether left, no chloroform. Dear God, if he has to cut her without anything to ease the pain, the shock of it alone could finish her.

She lay quiet a few seconds and I went to wash my

126

hands again. It was becoming an obsession, but I had only a few grains of knowledge learned from the nursing manual: cleanliness above all, it said, and then using fresh pads to staunch the flow of blood.

And if she did haemorrhage? What chance would Isabelle have in this primitive place, with every precaution sacrificed in favour of secrecy?

From time to time either the midwife or Gabrieli would examine her and I heard them muttering together.

'*Quattro centimetri.*'

'*Niente. No sta.*'

'*Ancora quattro.*'

I must have fallen asleep there with my head on the coverlet when I felt Gabrieli shaking me awake. '*Che accade?*'

'*Niente.*' The wretched man's eyes were like a beaten dog's. 'She does not open. And she gets very weak.'

'So do something. You are the doctor.' Dear God, had he wakened me simply so that I could watch her slip away? Is this what it had come to in the end? All that pain and the months of deception for this?

'You must help. Come and hold the lamp.'

'Where is the midwife?'

'She goes. Comes later.'

'But I know nothing about such things. I'm useless.' And then it struck me that that was why he preferred to have me there: because I would not know – and could not later give testimony – if he made a mistake, did something that could kill Isabelle.

He saw my hesitation and he snarled like a wild beast, 'There is no time. I must do it now. You must help.'

I looked hard at him. He seemed to have sobered somewhat. His hands were less shaky.

I went for the scoured bowl and poured boiling water

in and scattered potassium permanganate crystals. Then I cooled it until it was just bearable against the skin. 'Wash,' I ordered him.

He already had his sleeves rolled up and a towel round his waist, tucked into the band of his trousers. He hesitated, met my eyes, shrugged and complied. Then, into the same water he threw his instruments. I had no idea if that was safe or not, but he seemed in such haste that I dared make no objection.

I started spreading old newspapers under Isabelle's exposed body and on the floor around. Then I turned up the wick on the oil lamp and carried it to where it would best throw its light on his hands as he worked.

At that moment Isabelle gave a little despairing cry and he shouted, 'Push! As hard as you can, push!'

Then he bent over her straddled knees, feral and sweating, with a scalpel in one hand and in the other a terrible instrument shaped like a pair of fire-tongs.

Eleven

The child survived. A girl, tiny, but compact and beautifully formed. Apart from two bright red marks above the
ears and another behind the neck there was no evidence
that instruments had been used.

Isabelle was less fortunate. Her final screams will ring
in my ears till the day I die.

The child was thrust upon me and I was shouldered
away from the carnage. I had never seen blood like it.
The child was smeared with it and, beneath that, covered
in a waxy whiteness.

I bound her round tightly in a blanket and hugged her
close, offering my strength and warmth as a substitute for
the safer place she'd come from.

Poor little morsel. How much better off she had been
inside.

She didn't cry for long, but lay with eyes and lips tightly
pursed and her little fists clenched as if deliberately cutting
herself off from all around her. She looked rebellious, even
pugnacious. I hoped she'd prove as determined as she
looked. She would need plenty of spirit to thrive in the
world she had been born into.

Only when Isabelle was bound up and left to rest did
the nurse come for the child to clean and dress it. She
was granite-faced as ever, and I had enough Italian by now

to guess at what she muttered: that it was good that the *signora* would never go through that again.

'You can't mean she will die?' I demanded.

'If God wills, no. But inside – she is ruined. There can never be another child.'

I couldn't believe that Isabelle would regret that fact just then. How could any woman choose to suffer in such a way more than once? But in the next few days she amazed me with her ability to recover.

A woman came in, mornings and evenings, as wet-nurse, but in between and during the night either Margherita or I fed the little creature from a bottle with diluted cow's milk. She was always hungry and sucked away vigorously.

Now she had been cleaned I could better see her. Her fine hair had a tawny tint. She was brownish yellow all over, and her blue eyes were a little on the tilt, which gave her face a special piquancy. Privately I wondered whether her father had oriental blood, but when I questioned Margherita about the colour of her skin she threw up her arms and kept repeating '*Itterizia!*'

When I looked the word up in my Italian dictionary I learned that the baby had jaundice. And that, apparently, was because she was premature. In time, Margherita told me, the discoloration would go.

Isabelle would have none of her. She recoiled when the baby was placed in her arms, and the slightest cry from the child would drive her almost distracted. All the nurse's determination was needed to make her allow the little mouth on her breasts, and then she would cry that the monster was biting her.

'It can happen so,' Gabrieli said with a slumping shrug. 'In time she will become used to it.'

But if Isabelle had no motherly instinct, and with

130

the baby constantly cared for by others, how could she develop any fondness for it? I tried placing the cradle beside her couch during the afternoons, when I was close by to see that nothing went amiss, and I hoped that gradually Isabelle would soften towards the helpless little creature.

One evening about a week after the birth we were all three resting in Isabelle's sitting-room when I was called below to see a tradesman delivering our order of fresh vegetables.

'Before you go, Genie, just open the window to freshen the air,' Isabelle called from her couch.

I went across to feel her forehead, fearing the start of a fever, but she seemed only cosily warm. The fire was banked high, so the room would lose little heat before I was back. 'Just for five minutes, then,' I said.

Each morning the room was aired before Isabelle moved in there from her bedroom. I had discovered that the two long windows were permanently sealed by age, so the only ventilation possible was gained by opening the double doors which gave on to the balcony, and which I otherwise kept locked because of the dangerous state of the balustrade out there.

The room was peaceful, silent but for the mesmeric tick of an ormolu clock on the marble mantel. The baby was already cosily asleep, Isabelle drifting gently off. I quietly took the key from my waist-pocket, unlocked one balcony door and propped it ajar to admit the minimum draught. Then I picked up my accounts book and prepared to go downstairs.

Half-way there I remembered I would need my silver pencil, and I turned to go back. I thought I heard a little sound from the baby. As I paused it came again, a choking wail loud enough to be distinguishable through the thick

131

door. If she started crying in earnest now it would disturb Isabelle.

I slipped back, ready to lift the child, but as I opened the door I was thrilled to see that Isabelle herself was seeing to her. She stood in the middle of the room, head bent over the child in her arms, a sweet picture of motherhood, and I halted on the threshold, unwilling to intrude on the precious moment.

I wasn't prepared for Isabelle swiftly crossing the floor to the open balcony door. Before I could move she was out there, stooping towards the greasy canal water some twenty feet below.

And then there was no doubt about what she intended as she held the child out. I have no recollection of leaping after her and pulling her back. I only know I didn't cry out. In that short moment of panic, at least I knew that it could have been fatal. Startled, Isabelle might herself have gone over.

As it was, I had them both safe in my arms and we stood there for a moment that felt like eternity before I could draw us all back into the warmth of the house.

I loosed Isabelle while I comforted the child, rocked her and crooned her quiet, until it was safe to put her back in the cradle. Isabelle had collapsed on the carpet, half prone, her hands pressing against the floor, her body shaking with stifled sobs. Then it was her turn to be comforted.

She hid her face against my breasts and after a few minutes her muffled voice came out. 'I only wanted a little air.'

'If you say so.'

But with my free hand I lifted her chin so that our eyes met, and I let her know that I knew the truth.

Her sobs then were terrible. We sat on the floor holding

on to each other, Isabelle desperate, I almost petrified with distress. Eventually I said, 'We must tell *il dottore*. Clearly you are not as well yet as we assumed.'

'No! You can't betray me!'

'Isabelle, he will be able to help you.' But I doubted that myself.

However, he was unsurprised, which may have been some solace to her. 'It happens,' he said gloomily. 'Sometimes it happens, and these are early days yet.'

'We should have discussed all this before,' I said. 'Isabelle has never made any plans for the baby that I know of. She has refused to look that far ahead, and now events have overtaken her and she is almost out of her mind. Will you talk to her, *Dottore*?'

He said he would, and certainly I came across them several times over the next few days with their heads close together. Isabelle would start away at sight of me, as if she feared I might eavesdrop. Eventually Gabrieli approached me with a proposition.

'The *Contessa* is still unwell, as you appreciate. Until she has regained her health, it would be well for you to become – as it were – the *bambina*'s mother. If that is agreeable to you. Take your time to consider this. And meanwhile the *Contessa* has agreed to think of a name for the little one. She invites you to choose the second one.'

Isabelle was for calling the baby Margherita. The very act of naming seemed to mark some kind of progress in accepting her, but she might have hit upon a more gracious model than the granite-faced nurse to borrow it from.

For myself, there were plenty of pet names which I whispered to the sweet girlie when I bathed or fed her, but I searched now for something formal yet appropriate. Venezia would be a little too special. (I suffered, myself,

133

from too grand a name.) But remembering our first arrival here, at the Stazione Santa Lucia, I settled for the Italian form of Lucy.

'*Bene*,' said Gabrieli. 'Then I will go and register the birth.'

When he brought back the certificate, Isabelle seemed pleased and tucked it behind the ormolu clock. I thought she showed some sign of being reconciled to the baby by ringing for champagne to be sent in. We all drank to little Margherita Lucia, wishing her long life and happiness, but still her mother would not hold her.

'For fear I should drop her,' she said. 'I am so trembly these days.' And she stared at me with something like defiance.

I told myself fervently that the scene on the balcony had been an isolated moment of madness, and there was no possible chance of anything similar happening again. It was still too early to enquire what plans she had beyond the date in March when I was due to leave her. Surely by then Isabelle would be more stable and ready to find delight in the child's progress. I profoundly hoped so. Certainly I was bound to stay on all the while there was any chance the child could suffer at its mother's hands. Such a delicate and pretty little creature, her vulnerability must itself draw them close in the end.

But sometimes when I closed my eyes I seemed to see Lucia wide-eyed with fear against a background of dark water, and I remembered the kitten Gilbert had given me, which ended in the Nile. I longed to ask Isabelle what I should have asked months before this: 'Did my kitten scratch you? Was that why . . . ?'

Yet I dared not. And really did not need to ask, because hadn't she hidden her torn face in the dark of the cabin, and next day blamed me for leaving a pin in the dress I had altered? But the marks on her cheek had come from more than one sharp point.

I tried to see everything from Isabelle's viewpoint. If she could feel such anger against a kitten over a playful accident, how much more might she resent this child who – as she saw it – had put her through long hours of agony? A child who at present seemed to compete with her for everyone's attention. According to Gabrieli such hostility could be long-lasting and lead to repeated physical abuse. I must watch out for sudden spitefulness from Isabelle, while taking over the main burden of care for the infant. But I hadn't any doubt that eventually the little one would find a way into her mother's heart.

Every day now Isabelle was becoming stronger. 'And more slender,' she insisted when I remarked on this. She always kept a measuring tape to hand and spent long hours lying flat on her stomach to improve her figure.

Remembering how my mother used to rest her feet above the level of her head after she had stood too long, I persuaded Isabelle to lie in reverse, face-upwards on her bed for twenty minutes each morning and evening, with both legs stretched up the silk headboard.

Gradually it was having the desired effect. Although some puffiness returned after an hour or two, her legs were coming back to their normal shape. Her upper body needed stricter discipline to counter her self-indulgence and lack of exercise while carrying the child. Isabelle still found it difficult to resist the wonderful pastries and iced confections in shops and restaurants, and I had to order Cook to replace with lemon juice the olive oil she preferred to bathe every savoury dish in.

Isabelle's complexion too was returning to its previous soft glow, apart from a few small brownish marks which could be covered by a tinted cream which I obtained from a local pharmacy. At her insistence I smoothed glycerine and rose-water into her skin each evening before she retired. She was rigorous in this discipline, and it wasn't hard to imagine that she was working towards some unstated goal. I wondered if she intended presenting herself, with little Margherita, to the child's father in the expectation that he would – tardily enough – marry her.

I had too little experience of the world Isabelle had come from to know whether she would have more appeal to such a gentleman now than when she had first, unexpectedly, found herself carrying his child. One thing I did know was that in the middle-class society of St Leonards-on-Sea an earlier marriage would certainly have been arranged through family pressure, unless the gentleman already had a wife. In which case a second establishment would discreetly be set up and the unofficial family installed amid a great deal of pretended ignorance by the offended wife and her intimates.

In court circles it seemed there was a deal more laxity, and although the old Queen strongly condemned immorality, Princess Alexandra had come to accept the Prince of Wales's infidelities and would sometimes graciously receive the ladies he favoured, even appearing to find one or two pleasant companions. Since these were all married ladies there was never any scandal about their offspring. Whether this was more civilized, or simply greater hypocrisy, I was in no position to judge.

Whatever her intentions, Isabelle – now coming free of her mourning for Hugo Delmayne – was taking an eager interest in the fashion and society pages of English periodicals. There was a whole trunkful of colourful fabrics bought during our weeks in Milan. Now she had them all pulled out and required me to find her a tailoress in Venice or on the nearby mainland. 'Someone in the nature of your mama,' she ordered.

I spent almost a whole day visiting local establishments and examining minutely the examples of their work on show. I found two cousins, in their late thirties, with an eye for style and a competent workroom, who were happy to visit Isabelle for her fittings.

So it was that one afternoon in mid-February I returned to the *palazzo* to find the furniture in Isabelle's sitting-room covered in cut-off swathes of peach taffeta and aquamarine moiré, with scraps of *toile* still unswept from the floor.

'Oh Genie,' Isabelle complained instantly, 'that wretched housekeeper woman has gone down with stomach cramps and Margherita's away to visit her sister. Just look at the state of this room! For heaven's sake, clear it, will you?'

Of course the seamstresses should have done so, but knowing Isabelle I guessed she had magnificently dismissed them after the fitting, content to sit and play with the silk pieces and revel in their colours on her own.

When I had picked up all the evidence of the visit there were a few other things to be tidied away, even the baby's birth certificate, still tucked behind the fat cherubs on the ormolu clock. I pulled it out and went to place it in Isabelle's writing-box which was open on a side table.

'What are you doing?' Isabelle called sharply.

'Putting this in a safe place. Is there somewhere else you would prefer?'

'I don't want it.'

'It's Margherita Lucia's birth certificate, Isabelle. You need to keep it with your other papers.'

'I don't want it,' she said again. Then a tight little smile puckered the corners of her mouth. Her eyes were wary. 'You haven't read it, have you?'

Suspecting something underhand, but not the enormity of what she'd done, I asked, 'No. Should I?'

'It concerns you.'

I unfolded the sheet and my own name jumped out at me: Eugenie Catherine Fellowes. But not as any witness. She had had me entered as the baby's mother.

'Isabelle, you can't do this.'

'It's done already.' She moved across the carpet towards me, her skirt dragging with a soft *frou-frou*. I had the impression that she was enjoying my discomfiture.

'Remember Milan? Ask anyone who knew us there and they will tell you. It was the companion – the one with dark hair – who was expecting a child. Not I.

'Remember too that you agreed, just a few days back, when Vincenzo begged you to take over as her mother.'

'*In place of* her mother. Temporarily, while you were still frail.'

'It is no use making excuses now and trying to go back on your word. As I said, it's done. Anyway, the birth is only registered here locally. There has been no notification at the British Consulate.'

'But you have deliberately falsified an official document. Quite apart from knowingly putting me in a false position.'

Isabelle drew herself up and stared haughtily back. 'How dare you imply I did it! It was Vincenzo's idea, and Vincenzo who carried it out. And no official ever questioned it, because it is normal for the father to register the birth, on the authority of the doctor attending at the birth.'

For a moment I didn't grasp the full import of this, then the word 'father' struck at me. I read the certificate all through, and there was his name – Vincenzo Paolo

138

Gabrieli – in the space opposite mine. The wretched man had signed that he had fathered a child on me!

The whole scrap of paper was an insulting lie. I couldn't understand why they should trouble to have it issued, since it could only bring disaster later when we tried to get the matter straightened out.

Isabelle just stood there, her head tilted in the familiar way that meant she waited for someone to appreciate her fully.

'You see? The baby's yours,' she said simply. 'For ever. I want nothing at all to do with the child.'

Twelve

My mind was in turmoil. I, who thought I had been managing affairs for Isabelle so as to make her life simpler and less stressful, had been further trapped in the intricacies of her deceptions. Now I was like a fly in a spider's web, hanging trussed and paralysed, ready to be sucked dry. It was truly hideous.

'I cannot believe you would use me like this,' I protested. 'This is nothing short of criminal blackmail!'

She had the grace to look defensive. 'It's not really so bad, Genie, is it? You said once you could forgive me anything. Besides, admit it, you're fond of the child. Anyone can see that. You will be in a position to mark out her future, and, after all, that's the sort of thing you'd be very good at.'

'The *future?*' I marvelled at her blindness. 'How far ahead have you looked? Not at all beyond assuming that you can abandon all responsibility yourself. A child is not a sack to be foisted off on to other shoulders because you wish to flitter about free of any load. She is a part of you, Isabelle. It is your blood in her veins. Nothing can alter that. No one else can establish a valid claim on a child's life while its own parents are alive.'

She turned pettishly away. 'You should think hard about it, and maybe you'll see how this arrangement is by far the most suitable. I shall make you a generous allowance, of course. Not as much as Grandfather has probably been paying you, but who knows? I may yet marry well and then your maintenance will be amply covered—'

My maintenance would be covered. That is what our relationship was reduced to! After all these months of irksome dutifulness, I would be paid off, licensed to farm her child. I felt such rage then on my own behalf that I had no thought for little Margherita.

'Never!' I told Isabelle. 'This is the final insult. I adamantly refuse!'

In my own room, still shaking with anger, I pulled out my tin trunk and the pair of matching leather cases which I had bought in Alexandria, and I began my packing. Apart from the birth certificate which I had flung down somewhere in Isabelle's sitting-room, my affairs were in order. I had no idea how much my return to England would cost, but I still held the balance of the housekeeping money and felt no scruples about using it now for my own ends. Deception for deception, I told myself. *An eye for an eye; a tooth for a tooth.*

But like all primitive revenge, that was oversimplified. Single-tracked rage can discharge itself in instant folly. But if there is a moment of reflection other aspects become apparent. And I was due to feed and change the child, since the nurse had her afternoon off.

I found the cradle in the gloomy kitchen, and the baby no more upset by the clanging of saucepans and slop of dish-clothes than by the rough voice of the cook who was croaking some unrecognizable and monotonous rhyme of her own as entertainment.

'*Le piace,*' the woman claimed dotingly, grinning to display a wide gap in her upper front teeth. '*E una canzone molto bella. non è vero?*' Unmistakably a mother.

141

'*Molto bella,*' I agreed, but she was speaking into the cradle, not to me. Now she poked a reddened finger into the baby's ribs and cooed rapturously. Little Margherita turned solemn, round eyes in our direction and seemed to focus on her.

'*Quanti bambini ha Lei, Marina?*'

She straightened, rubbing her hands on her apron. '*Due belli ragazzi, signora.*' She bent over the cradle again and screwed her neck to squint up at me. '*Per favore, signora?*' and when I nodded she lifted the child and held her close a moment against her damp apron before handing her over. The gentleness of her roughened hands transformed her.

She brought the bottle, itself not unlike a fat gondola, wrapped in flannel to retain the warmth, and I sat on a kitchen chair to give the feed. It was the first time I'd done it there, but it felt homely and I guessed it would give Marina as much pleasure as it did to me.

By the time it was finished she had the wooden table scrubbed and covered with a blanket so that I could change the soiled clothes. While I did so Margherita hiccupped back a flood of milk and Marina clapped her hands in applause.

In a rush of Italian that I had to have repeated twice she advised me in future to change the child before it was fed. Which made admirable sense, and I thanked her for the suggestion. Then, stroking the little back to bring up any more wind, I carried the baby back into the sitting-room I shared with Isabelle.

She was there with Gabrieli, and it was clear she had reported to him on our disagreement earlier. The rejected birth certificate was also there, lying beside Isabelle's left hand on the chair arm. It was evidence of their duplicity, so as I passed I reached out and picked it up.

They were watching me closely, apprehensive of what

I would now say. I found a seat for myself, since *il dottore* had not chosen to stand and offer me one. There I sat apparently absorbed by the baby's reactions to my gentle rocking and humming. 'She is five weeks old today,' I observed. 'It's not long now before I am to quit your service, Isabelle.'

I still had made no decision, whether to leave at once or stay the course, but let my mind run over how each of us was affected. There was no question of what would best serve the baby. Over the next few weeks, until my departure, there was still a chance that Isabelle could be won over by her little daughter. So I must not be hasty and rush away at once. Not that, on calmer reflection, I really wished to. I would miss the child sorely, and miss the new part of myself which she seemed to have brought alive.

I owed Isabelle nothing and determined to preserve an attitude of cool detachment; and I despised the sly Gabrieli, but I could tolerate them both for the short period that remained. Until Quarter Day in the next month.

Gabrieli was biting at his lower lip, scared perhaps that I would make trouble for him, perhaps report to some consulate official that he had made out a false document in my name. I had no idea what defence he could raise, except that he was confused and made an error. I knew Isabelle would deny any involvement and leave him to take whatever consequences their joint deception brought about.

She rose languidly, walked across to a table near the window and helped herself to a cheroot from the mother-of-pearl box there. As she came past me again she reached out to recover the certificate, but I was too quick for her.

'I thought you wished me to read it all through and consider it carefully,' I said softly.

She was unsure of me, perhaps catching the residual anger in my voice. No doubt she was realizing that two could play at blackmail. And hadn't I far more on her to her disadvantage?

'There are options you could consider,' she said cautiously.

I nodded mockingly. 'It's kind of you and your minion to have given so much thought to it.'

'Genie, don't sound so cold,' she pouted, changing tack yet again. 'You know what a perfectly diabolical experience I've been through recently. You could be more sympathetic.'

There had been demands on my sympathy for a while now. Its funds were running low.

Over my knees Margherita lay staring up unwinking, her arms and legs pumping away with that frenzied, involuntary agitation of the limbs that babies are subject to. In a few weeks – or was it months? – she would gain control over them, begin to respond to those around her, notice and copy, try to babble as well as scream for milk. She would smile and frown; she would roar with anger and frustration, reach out for some things and push others away, recognize people.

She was a small, whole person, as I was a large one. It seemed significant that I should suddenly see that.

I got up, folding the shawl about her and cradling her against my shoulder. This time Gabrieli was careful to rise too. I nodded coolly to him. '*Si chiama Lucia*,' I told him, and added for Isabelle, 'her name's Lucia.'

Then I took her off to my own room.

Isabelle and Gabrieli made no further reference to the birth certificate. I left them hoping that I had fallen in with their plans, but also uncertain of my motives. They

144

were certainly disturbed, and intended leaving it to me to renew the debate.

For myself, I was alarmed at the situation yet at the same time excited by my own ability to keep them guessing.

Two days later it was Isabelle's birthday. She would be twenty-one, and it seemed sad that so much had already happened to her – married at nineteen, widowed at twenty, giving birth to an unwanted illegitimate child a year later – yet she was still comparatively young. I doubted the experiences had left her much wiser.

I found a modest present for her in a haberdasher's near the Rialto: a plump red velvet pincushion shaped like a hedgehog, with a little face embroidered on and tiny black beads for eyes. The card with it was one I had painted, of a spray of autumn berries. Inside it I wrote 'To Dear Mama', and left it unsigned.

There was a small celebration for dinner that night at an ornate restaurant where *La Contessa* was fêted by the manager and staff in the manner she always enjoyed. Gabrieli brought along a gentleman of his acquaintance to balance the numbers. Remembering our wretched quartet at Potsdam I hoped he had no further intention than that.

Signor Dimarco was in his late twenties, smoothly confident and full of amusing anecdotes. He shared his conversation equally between both of us ladies, as I am sure he had been instructed to do. He was handsome enough with his swarthy complexion and plentiful black hair lying thick on his neck like a door knocker, but the unfortunate young man had cut himself when shaving and the congealed blood jiggled on his Adam's apple in a horridly fascinating way as he talked. His evening suit was well pressed, but the cuffs were as worn as Gabrieli's originals.

While we were being returned by gondola to the *palazzo* he sang to us in a sub-operatic tenor, lying back on the cushions, and Isabelle drifted her fingers romantically through the water, until she found how icy it was.

'What a really charming fellow Franco is,' she said when we were back indoors. 'And such entertaining company. I think we should see more of him. Don't you, Eugenie?'

When I only smiled she closed her lips tightly and pretended not to be put out. Next day young Signor Dimarco was invited for tea and repeated his charmer's repertoire. It was three evenings later that Isabelle suggested how much more impressive – and inviolable – my eventual return to St Leonards-on-Sea would be as a married lady with a handsome Italian husband and a dear little girl.

So at last she had broken our unspoken truce and come out in the open. 'Really, Isabelle, you are so transparent,' I said, not troubling to suppress my bitter distaste.

Isabelle stood rigid with anger. 'How dare you speak to me like that? Remember who I am. You owe everything to me. It was I dragged you out of the gutter.'

It left me speechless a moment. Perhaps I should have taken that chance to draw up some balance sheet of who owed what to whom. The fury I felt could hardly be contained, but my voice when I spoke at last came out coldly detached.

'That is a vicious phrase you've picked up, and inappropriate in this instance. You have used me shamelessly, Isabelle. We both know you offered me honest employment, which I accepted. Since then you have pleaded with me time and time again to become embroiled in your deceptions. As for my origins, there was never any *gutter.* You know I was raised as a gentlewoman.'

She was disconcerted, her face flushed, but her voice still held some scorn. 'A gentlewoman, I'll grant you then, but not by any means a lady.'

'We are not discussing rank, Isabelle, but whether I am ill-bred. If one judges by recent conduct, I should like to know which of us qualifies better as that.'

Stung at last beyond endurance, in a single movement she turned on her heel, swung the train of her dress and flounced out of the room.

I stood marvelling at what I had done. Actually defied her. Even more, I'd planted an insult full on target. She could have no doubt now about my hostility towards her. After that could she have any further use for me?

In her place I would instantly have written out a cheque for any outstanding debt and dismissed the rebellious companion forthwith. But of course, she paid me no wage. There was just the unspecified amount her grandfather had decreed should be sent each month and banked for me by my mother. Apart from that, Isabelle disbursed pocket money for me when she thought fit. I had not enough of my own here to pay my way back home.

And where was home? So much more worldly-wise now, I could not conceive of returning to the non-life my mother had inflicted on me before. And without dear Papa, there was nothing for me any more in St Leonards. Truly I had burned all my boats. Soon I would have to contemplate a future in employment, perhaps – grim thought – as a governess with testimonials from the Misses Court-Withington. But for the moment at any rate, I could revel in having countered Isabelle's next intended move.

And then there was the child. What would become of her if I walked away? She would retain no memory of me at all, but I would forever be reminded of her vulnerable smallness and the emptiness of my own arms.

Suppose I did accept her as my own? It seemed that in some indeterminate way this little creature who already seemed to leech on to me could become my liberator from Isabelle, who would be glad to see the last of us both. But that, sadly, was out of the question, because what decent family would employ an unmarried mother as tutor to their children?

I gave up on the unanswerable questions and determined to live each day as it came, working in a new state of truce towards my Quarter Day release.

We had a brief interlude of fair weather, without icy blasts or unremitting rain: only a false spring, because surely there was more winter to come at us yet. Gabrieli had left for the mainland and Isabelle seemed uncertain when he would return. We had only a fortnight more of tenure at the *palazzo* and I assumed *il dottore* had been dispatched to look for alternative accommodation.

Three days after his departure Isabelle announced that she would be away on a trip inland for at least one night and required me to accompany her. I declined, because I feared to leave the baby behind insufficiently looked after.

'Then bring her with you. Do as you please. But you know I cannot stand her noise. You will just have to keep her very quiet.' She sounded disagreeable, and I could imagine how it would be, with my hand constantly over the little one's mouth. Still uneasy about the plan, I packed an overnight case for myself and the child, as well as one for Isabelle.

We took the train across to Mestre where a magnificent Italian motor car was waiting for us with a chauffeur in cap and goggles at the wheel. We set off northwards, ever uphill towards the distant Dolomites. Having slept badly the previous night, I was lulled by the movement and the monotony of the engine as we ground on, only to be jolted awake on our arrival at a country *albergo*.

The air was fresher up here, the ground streaked with dry snow which had blown thickly into ruts and up against the stone walls, but indoors huge fires of pine logs made the small rooms pulse with welcome heat.

Gabrieli was there to greet Isabelle with a smile of smug satisfaction. He kept whatever news he had to impart until I was shown to my room under the eaves, and this did nothing to dispel my suspicion of a conspiracy against me.

I removed a deep drawer from the wardrobe there and lined its rough inside with blankets to make a nest for Lucia. The innkeeper had not been warned, so there was no crib provided, but a girl was sent for from the village to mind the baby.

At supper, which everyone took in the communal living-room downstairs, I asked how long Isabelle intended our stay to be.

'That rather depends on you, Eugenie,' she said sweetly. 'There are things we must discuss, but let us leave it until later. I should like to rest a little first.'

The food was simple but adequate, with local cheeses and a lot of coarse red wine. I refused coffee afterwards but felt obliged to swallow the fiery local liqueur which the landlord offered from his cellar. And prompt on that we broke up to retire, I going with Isabelle to wrestle her from the pernicious stays she was disciplining herself back into.

When she was freed she sank exhausted into a low chair by the stone hearth and I saw silent tears glistening on her cheeks. 'Oh Genie, I've made such a stupid nonsense of my life. How fortunate you are, never to have been tempted into folly like mine.'

I said nothing, having experienced temptation but not been allowed the opportunity to snatch any forbidden fruit. Which I was sure I would have tasted, had fate permitted Gilbert and me much longer together. And then I might have been in Isabelle's shoes, with a baby born outside wedlock, and all the world censorious of me. But with some precious part of his flesh and blood still to warm my heart.

I lifted her heavy silver brush and began long, calm strokes through her unpinned hair. It was comforting for us both. The act of touching seemed to dissolve the barrier between us. We were closer then to the two unscarred travellers who had started out from England some seven months before.

'We have endured a lot together,' she said, finding the level of my thoughts. 'You have been a good friend to me.'

And must pay for that? the cynical part of my mind still objected. I knew she was about to demand more of me, but I did feel some pity then.

'I am truly sorry,' she said, and her face screwed up like a child's that tries not to weep in public. 'Truly sorry to have thrown that most – *unsuitable* young man at you. I was badly advised, but so desperate, Genie. Can you understand that?'

'I understand enough to know I would not have suited him once he learned I'd no adequate dowry.'

'That could have been arranged, but you would have been tied together for ever. I see that now. It was wrong.'

'A lifetime without love,' I reminded her.

'Yes. That is something I've thought about further. And I think I have the solution.'

My hands slowed and stopped. What enormity would she propose this time? 'You have another husband for me?' I asked with cold sarcasm.

'Vincenzo has found one, here in this village!' She turned to me, hands clasped in delight, her face shining in the firelight. 'He lives quite close. You shall see him tomorrow. But we need to have everything quickly arranged for fear his life gives out before the ceremony.'

150

It was preposterous. I sank back on the hearthrug and stared, unbelieving.

I could see she had trouble curbing her impatience with me. 'Eugenie, the man is *dying*. Leaving his family impoverished. I will pay him well. In this way we shall be helping everyone. He is a widower with children and grandchildren. Now he can die happy knowing his home is safe and his family will not starve. I shall be generous, you may be sure. I shall make it my favourite personal charity, and you would do well to see it in the same light. You will be free again straight after, but a safely married woman. And it will cost you nothing; not a single penny.'

'Only my family name.'

'Well, you will become the Signora Facci instead. That sounds quite impressive, don't you think? It should go down well when you return to England. We're always such fools over foreigners.'

I looked away, ashamed for her hypocrisy. Talking of the advantages to me, to that poor man's family, she considered no one but herself.

'And then your right to the child will be undisputed. We'll have her surname changed by deed poll to match your new one. Within a very short while you will *genuinely* be a widow, because he is truly drawing his last breaths. And if some day you choose to remarry there'll be no obstacle, but *voilà*! a copy of the Italian marriage contract and your husband's death registered with the local officials.'

'There is no way,' I said, 'that I would allow you to push me into such an underhand contract. Goodnight, Isabelle. I am going to bed now.'

'Sleep on it,' she called after me. 'You will see how right I am.'

There was no sleep for me. Or not until the weak winter

151

sun began to lighten the sky. Then I turned on my shoulder and briefly gave in, because with a heavy heart I had already given in to Isabelle's invention.

My eyes closed on an image of the child wildly exercising her puny strength as she lay on the blanket, free of her long clothes, tiny fists and feet punching the air in involuntary jerkiness, and mewing like a kitten.

Fatherless and rejected by her mother; if I did as Belle asked, she would at least have me. She would become solely my charge. My daughter, my Lucia.

I would make myself into the Signora Eugenie Facci, mother of a small female infant, and in God's time a widow. Not at Belle's bidding, but at the helpless little creature's.

Yet it was not an easy choice to face. After a bare half-hour's sleep I dressed and took her makeshift crib downstairs to the village girl. For all that I was quiet, Isabelle heard and followed me down, standing in the doorway in her night wrapper to watch.

I turned my back on her in answer to Lucia's first little mew on waking. More used by now to babies, with their squirming bodies and unceasing wordless demands, yet I was afraid. I bent closer and looked down on her. At that moment I hardly dared gather her up and hold her to me.

She ceased her noise and the puckered lids came unsealed for a moment, showing eyes round and blue as Isabelle's own. I had no idea how much they could actually see, but they seemed to stare up into mine with a challenge. I felt then a quite new sensation, as though for the first time I became aware of warm blood coursing through my veins.

Overcome by emotion, I handed her to the Italian girl, pinned my hat on, seized my cloak and went out without

152

another word into the still dim village street. All the time I could feel Isabelle's eyes boring into my back. I imagined the expression in them, the hard gleam of determination, the tightened mouth as she forced herself not to remark on my rudeness in ignoring her.

I tramped across stiff-frozen grass and past a cracked fountain basin, contemptuous of ice pools in the stony road, the dirtied white of the wretched, sparse houses made more unlovely against the glowing purity of fresh snow. I walked far into the country. I was gone almost two hours and my feet were numbed, but by the time I turned back towards the inn I knew I could do it. If I was to raise Lucia, then I needed all the official protection I could get, however false.

After breakfast we went to meet my future husband. And two days later the local priest joined us in marriage, with my two witnesses and the poor man's entire family crowded round his deathbed.

Thirteen

'The police have come back,' said Geoffrey, bustling in to where I was writing letters in the morning-room. Laurence was in London and presumably his brother-in-law saw himself as in charge.

'Where has Hadrill put him?' I asked.

'Them, not him. There is an Inspector McGill with the sergeant who came before. They've been shown into the library.'

'Sergeant Best,' I remembered.

'Well, whoever. What do you want me to tell them?'

'Nothing, Geoffrey, thank you. I shall see them myself. I've almost finished here. Where is Isabelle?'

'She was with me in the rose garden, but I think she's gone upstairs for a little while. A headache, she said. Perhaps I'd better go and see she's all right.'

'Yes. And give her my sympathy.' I re-read the last paragraph of the letter to my mother, signed it and placed it in an envelope, which I left to be stamped. Crossing the hall I saw the tips of the children's shoes projecting beyond the nearer upright at the foot of the staircase.

'Mummy,' Edwin called delightedly, ducking forward and beaming when he recognized my step. Lucy's toes were swiftly withdrawn.

'Darlings,' I said, 'where is Nanny?'

Seeing that I'd already spotted her, Lucy acknowledged her presence. 'Gone to talk to Cook,' she informed me crisply. 'And she said we couldn't go with her because Cook always offers us something unsuitable to eat.'

'Silly blub,' Edwin put in. 'And I like silly blub.' He sounded regretful.

'I should think that syllabub was most suitable.' I bent and gave them both a little squeeze. 'Perhaps Nanny wants to have a private word with Cook.'

'Secrets.' Lucy condemned them. She was going through a phase of scorn for any action that denied her own presence or discounted her importance.

'So what are you both doing here?'

'Waiting,' Edwin answered, and 'Counting,' Lucy said at the same instant.

'Edwin only got up to twenty,' big sister claimed witheringly.

'Very good,' I told him. 'How did you manage that, with only ten fingers to count on? Did you take off your shoes and add your toes in?'

He gave a fat chuckle. He wasn't a great talker. I feared his sister's agile tongue had rather put him off competing. Perhaps the time was close when they should be educated separately.

I stood up and smoothed my skirt straight. 'I have visitors to receive now, but ask Nanny if later we can all go for a walk,' I said. 'Perhaps straight after luncheon.'

Lucy clapped, bobbing up and down. 'To the watermill!'

'Not today. We'll go to Ploversmead. It's my turn to choose.'

'But you're grown-up.'

'What difference does that make?'

'It's us children get to choose. Grown-ups can do as they like at any time.'

155

I thought I saw her point. 'Not "us children choose", but "*we* children choose",' I corrected her. 'But I really must go now.'

Behind me the library door had opened and a tall man stood looking out. Lucy flushed with shame at a stranger overhearing her put right.

'Inspector, Sergeant.' And I went to join them, the inspector closing the heavy door firmly behind us.

'I'm sorry my husband is away at present. Would you like him to call in on you when he returns, or will you talk to me to save time?'

'I think Your Ladyship can help us with anything we need to know,' the inspector said.

'Does this concern the man who went missing during the storm?'

He looked squarely at me from deep-set dark eyes, his bushy moustache and flattened hair startlingly black against a marked indoor pallor. 'The foreigner, ma'am. An Eyetalian, as we now know.'

'Then he came a long way to get lost here.' I waved towards a group of chairs.

'A long way to be murdered here.' This time the man's speech was curt, almost threatening. Keeping his eyes on me, and still standing while he drew a notebook from an inner pocket of his dark overcoat, he opened it and creased a page flat with a spatulate thumb. I felt my heart beating fast in my throat.

'Facky,' he said, watching my every reaction, and it was all I could do to stop myself correcting the pronunciation. 'A Sig-nor Facky. That was his name, milady.'

'So you've recovered his papers, then?'

'No, ma'am – Your Ladyship – but foreigners get took note of when they arrive at Dover, especially in this Eyetalian's case because he had mislaid his luggage on the boat. We'd had the cadaver photographed, and his face was recognized by an official at the harbour. He had a paper the man had signed when they returned his belongings.'

'That must be very helpful.'

'And we are hoping to trace an English gentleman who travelled to London in his company on the train. It seems the Eyetalian was trying out his few words of English on him, a gentleman who had himself once visited Italy.'

'So, if you know so much, you already have a witness who can give some idea of this foreigner's background.'

'We haven't as yet discovered who this English person was. It was a railway porter, ma'am – Your Ladyship – who overheard the beginnings of their conversation. If we can trace the gentleman concerned, I have every hope of learning just why this Eyetalian came to England and who it was he intended to get in touch with.'

'Yes, I see. Thank you, Inspector. It's good of you to keep us informed. I will certainly see that my husband learns of this on his return.'

'Thass not all,' he said abruptly, as if afraid I would hustle him out. 'I have to inquire, Your Ladyship, if the name is known to anyone in this household.'

'*Racky*, was it? I can't say I've ever heard of it myself.'

'Facky, ma'am. Heff-hay-see-see-hi, Facky.'

'That's quite an unusual name, Inspector. I'm sure you'll have an instant response, if anyone has heard of it. How would you like to question us? The family first, perhaps, and then let Hadrill summon the staff?'

'If you will be so kind.'

I went across to the tapestry bell-pull and rang. 'I take it you will not require the children?'

'Certainly not, ma'am. Those would be the only ones, the pair I saw just now?'

'Yes, Inspector. Lucy is seven and Edwin just four. We have managed to keep this unpleasant business from them so far.'

'Quite so. I have a lad of seven myself, ma'am, so I understand.'

Francis was the footman on duty. I explained to him when he arrived and within five minutes Geoffrey and Dr Millson had arrived, then Mildred pushing Lord Sedgwick's wheelchair. Isabelle drifted in last carrying a *petit-point* embroidery tambour which I knew she hadn't stuck a needle through for at least three years. I introduced Inspector McGill and left him to explain.

The others' faces stayed blank at mention of the Italian name, but I didn't dare to look directly at Isabelle for fear the watchful sergeant caught the direction of it.

It was even possible she had forgotten the name of the wretched Italian family up in the hills whom she had paid off in cash. Certainly by the time I returned to England theirs was not the surname on my marriage lines. *Il dottore* – whatever his lack of medical skills – had been adequate to doctoring that.

A final question closed the interview. Had the family at any time entertained Italian guests at Stakerleys?

This scarcely concerned me, as a newcomer of some mere seven years. Mildred hesitated. 'I am sure there have been a number of Italian guests at some time or other. My grandfather was much involved with Lord Salisbury in his day, and was himself briefly responsible for the Foreign Office. We frequently received European dignitaries here when it wasn't convenient to house them at Hatfield. This would go back to a time before I was old enough to participate, but I'm almost sure I could produce recent lists of people visiting. We always ask our guests to sign their names in our daybook.'

They arranged between them that Sergeant Best should return next day for these lists when Mildred had looked them out.

Lord Sedgwick, who had begun by looking slightly perturbed, had now dropped off to sleep in his wheelchair.

'Very interesting,' Inspector McGill said suddenly, addressing me. I was startled, my mind elsewhere. Then I saw his chin was raised, exposing a scrawny, turkey-red neck, as he scanned the classical figures on the deep frieze of relief moulding above the library panelling.

'They're thought to be very fine,' I told him.

He seemed to be considering what the nymphs and satyrs were actually up to in their fleeing games and floating draperies. 'Eyetalian, would they be, milady?'

'Indeed, I believe they may be, Inspector.' Surely he wasn't looking for some obscure connection there?

'Over a hundred and fifty years old,' I told him, to dispel any absurd suspicions. Did he think we kept a team of foreign artists secretly at work here?

'Ah.' His eyes dropped from the white and cameo-pink figures against their Wedgwood blue background, to take in the bold hunting prints grouped on the blank wall between the windows, and they clearly pleased him more. The British uniformed pursuit of vermin was more acceptable to his police ethos than dalliance in Arcadia.

'Right then, milady, we'll be seeing the servants now.'

The two policemen, one in uniform, the other with his dark overcoat rebuttoned and bowler hat in hand, were led off to wherever Hadrill had the staff assembled. I met Isabelle's eyes and she looked quickly away.

'Please don't expect luncheon to be on time today,' I said generally. 'Goodness knows at what stage preparations have been interrupted in the kitchen. I'd better go down myself and see to things.'

I collected the children from the staircase, where they had returned when Nanny was required to join the servants in their hall. Hand in hand we crept down the stone-flagged passage, past the door where Inspector McGill and the sergeant were holding court, and reached the warm heart of the house enticing with the scent of rising bread. It was a rare treat for all three of us to be left there to our own devices with so many diversions to hand. Edwin made a beeline for a tin of iced biscuits while Lucy unearthed a stone jug of lemon barley water from the marble shelves of the larder. We perched on stools as high as you'd find in any lawyer's office and played at being Queen Alexandra serving tea at Sandringham.

The warm dough scent was slowly being penetrated by the succulence of roasting lamb, with occasional feral spittings from behind the great oven door. On the hob the flame was turned low under a pair of bubbling steam puddings. I removed the lids and lifted each child in turn to watch the bowls chattering, plumply tied in knotted muslin bonnets. They sniffed the steam, to guess what flavours the puddings were. Lucy rightly identified both marmalade and sultana, while Edwin's wistful 'Chockerlit', each time, was the vain hope that it sounded.

We invaded the scullery and even dared to trespass in Hadrill's pantry where ranks of silverware filled the cupboards, and rows of shiny keys hung, each on its appointed hook, inside a glass-fronted mahogany cabinet.

'What are they all for?' Lucy wanted to know.

'Doors and rooms and cupboards,' I told her. 'I've no idea which is for what, but Hadrill knows every one. He would scorn to have labels on them to remind him what they open.'

'I think,' Lucy said solemnly, 'that Hadrill must be a very clever man. Nearly as clever as Papa.'

160

'You're probably right, darling.' And I hoped – felt almost sure – that Hadrill was also very discreet; enough so to ensure that any of the staff who remembered would never actually mention that briefly, before I married Laurence, I was known here as the *Signora*.

Inspector McGill did not depart from Stakerleys entirely unrewarded. His stern interrogation produced a confession. Robert Travers, under-footman, had an uncle who'd been valet to my father-in-law until he'd grown restless and gone to sea as a barber. And when he came home he brought a wife from foreign parts, Giannina from Trieste, but she had died from whooping cough some five years back, aged thirty-four. Her headstone was to be found in the parish graveyard.

This, I hoped, together with the guest lists Mildred was to provide tomorrow, should prove matter enough to sidetrack the police inquiry for a while at least. And perhaps by then the case would have started to recede in interest and memory.

In the meantime I yielded the children up to Nanny and went to my desk to check that the Italian certificates were safely locked away.

There were three papers folded together in one large envelope, and two in another, both dated on the outside. The more recent held Edwin's birth certificate and my marriage lines as wife to Laurence, Viscount Crowthorne. The other's contents went back seven years.

The birth certificate for my daughter Margherita Lucia appeared genuine enough, the additions having been skilfully completed in black Indian ink indistinguishable from the original. The father was now named as Ernesto Fabrizio Vincenzo Paolo Gabrieli; the mother Eugenie Catherine Fellowes Gabrieli. Only three words had been inserted, the first two forenames for the father and the final surname for the mother. The date was unchanged, at 14 January 1901.

The other certificate had originally shown Eugenie Catherine Fellowes married to one Ernesto Facci and was dated 5 March 1901. A little more ingenuity had been required there. Gabrieli's forenames and surname now followed the real husband's, while my own name was left unaltered. The final figure of the year's date had been rounded into an 'O', thus legitimizing my daughter.

But what gave most cause for relief then was that the word Facci had disappeared, converted into the forename Fabrizio, as shown on both papers. On the marriage certificate a slight thickening of the 'r' on its upstroke could well have been caused by some speck of foreign matter in the ink.

At the time there had been no need to conceal the name Facci, which would have done as well as any other, but since Gabrieli had entered his own name as father to Lucia, the same name had to appear as my husband. And this he had contrived, converting 'Facci' into a further forename for himself.

So I was safe, widow of a composite person who had never existed but was the father of my legitimate child. And surely, after all this time, no one would check back to the Italian records, or remember that in March 1900, far from marrying abroad, I was still in my last term as a schoolgirl at St Leonards-on-Sea.

I carefully put the certificates back and smoothed out the remaining sheet. It was the programme for a concert of music given at London's Royal Albert Hall in May of 1901, and included the Violin Concerto by Max Bruch.

Again the printed words swam together as I lived that evening over again. How fitting it was that I should have wept over the *adagio* that night, which proved to be the watershed of my life.

Fourteen

The ceremony had been short enough. Isabelle, Gabrieli and I left first, the sly-faced old priest following us out to the car for his payment.

Halting in the doorway I looked back to see the dying man – my legal husband – lying under his covers like a plucked and shrivelled eagle, fleshless between brown papery skin and jutting bones. His filmy eyes opened, briefly alive under wrinkled lids set in hollows that were a greeny purple like bruises, and stared at me accusingly.

As I had held his clawlike hand and the words were said, I had forced myself not to believe that mortification had already set in and I was wedding a corpse. By which I did him an injustice. In fact he was to linger on another nineteen days. And by then two other men, in apparent good health, were to predecease him.

There was no question of my deserting Lucia now that I was in fact a married woman and formally, if not physically, her mother. We returned to Venice in the magnificent motor car as soon as the ceremony was completed and the fee handed over to the next in line of the Facci family. I wasn't happy about the transaction, but every time I looked at Lucia's tiny sleeping face I felt a shade less guilt. She was the future; the old man the past. I hung in some indeterminate stage between the two, but not really the present. To exist in the present I should have some sense of vitality.

Isabelle was planning our transfer back to Milan. There, resuming her own identity, she would be free to pick up once more her career of captivating all who came near her. I was sure this Italian re-entry was to be the rehearsal for her next onslaught on English society; but fate has a way of trampling all over one's intentions when one least expects it.

Again mention of Isabelle's grandfather arrived by way of the London newspapers. Driving out from the House after addressing the Lords on some mundane domestic matter, his cab had passed through the customary little knot of petitioners waiting at the gates. As the horse turned, a woman had thrown herself at it, shouting some incoherent slogan and snatching at the bridle. She was dragged several yards as the terrified beast reared, savaging her with its hooves as it plunged.

Lord Sedgwick had alighted in great concern once the animal was under control. A doctor, summoned to see to the woman's injuries – which were less severe than at first appeared – quickly transferred his attention to His Lordship who had collapsed, clutching at his chest, but it was in vain. With the kind of irony that made the Greeks believe the gods mocked mortals, Lord Sedgwick, born to riches and fame, was literally to die in the gutter.

Isabelle could barely believe that this insurmountable obstacle to her full enjoyment of life should suddenly cease to be. As long as she could remember he had dominated the family, so that every small move had to be given his approval (or more likely the reverse). Her father, a less assertive man, had been reduced to a mere cipher, disallowed strong opinions of his own and restricted to concern only for the house and estate of Stakerleys, which the older man's passion for politics left him no time for overseeing in person.

All this I had learned over the months in Isabelle's company. Her eagerness now to return for the funeral arose less from respect for her grandfather than from the opportunity to demonstrate her new independence.

I helped her pack. It was farewell to the soft and vibrant colours she was again delighting in, and a return to black for all her outer wear. I shook out the creases from costumes and frocks made for her almost a year back at St Leonards as Hugo Delmayne's widow. They might not be *du dernier cri* but not everyone had the strict eye for fashion of my mother. Isabelle would grace the clothes so touchingly that no one would notice their details, only her veiled tears and sweet sadness.

I had some misgivings about being left alone abroad, but Isabelle declared this was no time for her to descend on Stakerleys with a circus in tow, and I had made no plans of my own by then. I was to go to Milan and wait there, where she would either come herself or send for me. She took with her only a young Venetian girl, her personal maid since I had become more heavily occupied with Lucia after the nurse was discharged.

Gabrieli, who was supposed to facilitate my journey across country, had disappeared by the time I made the move, claiming he had 'family problems' elsewhere.

I returned with Lucia and the main part of Isabelle's and my own luggage to find the Milan apartment shuttered and empty. The van with our baggage was obliged to camp at the pavement's edge while I ran to earth the woman who had been housekeeper-cook before. She was full of complaints against us, having received no wages from the bank since we left, nor any replies to the letters she had sent to Isabelle in Venice. I could not understand what

165

had happened. When she grudgingly unlocked the apartment we found a heap of unopened mail there including Isabelle's letter of instructions to prepare for our return.

It could only be Gabrieli who had stepped in to countermand the bank's instructions, and who had also suppressed the woman's letters of complaint to Isabelle, on their arrival at the *palazzo.*

Now, left alone in Italy to fare for myself and the child, deserted by Isabelle and cheated by *il dottore,* I was almost in despair. Temporarily relodged, with the unpaid housekeeper grudgingly in attendance, I visited the bank and examined the document allegedly signed by Isabelle that transferred the servants' wages to a separate account now emptied.

I was able finally to persuade the manager that it was a forgery, and he should await new instructions from England following my telegram to Isabelle explaining the circumstances. He was not at all happy with this arrangement, and I was left praying that Isabelle would not suddenly decide to cut me loose as an unneeded encumbrance. In which case there could be real trouble for me, even a criminal charge. I was uncomfortably reminded that I had myself signed the original instructions on Isabelle's behalf. If she was ever required to disclaim Gabrieli's forgery, she would be free to do the same for mine.

It took four days of telegrams and an assumed face of easy confidence before help came and I felt secure enough to order in fresh food and fuel. Until then we were obliged to wear heavy outer garments in the house and eke out what lire I had on scratch meals in a cheap eating-house.

The bank forwarded a hundred pounds on a money order from the new Lord Sedgwick's London account. A short note from Isabelle, written a few hours after the funeral, assured me we were in her thoughts and she would return some time after Easter. In the meantime I resolved to track down the whereabouts of the rascally Gabrieli.

I had barely wrested from the housekeeper the name of the intermediary whom the wretched man had originally used to hire her, when a fresh telegram arrived. Isabelle and her maid were to be met from the train at Milan railway station in three days' time. She had certainly not intended so rapid a return, and I assumed – wrongly, as it happened – that her change of mind was due to rage at Gabrieli's absconding with her funds.

The Isabelle who alighted from the first-class carriage at Milan was markedly different from the confident one who had left me in Venice some ten days before, revelling in her accession at last to the title of 'Lady'. She was pale and appeared to be suffering from shock. As soon as we reached the apartment she asked to be taken to see Lucia, knelt by the sleeping child's crib and laid her head against the frilled muslin of the canopy. I was disconcerted to see her shoulders shaking as she tried to fight back real tears.

'Isabelle?' I put my hands on her shoulders as she turned, and she clung to me, speechless with emotion. 'Isabelle, what on earth has happened?' Surely her grandfather's death had not suddenly struck her into a new realization of her own frail mortality?

She went on weeping, and it was not until a full hour later, after she had eaten and been revived with brandy, that the words came tumbling out. She had twice fainted at Stakerleys and, as a result, consulted her late mother's specialist in Harley Street, London. He had examined her thoroughly and insisted she must attend hospital within a month for further, surgical exploration.

'Something has gone very wrong,' she said. 'It's the

fault of that monster Gabrieli. The damage must be seen to without delay if I am to regain full health. And in any case—'

'What, Isabelle?' I waited for her to muster the courage to say more.

'In any case – it seems – I can never bear another child.'

She fought with emotion before she could go on. 'So you see, Lucia is all I have; all I am ever able to leave behind.'

But Lucia was mine: we were inseparable. Hadn't that been the whole point of Isabelle's machinations? Now was she to make an about-turn and demand the child back?

No, she said; Lucia was to stay mine, but never out of her own reach. We must both return to Stakerleys with her, I as a widowed mother retained as her companion.

I was appalled. If I were to grant what she asked, then I would never be free of Isabelle. She was demanding an extension of my bondage to her, because there was no way in which I would yield my baby up to her now and quietly go away.

It seemed that despite her earlier willingness to cast off all obligations she was proposing something like the situation with the Bey's two wives at Qasr el Mastaba, women so close and interdependent that no outsider could guess whose any child was. I was in a torment, unsure that I could rise to such selflessness. And yet Isabelle was the natural mother, and seemingly distraught now at her loss.

For the sake of peace, there was nothing for it then but to let a few days pass in apparent acceptance. But Isabelle had plans to make about her coming surgery in London, so we put arrangements in hand for our final passage home. It was then I explained to her the full extent of Gabrieli's treachery.

'He'll be in Venice,' she decided. 'We'll catch him there.'

'Do we need to, Isabelle? Such a disagreeable man; I know he has cheated you, but can't you leave it at that, and wash your hands of him? He's so untrustworthy. Just suppose he threatened to expose the truth. Could you bear it?' I looked at her. With her head tilted, she was watching me from the corner of her eyes. I knew that look. It meant trouble.

'No, Eugenie. What he has done to me I can never forgive. He shall pay for it in full.'

It was not the stolen money she meant, but much more.

'If you won't come with me I shall go alone and speak to the police there.'

'Of course I'll come.' Alone she might do something outrageous which would get her into deep water. The *carabinieri* might not be so compliant to English peeresses as our police at home, and Isabelle could be offensively arrogant with anyone she considered her social inferior.

There was nothing for it but that we must travel to Venice next day, catching a train without even making reservations, and leaving Lucia behind with the servants. I wasn't happy about this but Isabelle insisted that children rarely saw their parents in her walk of life.

I had not expected to be travelling to Venice again, and as the train rattled across the causeway from the mainland I regretted that we should not be staying longer in the languorous magic of its elegant dilapidation.

When our boat reached the *palazzo* steps Isabelle ordered the gondolier to take us two buildings farther along, where she paid him off and took my arm for walking the little distance back on the narrow landing path.

'There is no call to advertise our presence,' she said, 'or the wretch will try to escape by the rear.'

The great door was unlocked, and opened to my touch. We passed the dim offices that took up the ground floor, and mounted the grand staircase in silence. Corridors led to the front and back of the building from the tiled landing. We listened and I heard the cook's voice raised in the wordless grunting that was meant as song.

'Go and ask where he is,' Isabelle ordered.

Marina was astounded as I appeared in the kitchen doorway. She stood beaming, in grubby apron and down-at-heel shoes. '*Signora! Come sta? E la bambina?*'

I closed the door on our brief conversation in case we might be overheard and our quarry warned. By the time I had explained why I was there and she had informed me that *il dottore* was in residence, '*comodo com' un principe*', Isabelle must have come upon him. From the landing again I could look through two doorways to a pool of light where they stood talking together, he trailing in one hand the rug that must have covered him as he sprawled on the scroll-ended sofa.

'. . . would not have you think I was ungrateful,' a smiling Isabelle was silkily saying as I approached. 'So I am making this brief visit to ensure you are adequately rewarded, *Dottore.*'

She turned. 'Ah, here is the Signora Fellowes. Or perhaps I should say Facci?'

His laugh was a short bleat. 'Gabrieli, surely? That was neatly arranged, *non è vero?* My beautiful English-milady wife. Has she come to claim her rights with me?' He leered in my direction.

He had been drinking or he would have been more on his guard against Isabelle's dangerous affability.

'Ah,' she said softly, her head tilted, with that sinister

170

sideways look in her eyes. 'Yes, of course. You will need some compensation from Eugenie too. To maintain you in the manner to which you have became accustomed with us.'

I looked at him and shuddered. He wore the same clothes Isabelle had bought for him in Milan, but the waistcoat was stained with grease, and white flakes of dead skin powdered his shoulders from his unwashed scalp. I doubt he had shaved at all since last we saw him and there was no shaping to the mass of greying whiskers on his chin and cheeks.

'Eugenie, my dear.' Isabelle turned to me with a handful of banknotes she had pulled from her muff. 'We must not overlook the staff. Will you give this to Cook? With my warm thanks, of course. As a special and final settlement. Explain, if you will, that you are not staying.'

'Meanwhile my dear Vincenzo will escort me below.' She beamed on him. 'Perhaps we can enjoy a last glass of wine together before I take a gondola to Santa Lucia. And I will have the chance to show you some little gratitude as well.'

I hesitated, but knew she could not get far before I caught up with her. Gabrieli was fool enough to accept her sweetness at face value but she could hardly entice him into the police post against his will. Marina delayed me a few minutes more and then I ran downstairs anxious to see which direction they had taken along the narrow quay.

They were walking ahead, had almost reached the turning to the next canal, and Isabelle stopped, waving an arm as if to illustrate some remark she made about the scene gently sparkling before her in the springlike sunshine. A gondola with closed red velvet drapes went gently past, but there was no other sound just then, no other movement.

My eyes travelled back from the slow, rhythmic flow of

171

the gondolier's graceful figure as he took the turn and went out of sight. Then with horror I saw Gabrieli staggering, seeming to lean out sideways on empty air, poised a moment with his back arched and one leg outflung, then the other buckled under him and he fell, his head striking the stone landing steps before he tumbled sideways, entering the water with barely a splash. I started to run and came up with Isabelle who was staring wide-eyed at the widening circles where he had disappeared.

'He was drunk, wasn't he?' she said. 'You surely noticed. They will find that when they come to fish him out.'

There was no sign of a body in the dark-clouded water, just a little rush of bubbles upwards. I looked around for something with which to reach out and prod the depths, but there was nothing.

'What happened? Did he slip?'

Isabelle raised her glazed eyes from the canal and stared through me. 'He simply seemed to lose his balance.'

'Couldn't you have saved him?'

'I reached out, but it was too far. And besides—' She shuddered theatrically '—he was so dirty. There could have been creatures in his clothes.'

Fifteen

I have never understood why I allowed her to hustle me away. In horror I looked back over my shoulder but there was nothing to be seen of the man.

'He was a good swimmer,' Isabelle had claimed confidently – but how could she have known?

'He will have dived down and let the water carry him under the bridge. So he has escaped us in the end. Never mind. We have more pressing things to see to.'

But there had been those bubbles, and hadn't he struck his head in falling? If the water hadn't revived him . . .

'Isabelle, we must tell someone. Suppose he can't manage—'

'The devil looks after his own. Don't worry, Genie. It's just another of his devious ways of getting out of trouble.'

Although I could scarcely believe he would recover, Isabelle's calm assurance made any more terrible alternative seem impossible. Later in the train to Milan I still fought against the horror of the sight, knowing we had done wrong to leave him. However repulsive a person and however much his incompetence had ruined Isabelle's life, he was a human creature and instinctively one had this urge to protect.

Isabelle was aware of my silent torment and laid a hand

on mine. 'Genie, what a worrier you are. The man was drunk. You saw how unsteadily he walked. Cold water will instantly have brought him round.' Her eyes brimmed with laughter. 'Haven't you heard that alcohol is a great preservative?'

If she could make a joke of it, could matters be really so very dire? Life was black enough then with my own and Lucia's dilemma. I was at my wits' end. A lone woman, and a foreigner, I could not hope to support us both in Italy. There was no option but to travel with Isabelle back to England. I wasn't ready to face my mother and the sad emptiness of what had been my home. And so, too feeble to swim against the current, I let it carry me in Isabelle's wake, to Stakerleys and a continuation of my subservience to her.

There were certain adjustments to be made, but surprisingly I had seldom lived so free of cares as in the first few weeks of our return. The new Lord Sedgwick's delight in his daughter was all-embracing. As principal of her modest entourage I was warmly welcomed, and although he seemed momentarily startled by my baby's inclusion he gave instructions that we should be accorded every facility.

Isabelle was for us all having our rooms together on the same floor of the east wing, but His Lordship was quick to perceive my coolness towards this idea. 'The *Signora* is right,' he decreed. 'You could find the baby's crying tedious, my dear. Far better they should be housed on a higher floor, where they can spread to three or four rooms, with accommodation besides for a nanny.'

'But I need my companion close to hand,' Isabelle pouted.

Her father, however, was adamant. Newly released from

an autocratic rule himself, perhaps he recognized that I needed a little freedom from Isabelle's constant demands. His new-found authority surprised her, but she was obliged to accept this further distancing from her child.

It suited me well that I should have this much privacy, and that outside my set hours of duty Isabelle would need to walk up another flight to visit us, or send a message by a servant.

Fascinated by the change in our way of life, I began indiscernibly to settle in, succumbing to Stakerleys' enchantment. I now recognized the great house, which on my first visit had overwhelmed me, as similar to many fine buildings on the continent. Better informed on architecture, I could appreciate the classical proportions of the golden stone elevations with their three storeys of identical tall windows topped by a further one of perfect squares.

On the west face a vast arched entrance under the central pediment is approached by a raised carriageway with balustrades and twin stone stairways leading down to lower terraces. The formal gardens lie on the south side, separated by high hedges or brick walls as if into individual, connecting chambers, and here Lord Sedgwick had indulged his enthusiasm for flowering shrubs and pergolas with rich patterns of coloured blossom.

The ground falls away from the house in all directions, on three sides in open parkland to a wide loop of the river, and on the fourth, beyond the gardens, to ancient beech woods. The gradient is quite steep, so that from ground level only the tips of the many chimneys are ever visible above the hidden, balustraded roof. Lord Sedgwick told me that a Venetian architect had designed the house in 1737 to replace an earlier Jacobean one destroyed by fire.

After the frenzied months of travel and anxiety for

Isabelle's health, the calm of the quiet Buckinghamshire countryside was bliss. In that late spring the beech woods were enchanting, the tiny leaves unfurling into a delicate translucent green against silver trunks smooth as cathedral pillars. And underfoot, damp and yielding, there still lay a soft copper carpet aromatic with the subtle scents of English earth. We enjoyed long walks together, with Lucy – we had completely dropped the Italian pronunciation – trundled in a baby-carriage on solid rubber wheels.

There was little sense of mourning in the great house although we all wore unrelieved black and for a while received no guests. When we gathered for meals, but for the presence of so many servants, there was an informality about the family reunited from their respective occupations elsewhere.

Before we ladies retired from the table one evening, Lord Sedgwick looked round our circle with a sad smile, his eyes coming to rest on Isabelle and her brother. 'Ah, my dears, if only your sweet mother could be with us. How happy and proud she would be.'

He put down the glass he had raised and with humble apology laid a hand over his elder daughter's as she sat alongside. 'I meant, of course, your dear mothers, both of them, bless them.'

Mildred took it well, equable as ever. She was the daughter of his first love who died at her birth, although Isabelle claimed later it had been a dynastic match arranged by his father and he had had no choice in it.

Usually quite quick to pick up on people's character, I had initially discounted the older woman. There had been so much breathtakingly new at Stakerleys, and other distinctive personalities challenging my attention, so that this quiet spinster, draped in shapeless garments and seemingly always beyond the perimeter of the chandeliers' bright illumination, I had unthinkingly set aside for later consideration.

At table her voice was low and gruff, her chin bedded on the boned net choker of her high-necked blouse, her conversation minimal and inconclusive. When, as elder daughter, she served coffee for the ladies after we withdrew, she remained silent. So her interruption of the complaints Isabelle aired of some guest 'quite unsuitable to be given dinner the following weekend' was startling.

'Unsuitable people,' Mildred said in a new, well-modulated voice, 'are sometimes gifted in some outstanding way. And that makes them totally acceptable. We shall be receiving Dr Millson, Belle.'

Her quiet tone of authority was not all that astonished me. Something showed briefly in her eyes which revealed she spoke with irony. An irony quite lost on her younger half-sister.

Mildred, I was to learn, was an intellectual, well considered by other ladies who had attended Oxford University at the same time. She was accustomed to being discounted, even took a perverse kind of pride in it, having long been the butt of witticisms and elephantine asides from some of the most elevated academics there, gentlemen who first opposed and then ignored the presence of women at their lectures. She admitted to an amused contempt for the boasted superiority of the male sex (outside her own family) – a fact which Isabelle attributed to her acceptance that no man would ever woo a female of such ovine features and graceless carriage.

While unable truthfully to call her a beauty, yet I found Mildred handsome in her own way, strongly resembling her father's line. The long jaw, aquiline nose and straight, heavy brows were frequently to be recognized in family portraits dating from the first baronet created by King

James in 1610. If indeed she did slightly resemble a sheep, it was a good beast and well bred.

I soon learned to respect Mildred's judgement and the austere silences which marked her disapproval. It took a little longer to decipher all the subtle references accompanied by a glint of humour behind her severe pince-nez. While accepted as unremarkable by her nearest, she was the undeniable final arbiter in all family disputes in which her father and brother chose to accept a lead. She should, Isabelle grumbled after some such defeat, have been a man and been done with it.

The 'unsuitable person' of Isabelle's censure was a local doctor whose shabby pony and trap was to be seen any day outside the meanest cottages in the village. He appeared kindly if slightly austere, but I soon found this severity was a shield for his natural shyness. It disappeared at once when he felt himself needed or among people of his own kind. He was above all modest and from a humble background, having been put through medical school by a London professor of surgery who had recognized his interest and potential as a very young man. He was now approaching fifty and I assumed he was a widower until Mildred mentioned a delicate wife in a nursing home in Windsor.

Dr Millson had become a quite regular visitor to Staker-leys since the old Earl's death, and was now regarded less as a guest than as part of the extended family. I watched Isabelle's growing disdain as it became evident that he would be staying overnight. I could only guess that she found him unwelcome because he had infil-trated the family during her absence. But there was also the possibility that she feared the closeness of a medical man who might observe and rightly diagnose her present weakness.

She had covered the planned visit to a nursing home at Marylebone with the excuse of a shopping excursion, and expected me to put up in nearby lodgings, leaving Lucy with our new nursery maid, interviewed by – and under instruction from – the semi-retired, semi-lodger on the top corridor south, whom Isabelle and her brother referred to as 'Nanny T'. This formidable lady was in most respects regarded as a family member but, suffering from badly swollen legs, she seldom descended to ground level and took all her meals in her rooms upstairs.

I have omitted to mention Isabelle's brother, and this is because I seldom saw him. He would be away in London for days at a time, often returning late, after we had dined. Then he would usually spend the remainder of the evening in the library with His Lordship.

I learned from Isabelle that he was soon to return to the Far East, this time to China to join an international body overseeing the reformation of the *Tsungli Yamen*, China's discredited Foreign Office which had been strongly pro-Boxer and itself inflaming anti-European feeling. I over-heard him once in conversation with Mildred who feared for his safety from secret societies out there.

'I try to take a sensitive line in mediation,' he said. 'There are faults on all sides, and innumerable sides for there to be faults on. We allies have much to regret, our-selves. The pillaging and torching after final victory were deplorable. For a long while the Chinese will continue to see us as "Foreign Devils", rapacious in trading, and arro-gantly intent on imposing an alien religion on them.'

Mildred had nodded, quoting Lord Clarendon: ' "Mission-aries require to be protected against themselves . . . a constant menace to British interests".'

'I hope,' Laurence said, 'to steer a path that is favourable to us and to the Chinese as well. But I hardly think it will be an easy task while the Manchus keep absolute power.'

On the evening of his last day in England Laurence invited the whole family to a concert of music at London's Royal Albert Hall. He had arranged for a private box, and I was included. We put up at a small hotel in Dover Street from where he would depart next morning to catch the boat train, travelling overland from Calais to Brindisi – a duration of less than two days – and so saving a week on the longer sea route.

Being still in mourning for the late Earl, we were sombrely turned out, and Isabelle's papa gave the briefest of formal bows in reply to the audience's acknowledgement of his accession to the title. This was my first musical outing since the disastrous night at La Scala, but I felt secure enough by now not to make a fool of myself. Until the Violin Concerto by Max Bruch.

From the start it seemed to have an uncanny power over me, the solo instrument shadowed by a phantom cello, and half-way through the *adagio* I could no longer contain my emotion but felt the tears running down my cheeks while inside I cried silently for Gilbert and his haunting music in the garden of the Qasr el Mastaba.

Even before the interval and the lights coming on, I felt the firm hand on my wrist, with its sympathetic pressure. I did not dare to look across but nodded slightly, acknowledging the need to keep myself under control.

When Isabelle rose, gracefully bowing to some acquaintance in the stalls, we all stood, but the hand still held me back from following the others to the foyer.

'We don't all need to mingle,' Laurence said lightly. Then, more softly, 'Perhaps you would prefer to return to our hotel. If so, I will be happy to accompany you there.'

I kept my eyes down. 'I am so ashamed. But I fear I'm

not yet ready for such . . .' No word came, but he seemed to understand.

'Raw wounds are not our fault,' he said. 'We should never apologize for them.'

He stayed silent in the cab, offered his arm as we alighted, and ordered the driver to stay until he had seen me inside.

'Please make my excuses to His Lordship,' I begged.

'Of course. Rest now. I shall see you perhaps at breakfast tomorrow?'

Next morning he was waiting in the hotel foyer as I came downstairs. 'It seems a pleasant enough day outside. A purely London sort of pleasantness, of course.'

I followed him to the door and we stood there in the morning light. 'Pain never quite vanishes,' he said softly, watching the street, 'but one learns to live with it. Music is perhaps the deepest probe, so full of passion and pathos and unfulfilled love.'

I looked at him then, the bronzed face serious, brows contracted over eyes as blue as Isabelle's but with an added intensity. 'You understand,' I marvelled.

He took me by the elbow and hatless we began walking towards Piccadilly, surrounded by the normal sights and sounds of the waking metropolis. 'You must have loved your husband very much.'

It so startled me that I was off my guard. 'The man I married? Oh no.'

I managed not to say, 'I barely met him.' To cover up I muttered, 'There was a serving officer in Egypt. We were to have married, but he was killed in Sudan. Or, rather – such bitter waste! – he died there of typhus.'

Laurence must surely have assumed then that Lucy was Gilbert's love-child. If only she had been!

But no, his thoughts were elsewhere as he crossed

181

behind me to take the opposite arm and we turned to stroll back. 'I had a hopeless love,' he confided. 'An Indian lady, forbidden by her father to accept an Englishman, and then hastily married to an elderly prince.'

'But if you loved each other . . .'

'—we could have run away and defied both our countries?' He gave a short laugh. 'That would be admirable passion, and very poor judgement. The world isn't ready for it, except in stage tragedies. And we wanted happiness. But had to settle for a sense of duty done.'

He looked at me brightly, almost with a quirk of mischief. 'After all, I am a diplomat.'

'And I'm sure a very good one.'

We ran into Lord Sedgwick at the entrance to the breakfast-room. 'Eugenie, my dear, I do hope you're well recovered. How wise to take a little turn in the fresh air. I must do so m'self if there's time before Laurence goes off. Dreadful stuffy place, London.'

And Isabelle smiled seraphically over her toasted crumpet. 'Don't worry about Genie's disappearance, Papa. She simply finds highbrow music boring. Doubtless she had some alternative amusement in mind last night.'

Later that morning we went our separate ways, Lord Sedgwick to see his son off at Victoria station and then return to Stakerleys; Isabelle and I (ostensibly staying on at Dover Street) to settle her in at the Marylebone nursing home.

She was horridly apprehensive, despite the reassuring manner of her surgeon, so I returned to comfort her early the next day before she would be taken to the theatre. They were long hours until I was allowed to see her again, back in the narrow bed, tightly tucked under flat, starched sheets, her face almost as white below the linen operation cap.

182

'Is it over?' she asked vaguely.

'Completely. You're all tidied up now inside. Everyone's very pleased with you. You can go to sleep without any more worries.'

'Don't leave me, Genie.'

I promised I wouldn't, but the sister turned me away, saying Isabelle would know nothing until at least eight hours later, and I should come back then. When I did return she was propped up on her pillows, admiring the hothouse flowers I'd had sent in. Her manner was too bright, her voice high and rapid as she said, 'Just think, Genie. I'll have no more bother with periods. None of that boring old stuff again.'

'Are you sure?'

'The surgeon came in to tell me. He's taken all those stupid bits away.' She still sounded terrified, as though she expected to fall apart.

'Lucky you,' I said insincerely.

'Aren't I indeed?'

And I knew that if we were ever to discuss the matter again it wouldn't be for a very long time.

I was sent shopping, so that on our return there'd be some proof of our supposed activities. The difficulty lay in choosing what to buy, because family mourning for the late Earl restricted our fashion purchases.

I bought clothing mainly for Lucy; a set of fleecy towels and two silk cushions for Isabelle; several books which we would both be reading; a glass globe paper-weight as a present for her father; and a warm shawl of Shetland wool for Nanny T. Mildred was a more difficult person to choose for, because at that time I barely knew her tastes, but finally I settled for a beautiful little Spanish stiletto in an embossed leather sheath, which was meant for opening her letters.

When I showed Isabelle she seemed quite mystified that I had bought presents. 'How very modest,' she commented on the rest. 'Papa will think I'm suddenly a cloistered nun. But never mind. When I'm feeling stronger we'll take a cab to Bond Street and look at some necklaces. And isn't it time, Genie, you bought yourself a widow's jet ring?'

Sixteen

If, in those early months together at Stakerleys, I felt some resentment at still being tied to Isabelle, how much less comfortable must her feelings have been about me. It took a while for me to appreciate this. I was at the same time her only link to Lucy and also the immovable barrier. When this truth finally reached me – until then seeking some explanation for Isabelle's ambivalence, her rushes of exaggerated concern for me alternating with periods of cold patronage – I could feel some pity.

It was later that I became fearful, realizing how I stood in her path and so was vulnerable. Whatever she wanted she seized, unfeelingly, confidently. I remembered my terrible doubts over Gabrieli's death, which seemed strangely to echo my kitten drowned in the Nile.

And yet the two cases were quite different, if one was the result of a moment's anger when play together had ended in the little creature's claws raking her cheek. She might have flung it from her or unthinkingly squeezed it too tightly. I wanted so much to see it as an accident. The tiny thing would have been so easy to kill. Then Isabelle – this I found easy to credit – would immediately have panicked and tried to cover up what she'd done, because she so hated to be thought of badly. And how more conveniently to dispose of the little body than to drop it overboard and let the sluggish current drift it away? How could she have known that I would choose to walk downstream next morning and stop to watch the little boys throwing stones?

Gabrieli's death – if it was her doing – must be something more heinous. I remembered her stated intention to make him pay for wrecking her life. (His cheating her of money would have cost her only a brief fit of anger.) It was his drunken ineptness in dealing with the birth that rankled. And his leaving her mutilated. Even now she finds it unforgiveable.

I shuddered to recall that last day in Venice, how graciously charming she'd been to him, so sweetly treacherous, openly displaying her generosity to the servants, hinting at greater rewards to come for him, and suggesting the final glass of wine together ... Meaning perhaps all along a different kind of drink, the befuddled man's lungs swamped by an inrush of foul water when she would thrust him off the narrow path, and the canal's dark surface closed over his head?

I would never erase that image of her watching the clutch of bubbles rise, innocently as if she fed pet fish, one arm still extended, impassive, yet at that moment so evilly ageless, as she considered the good fortune of his having been drunk – reassured that whoever found and examined the body would discover the state he'd been in, doubtless unsteady on his feet and so liable to totter off the narrow edge. Such things had happened before. Not often, because Venetians seldom got into such a helpless state, but the idea was acceptable. More so than that an English milady could have murderous intentions.

And if she had done it that once, with cold premeditation, mightn't she do so again when feelings of outrage pushed her too far? I was now an obstacle to be overcome like any other. With me done away, who was there to deny her the whim of adopting the poor little orphan?

Her being a woman didn't make murder beyond belief; and only recently in a court case a condemned prisoner had admitted it was easier the second time. And that evil woman had gone on to kill eleven times more. All her victims had been unwanted babies whom she had advertised for, and been paid to take off their mothers' hands. She had killed them and buried them in her garden among the cabbages and turnips and onions. In her case, just for the love of money. Newspapers had shown a photograph of her, a comfortable, plump countrywoman in a neat dark dress and white, starched apron.

The gentler sex, hobbled by social and legal restrictions, allowed so little voice, but still not averse to violence when need be. And I had to remind myself how easily I too might have been accused as the same kind of demon, because of that horrendous night in the hotel garden at Potsdam when I had fought off Ralph Cruickshank and would have torn his eyes out. It was Isabelle who next morning assured me drily that what I'd done was short of bloody murder, so I would not be lodged in a German jail in fear of execution.

So, under the skin, were we the same, Isabelle and I? Should I confess to her my complicated feelings? Would that help her to accept me and my permanent place in her life?

Isabelle, who had been eager to get rid of the unwanted baby, had discovered too late that she needed, like any true woman, to be a mother. Deprived of the hope of it in the future, she now wanted Lucy with her. If the need became overwhelming, if by removing me she could be assured of possessing Lucy for herself, would she dare . . . ?

Surely not.

On one hand I could not believe that anyone, anyone at all, might deliberately mean to take another's life. But on the other hand I had the evidence of my eyes and a terrible premonition that Isabelle, once on the path to achieving what she most desired, would stop at nothing until she was satisfied. There was a single-minded persistence about her that seemed hardly sane.

I decided to consult a lawyer and make some alternative provision for Lucy. For *my* baby's safety.

With this in mind I let it be known that I should welcome a few days' leave of absence to visit my mother in St Leonards-on-Sea.

As soon as Lord Sedgwick heard of this – through Mildred, I believe – he was instantly apologetic that a holiday break hadn't been arranged before.

Isabelle was uncertain. 'Will you take Lucy?' she de-manded. Pehaps she feared I might abscond with the dear baby.

'Don't you think she'd be better left here with Nanny?' I reassured her. 'Trains are such noisy, sooty things.'

So Isabelle was content to let me go alone, leaving her free to monopolize Lucy, as far as the nursery maid and Nanny T would allow.

I took a ticket for one station beyond Warrior Square, alighting at Hastings, and walked down Havelock Road to the Memorial clocktower. There were still the same lawyers' chambers behind the Queen's Hotel as when I was a child there. I had no reason to expect any change, but it did already seem so much longer than a year ago that I had left on my Grand Tour with Isabelle. The legal profession has no reputation for rapid decision-making and these gentlemen were of the most conservative kind.

I made an appointment there for the following day

before taking up my reservation, already secured by post, at the hotel.

It was a balmy summer's day, and in the afternoon I strolled along the promenade as far as White Rock. The tide was out, and a wonderful iodine smell of seaweed came off the beaches. I was overcome by a strong sense of nostalgia, remembering my small hand clasped in Papa's as we watched just such a scene on the foreshore below.

There were women spreading picnics over rugs on the upper, dry shingle, and others watching over children in rompers at barefoot play on the sands, and poking in the green-slimed rock pools with their shrimping nets. When Lucy was older, I promised myself, we would do that. Long days in the sun, paddling together with the cool silky water rippling over our bare toes, and our skirts tucked up inside our bloomer-legs, with nobody over-proper there to think the worse of us for it.

I imagined the little bucket and spade we would choose together in the gift shop and stationer's opposite the promenade, which sold picture postcards and painted pebbles, and humbugs and strings of tiny, pink, pierced shells. And early in the mornings we would go to Hastings Old Town when the fishing boats came in, and see the catch landed, with the gulls swooping and screeching to pick up the guttings. And we'd eat whelks, sharp with vinegar, from the little stalls there, and smell the amazing mixtures of salt and bubbly bacon dumplings, and fresh creosote off the tall, black, fishermen's huts where the nets were hung up to dry. And everyone so natural and friendly and cheerful.

A long way from Stakerleys and the Sedgwicks. It came as a shock to me then to realise that I had become two persons facing in opposite directions. How could I ever persuade Isabelle to join me in hiring a beach hut here and mixing with these happy, ordinary people?

189

I walked back and took tea in the Queen's Hotel among the potted palms and pretentious nobodies who seemed more stilted and stiff than the Somebodies I was becoming accustomed to. And I reminded myself that I was a nobody too, as Isabelle had once pointed out, so I'd better take care I didn't put on airs just because I found myself in between.

Next morning I kept my appointment with the solicitor who drew up my document of guardianship for Lucy in the event of my early death.

'A very wise precaution for a widow, Mrs Gabriel,' Mr Lewis approved. (By then I had already anglicized my surname by dropping the final letter, having decided against the complication of a change by deed poll for both Lucy and myself to the original Fellowes.)

'Of course, you will require to obtain the agreement of the party named as guardian,' he cautioned. 'And in the event of your remarriage we shall be pleased to draw up a subsequent document. You have, I assume, covered all occasions by making a will in favour of your daughter?'

I hadn't. But I proceeded to do so there and then, to his barely concealed satisfaction. It was in the simplest possible form: '. . . of all I die possessed whatsoever and wheresoever . . .' with no tiresome bequests to individuals or charities.

Mr Lewis was a little troubled that I made no financial provisions for my daughter's guardian, but then he wasn't to know that I devoutly hoped the precaution I'd taken would never be drawn upon. The document existed only as a threat, a warning to Isabelle against allowing any accident to hasten my end.

Although I could not deny that she alone had any right to the child, by then I could not safely trust Lucy's upbringing to her. At least with the provisions I had made she would be protected until she was of age and able to choose for herself.

With assurances about his readiness at any time to prepare whatever codicils I should require, Mr Lewis bowed me into the hands of his lady secretary who showed me out. Both new documents would be made out and forwarded to me by post to Stakerleys within the week. I was advised to sign them on receipt, duly witnessed, and return them for safe keeping.

In the street again I drew a long breath of satisfaction. I could now enjoy one night more of lone freedom and return next day with my mission completed. Except that my quoted motive for this visit remained untouched on. I had spoken of a visit to my mother. Only at this last moment did it enter my head to consider actually making this.

A year had gone by since I left home with her approval. It was eight months since I had received her cold letter about dear Papa's sad end. After my reply to that, silence on both sides. Not that the blame for that rested with her: I had never sent on any address since the Gasthof in Heidelberg.

What must she be thinking of me? If she thought of me at all.

I had been harsh in condemning her insensitivity, but what of my own? She was my mother. As a mother myself – or feeling so – how could I bear my only child to cut herself off completely? Perhaps I should . . . At least I could take a tram into St Leonards and walk past the house.

I arrived at dusk. Standing between the twin stone pillars I caught the scent of roses and their white glow against the darkening garden. The driveway which led round the side to what had been Papa's print-shop was freshly made up with gravel. If I dared to walk round there I should risk being heard by anyone in the house. There were globe

191

lights shining to either side of the front door, and upstairs several windows were lit with the curtains not yet drawn.

I wondered if my mother even lived there any more, or if some alien family had taken her place. But surely she would still be keeping her workroom beavering away. Why should I imagine Papa's death, or my absence, should change such an immutable woman?

I hesitated over what I should call myself and how much to tell. If I approached her.

And then I found myself walking forward, over the crunching gravel, advertising my presence, and there was no turning back. I pulled the bell-handle and heard a clear ringing inside, but when I tried to turn the knob I found the door locked. A uniformed maid came to open up. 'Madam?' she said politely, and bobbed.

'Mrs Gabriel,' I said, 'to see Mrs Fellowes. A social call.'

I was shown into the tiled and panelled hall, which seemed to have shrunk in my absence. After a few moments the maid reappeared at the head of the stairs and came down alone. 'Madam says will you please leave your card.'

I explained. I hadn't one to offer: I was lately back from living abroad. Then I tired of the negative formality. 'Kindly tell Mrs Fellowes that it is Eugenie.'

The girl looked doubtful: the name meant nothing to her. Again she trailed up the long half-circle stairway and disappeared.

My mother exploded from the dim end of the gallery and stood above me staring down assessingly. When she appeared satisfied – or not discountenanced – she commanded, 'You may come up, Eugenie.'

She didn't miss the black dress and veiled hat. How could she? Costume played so great a part in her life. 'What name did you give?' she asked suspiciously.

'Mrs Gabriel. I had been married only a short while when my husband was drowned, Mother.'

Her eyes had gone black like damsons. 'And what did Lady Isabelle think to that, miss?' So she had not overlooked the social news and Isabelle's change of title.

'My marriage? She was very much for it. Indeed she was one of the witnesses. It took place in Italy. My late husband came from Venice. Of a good family. They have a *palazzo* just off the Grand Canal.' I spoke casually. It was not a really big lie; just a question of tense. In Venice so much was in the past. And my certificate proved me Gabrieli's wife. By now I was trying to forget poor dying Ernesto Facci.

Her gaze flickered again over my costume, which had been made in London by Isabelle's favourite dressmaker. 'Then I trust you are left well off.'

'Adequately so. In any case I'm still with Isabelle. We've settled back into Stakerleys, two widows together.'

All this while we had not moved from the head of the stairs. Suddenly my mother tapped me on the arm and offered her cheek, which I dutifully bent down to kiss.

'I was about to have some supper,' she told me. 'We work late on these bright evenings so I forgo dinner. It hardly seems worth while on my own. But come in and have something with me.'

We turned towards the private part of the house and entered the dining-room with its same red damask walls. Supper she might call it, but the table was still formally laid. Mother was not letting up on standards.

'So we must commiserate with each other,' she said rather grumpily, as the maid laid another setting at the oval table.

'For dear Papa's loss, yes. How are you managing?' I ventured.

Her mouth tightened and she stared fiercely past me at the gas globe over the chiffonier. 'When you have been someone's wife so long – for twenty-two years, as I was – you . . . It leaves . . . an enormous gap.'

She actually grieved, then. Now, too late, she had learned to value Papa for the marvellous man he had been. And she must have regrets, must feel guilt for missed opportunities. Isn't that the most awful part of a loved one's death?

We were served a mackerel terrine, followed by veal escalopes with duchesse potatoes, asparagus, and broad beans in a butter sauce. Afterwards there was a choice of baked lemon sponge or fresh fruit salad with Cornish cream, and a cheeseboard with crackers. It struck me that Mother's replacement of supper for dinner had caused little less work for the kitchen.

'We still get the odd pheasant or hare in season,' she offered. 'From Papa's friends on the shoot.'

'That's kind of them. Mother, what happened to Rory?'

'Your Papa's dog? Mr Fennell asked for him, to replace one he'd had that died. So I let him go.'

'Oh, I'm glad. So he's still hunting.'

'Did you think I'd have him put down?' Her eyebrows soared into the upswept bang of hair, which I now saw had a tell-tale streak of white. And her mouth had tightened again as she stared at me with angry eyes. I had misjudged her. However hard the outside, she could yet feel pain. I was glad I had come; only regretted that I did not know her well enough to dare to tell her everything.

She asked a lot about Stakerleys. I could see that my visit would be an event to publicize freely among her cronies, and details of my good fortune would be much in demand. A year ago I would have been ashamed of her snobbery, but it seemed so innocent now compared with some of the grovelling and pretentiousness I'd experienced in others.

194

In fact I began to feel a kind of pride in her sturdy independence. She would survive all, and without doing any great amount of damage to those around her. And to be honest, I believed I had not suffered in the long run from the severity with which she'd had me brought up. Not that I would wish the same for Lucy. Fatherless, she should not have to wait so long before being assured of her mother's affection.

We said goodbye almost warmly, nearly as friends. And I believe she was sorry that I had to leave. She promised to send on by a carrier the guns which were my legacy, together with a banker's order for the money the late Lord Sedgwick had sent as my pay.

I still could not bring myself to confess to her that I had a daughter, but I was consoled that if things went badly awry with me, then Lucy would be safe left in her charge. And I never doubted for a moment that my mother would agree – would be firmly resolved – to act as the child's guardian after my death.

Seventeen

'How much did you tell her?' Isabelle demanded as soon as I was back and she had found an opportunity to draw me off alone.

'That I was Mrs Gabriel, widow of an Italian gentleman introduced by you, and who had sadly drowned not long after our marriage.'

'And nothing about Lucy?'

'Nothing at all.'

She seemed relieved. Perhaps she saw it as one less person to deny my rights to in the far future. 'And how did you find your excellent mama?'

'Surprisingly mellowed. As with us, widowhood appears to become her.'

'You recommend it, then?' For once Isabelle had picked up my irony and responded to it equally blackly.

'I fear that in her case there is some real grief.'

I threw off my travel wrap and unpinned my hat. 'So what has happened here in my absence?'

'Papa has accepted an invitation to some dark and dank Scottish castle for August and we are to go with him. Personally I have no taste for shooting, but there should be some merry evenings of dancing and parties. We'll be only a reasonable drive away from Balmoral.'

'Is His Majesty to be there?'

'One imagines so. He'll hardly miss the chance of supporting his guns, especially since the Grim Presence is now no more.'

So perhaps strict court mourning did not proscribe the slaughter of innocent animals. It was known that the King and Queen would attend Cowes week at the beginning of the month, he in the uniform of an Admiral of the Fleet, but Alexandra and Princess Vicky in full black.

Queen Victoria's death, so long expected yet so shocking to the nation when it finally came about (while we were still in Venice) had produced uncomfortably warring emotions. One, of which I was mainly conscious, was a sense of impatience for the new reign to get fully under way. Once that doleful black pageant of the funeral was over – recorded for posterity on moving film – there emerged a general hope for something quite the opposite. There was still disappointment that our King had been so long denied his active role. It was a pity that everything new had not started together with the opening twentieth century.

And – although one felt a certain guilt at the disloyalty of it – how much more wonderful if the coronation were being planned for a young man of fresh ideas and ideals with a long future stretching ahead, rather than a portly man of sixty. Perhaps by now he was too set in his ways for us to expect such a change of character as when young Hal had been crowned as Henry V. But Edward had learned diplomacy abroad, and even in dealings with his mother, having come a long way since the cockfights in docklands, pretty actresses, and scandals over his card-playing companions. He was our King after all, a warm, sympathetic man of undoubted charm and goodwill. So he would be honoured and loved by the people as was his due.

Isabelle was having new costumes made in woollen

plaids ready for the coming shoots, and a severe white evening dress to set off the contrasting tartan sash. 'What can we do with you, Genie?' she demanded. 'You must produce some Scottish connection. Every civilized person has one.'

'I believe Papa had a cousin who served with the Black Watch, but closer than that – nothing.'

'Well then, that's your family tartan. It should suit you well: dark navy blue and hunting green. Thank God we Sedgwicks are distantly akin to the Buchanans, which allows us plenty of bright yellow and scarlet, at least indoors.'

We were to travel overnight by train from London with enough baggage to equip a Turkish sultan's harem. I had hoped that Lucy might accompany us, but His Lordship demurred. Nanny Tucker was past enduring the long journey, and there would be too many distractions for a young nursery maid. Besides, Isabelle stood in danger of becoming obsessed with the pretty baby. 'Shouldn't risk her going broody, eh what? Need you to spend all your time as her chaperon, m'dear. Find her a suitable young man this time for a husband, eh?'

So my role was determined in advance, and I gladly fell in with his suggestion. Isabelle in thrall to a new love should be sufficiently diverted from any attempt to recover Lucy.

Knowing nothing of the Highlands beyond what I had read in romances full of kilted lairds in dark halls hung with antlered trophies, Ossian gloom, misted glens and wildly tumbling cataracts, I was astounded on our arrival.

It was a perfect, cloudless mid-morning aromatic with the honey-scent of heathers on sun-baked peaty soil that showed all the signs of a considerable drought. Isabelle's 'dark and dank Scottish castle' was an extensive hunting lodge. Its grim prison frontage was mocked by slate-spired French turrets which hung over all its corners and recesses: granite excrescences set on inverted stone steps, giving the whole an incongruous and whimsically tipsy appearance.

The servants would not have lasted a week in fashionable London, but were characters of enormous sturdiness of opinion and homely comfort. Although I sensed a clash of cultures as our own were installed alongside and each set endeavoured to patronize the other, Hadrill – with us for only four days to facilitate the change-over – seemed to melt into a person uncannily native to both.

The Earl's guests included friends of Isabelle's absent brother, Viscount Crowthorne. They were mainly young officers accompanied by their wives. There were also contemporaries of His Lordship, several peers, two members of Lord Salisbury's government and a number of county gentlemen.

Ladies were in the minority; some of them languished indoors until the evenings' entertainments or took carriage drives to observe the grouse shooting from afar, but there was also a group of jolly, apple-cheeked enthusiasts who took to the deer-stalking scene as heartily as their horses would charge fences back home in hunting the fox.

I found that my late father's firearms had been transported along with the others, a twelve-bore shotgun and a modern hunting rifle. They awaited my claiming them in the gunroom. I could hardly insist that I would use them only for target practice, so I listened carefully at dinner on that first evening as the estate factor explained the policy of culling the deer herds.

In managing the estate he was responsible for the many farm tenancies, some raising beef and sheep, others mainly dairy cattle. A balance had to be kept between the domestic beasts and the wild herds and grouse which otherwise would overrun the grazing and devastate the crops.

There was an historical element: one good outcome of the old Jacobite rising had been that southerners discovered the Highlands, and ever thereafter were attracted to the hunting, bringing welcome wealth. Throughout the past two centuries war had been waged over tenant clearances, whole populations callously turned out to make way for the incomers' sport; but most landlords, thank God, were more merciful now.

Although the sporting season was short, beginning in early August, all year round it was necessary for professional stalkers to pick off old and sickly beasts to keep the herds healthily stocked. The factor spoke movingly of the severity of winter and the slow, agonizing end of even fit young deer struggling in snowdrifts yards deep. He was no sentimentalist, but I felt the passion of a man dedicated to his work. He was only forty-seven but, rugged and knobby-faced like a potato, he looked fifteen years older; a man of the earth, with a kindly heart.

Dutifully I kept watch over Isabelle's flirtations. In particular I favoured a group of three young bachelors as likely partners for her, but she soon poured scorn on my hopes. Alastair was altogether too thin and lanky. It would be like going to bed with a bicycle. 'No,' she corrected herself, 'a tandem!'

Geoffrey was wealthy but boring, wanting to travel the world and collect animals for a private menagerie. Her friends would mock her, suggesting she'd be kept in a cage. As for poor Ralph, however charming and handsome, his highest expectation was to become a baronet after his father's demise. Which would not do at all. Isabelle's heart was set on becoming a duchess, or a marchioness at least. One should, she informed me, set out to do a little better than one's parents.

It seemed she had forgotten Hugo Delmayne's lack of distinction. But this time, of course, she would not be marrying for love.

And by the end of the first week of our stay, with Isabelle throwing herself energetically into the boisterous festivities and hearty Highland dancing each evening, it looked as if her intentions would come about. The Marquess of Clune approached her father with a request for Isabelle's hand in marriage. I would have been most happy for her, except that he was fifty-four, a widower and not blessed with any great charm.

'It's not what I had in mind,' Lord Sedgwick admitted to me uncomfortably. 'But I felt obliged to give permission for him to speak to Isabelle. She is, after all, a widow herself.'

'But with such an age difference? Thirty-three years! Surely he can see it's asking a lot of her.'

'It's out of my hands, m'dear. We must wait and see what she makes of it. I've told her of Clune's intentions, of course; but I couldn't judge her reaction. Obviously she'll need time to consider all aspects. And I'm sure she will turn to you for any advice she needs.'

'What advice could I – should I – give?'

'That rests with you. It's not for a mere man to say; not even her father.'

He was in two minds about it, as I was. She was still his little ewe lamb, unspotted by the world. Perhaps he believed the Marquess could be a substitute for himself when he was gone, a father figure and protector for a young woman delicately raised. But also he might be fearful of the man's motives in seeking out a young wife, and of how she might react to her husband as he so soon became an old man and infirm.

He had spoken hopefully just a few days back of a *young* man Isabelle might find acceptable. And surely he had been thinking of her brother's friends. Maybe the two men had spoken together of this, and before leaving the country the Viscount had listed acquaintances from whom his father should make up a guest list acceptable to them both.

'I'll try to find out how she feels,' I promised.

Isabelle met my enquiries with a teasing air of mystery. 'I certainly have an admirer,' she boasted. 'I told you I would reach a rank above my mother's. Well, like as not, I'll rise by two rungs of the ladder. Provided I accept the old goat.'

There was only one marquess among the guests, and her description made it clear who she meant. 'Lord Clune?' I queried. 'Isabelle, can you seriously consider him?'

'I'd say he was sixtyish, wouldn't you, Genie?'

'A little younger, I think.'

'But not a lot. And women normally live to be much older than men. It might not be so very long that I'd need to put up with him. And such a relief to be a married woman again.'

Because then she could take a lover without being much talked of. Not that she needed such protection, since she could not conceive again and so find herself embarrassed by a lover's child. It left me a little breathless, the rapid calculation of her mind.

'Have you imagined what it would be like,' I pressed, 'to spend those years, however few, in his exclusive company?'

'Not exclusive. And he has a very grand house. There would be plenty of room there to avoid his presence if I found it distasteful. It would not be love in a cottage, Genie, as no doubt would figure in *your* rosy dreams. And

202

just think. If we marry quite soon, then as a marchioness I'll have great importance at the coming coronation. Won't I look breathtaking in my coronet, or even carrying Alexandra's train?'

A lady of the bedchamber, I thought crudely. But whose then? The other royal one? Isabelle was capable of monstrous ambition.

'I beg you to think beyond that,' I pleaded. 'Think of the three hundred and sixty-five days each year of facing him at breakfast, listening to that droning voice, watching that grim mouth for the disapproving downturn of the thin lips. Imagine more, that scrawny shape in his nightshirt, expecting . . .' I could not continue.

'Me romping with him in bed?' she almost squealed, teasing me. 'Really, Genie, how improper you've grown. Such visual imaginings. I declare you're quite lascivious!'

I looked long at her. 'Isabelle, I know you delight in mocking me. Don't, please don't, treat the matter lightly. All your future happiness is in the balance.'

But for all that, when the Marquess of Clune led her aside after the evening's entertainment she threw back a victorious glance over her shoulder at me. And I knew her mind was made up.

She didn't reappear that night, and it was Lord Sedgwick who told me as I left for my room that they had asked for his blessing, and the engagement would be announced on our return south in a fortnight's time.

I found it understandable that from then on Isabelle was changed. Since our return from abroad she had managed to keep her wilder side hidden from others, but now she indulged it in a form of self-display that might have given offence if I had not seen the defiance of near-desperation in it. It seemed as though she now seized on every occasion to taste a freedom which she must shortly be denied. While avoiding Lord Clune's observation – not difficult, since when he was not out stalking he was at the card tables – she flirted ever more outrageously with any man who took her fancy. She dressed one evening after dinner in a man's full Highland dress, bare-legged between calf and kilt, and insisted on leading out to dance all the prettiest of the ladies, and myself last. There was little point in protest because by then the whole party was half-way to a wild rout and most of the guests, after Lord Sedgwick's withdrawal, had drunk too well of the local malt.

I went to sit on the tower stairs, my head humming from the fug of peat smoke, the skirl of pipes and the sharp animal cries of the dancers. Before long I was joined by my friend the factor and his rosy little wife, Molly. 'The whole house throbs,' she complained.

'Aye, and we've an early rise the morn,' he said. 'I've a mind to pick out the mannies I'll be taking and haul them to their beds noo.'

'Do that,' she agreed, 'and there'll be fewer spewing their souls out all nicht long.'

It seemed that the great house had barely quietened when Isabelle was beside my bed pulling the covers off. Only the faintest streak of light showed over the eastern horizon.

'The main party's away shortly,' she told me. 'And I don't see why we should be left behind. There are plenty of ladies who are equally good shots as their menfolk. So we'll be trying that ourselves. Come along, Genie. You and I will make up our own party and go stalking together.'

She had persuaded an old ghillie to act as her stalker and Geoffrey (the despised animal-collector) to come along besides, so I was obliged to accompany her. 'We'll use your rifle, in case Geoffrey's are too heavy,' she said, commandeering it and strapping on a pair of men's gaiters.

Beneath her ankle-length tweed skirt she was wearing a pair of plaid trousers and she threw a similar pair at me with instructions to get them on. I had my walking boots from Heidelberg and they seemed stout enough for any tussocky rough.

The ghillie's name was Angus MacLeod. He was handsome in an elderly, craggy way. His profile was like rough-hewn granite with overhanging white eyebrows under his bonnet and a permanent drop of water at the nose end, whether from inside or from the foggy dew. From time to time he'd lift his head to sniff the air and then pull out his telescopic spy-glass to scan the surrounding countryside.

'They're stalking out west,' he said in his thick accent which Geoffrey had to translate. 'So we're for ganging east.'

'To pick up what's left behind,' Geoffrey explained. He was an affable man, a little embarrassed by Isabelle's arbitrary manner, but also flattered to have been chosen. He clearly found her enchanting, animated and charged with good humour as she appeared then.

We had ridden out on scratch mounts and then left them tethered at a little cairn, MacLeod gesturing towards a crag to which we were to climb on foot. It was rough walking but the early scents of wet bracken and bog myrtle and the misty brightness of a low sun trying to burn through made it a magic morning. It was not all uphill; every now and then the terrain flattened and despite the recent drought we were floundering in shallow, blackish water. At its crest the hillside fell away steeply before us, littered with great boulders. We moved down below the skyline so as not to be seen, then sat on the hummocky grass while the two men took turns at scanning the slopes below.

Small like toys, over to the left on the glen floor, was a string of huts that seemed to be moving. 'Tinkers' caravans,' Geoffrey said. 'Downwind. They'll not trouble us.'

'Where are the deer?' Isabelle demanded.

'Ahead and upwind,' the ghillie said. 'There's five I see. Three hinds, a young stag and one with fine great antlers.'

'Where, where?' Isabelle snatched the spy-glass as it was passed to Geoffrey. He pointed, and with the naked eye we caught the slight movement of fawn against fawn as the young stag rubbed its head on a rock.

'But they're miles off.'

'Far enough, and they'll move more yet. I'll point ye oot the way we go doon.'

We passed from rock to rock in a zigzag progress, stopping twice to drink water from our flasks and once to chew on oaten biscuits. By the time we reached the glen floor the sun was high over us and the distant range of mountains indigo against a white-streaked sky. We had lost sight of our quarry but MacLeod, sniffing, swore they were but half a mile ahead over the ridge and still moving away.

'We'll never catch up with them,' Isabelle complained.

'Patience,' Geoffrey advised. 'They'll not get any scent of us. We need now to get higher again, for a vantage point.'

Half an hour later we suddenly had clear sight of them grazing almost directly opposite on the facing slope. The men slid their rifles off their shoulders and we moved into the shelter of a waist-high boulder.

'Let me,' Isabelle pleaded. She had adopted my father's rifle, a .303 Purdey with almost noiseless report and no recoil to speak of. As Geoffrey pointed out the older stag she shouldered the rifle, supporting hips and elbow against the rock. I turned away as she fired, swung back at her sharp exclamation closely followed by Angus MacLeod's deep grunt.

'Again,' Geoffrey urged. 'It's wounded. Don't let it run.'

'No, no,' Isabelle said wildly. 'It's a hind, isn't it? I got the wrong one.'

'It's wounded, Isabelle!' I shouted. 'Finish it quickly.'

'I can't. Oh, poor creature! Just look! And it was so pretty!' She was totally overcome at the reality of it.

Fury seized me: Isabelle sentimental over an animal, when she'd likely caused the death of a human being!

I snatched the rifle, operated the bolt and reloaded. Following the limping arc of the little hind's progress, squeezed the trigger and discharged the second bullet.

I lowered the rifle an instant before the ghillie dropped his, unfired. The bright blue eyes stared at me from under the whiskery white brows. 'Aye,' he said. 'I tak it ye'll have me gralloch it.'

'Paunch,' Geoffrey translated apologetically. 'Will you both go down with him, and I'll fetch the horses. That's all for today. We can only manage one carcass as we haven't any carriers.'

There was no sign of the other deer which had run off as the hind fell. Our direct route down was full of potholes and covered with patches of scree on which we slid, floundering after the ghillie's more sure descent. By the time we arrived he had slit the dead beast's belly open and had a loathsome pile of entrails in his hands. 'I'll blood ye, mistress,' he growled at me. ''Tis the way it's done, ye ken.'

'Isabelle,' I said, 'it's your beast. You wear the trophy.' And after one sharp look at me the man complied, smearing her forehead and cheeks with the bloody mess.

Geoffrey looked startled but made no comment when he caught up with us. He laced his fingers to lift Isabelle to her saddle, then me to mine, and swung alongside. The trussed carcass lay over MacLeod's horse and he plodded on alongside, making good speed with little apparent effort.

We rode back through gentler country thick with birches where Geoffrey pointed out badger holes and a golden eagle hovering above. 'They shoot eagles here,' he said, sadly I thought, 'because they take young lambs.'

Isabelle wore the pride of her blooding until all had seen it. She did not explain that she'd hit the hind by mistake, and the body was removed to the domestic offices. She spoke of the fine stag we'd seen and how she'd been the quickest one to fire.

I still tasted bile in my throat and could barely bring myself to talk to her again that day.

Eighteen

After the Highlands interlude our return to Stakerleys' routine of tennis parties, soirées and regular church attendance was a relief to me, but Isabelle was restless. Her father seemed weary after so much socializing and uninclined to take on all the preparations involved in celebrating his daughter's engagement. Countless photographs were taken of the future Marchioness, appearing with views of Clune Castle to illustrate articles in *The Lady* and *The Queen* magazines.

Raised in a small town and educated by modest maiden ladies as I'd been, it seemed to me tasteless and even indelicate that society should so openly boast of a young woman's acquisition of wealth and rank through her ability to charm. But on further thought I saw that this was the entire *raison d'être* of an aristocracy: to secure continuous exclusivity, marking its members out as special as they moved ever upwards.

Isabelle was on display as the successful model to be envied and copied. All the pretty noodles were given no alternative route through life, unless, like Mildred, they were to be regarded as pitiably eccentric.

Was it so different for our middle-class families in St Leonards? Wasn't Mother's snobbery an inferior imitation? Hadn't she expected me to benefit from association with an Honourable, irrespective of that lady's unsuspected character? She must surely still hope that I'd make a second match – one more suitable, since foreigners were hardly proper – to exhibit that our family was socially on the upward path? What other ambition was left to her, a widow with a single child, who had already risen locally to the top of her chosen profession?

It came to me as a shock then, that I, as an apparent widow with a single child and a profession of companion, would shortly be freed by Isabelle's marriage. And I had no ambition any more except for dear Lucy. Was she in her turn to be exposed to the cattle market of social evaluation, or would woman's lot improve so that she could choose to follow her heart as I had once hoped to with Gilbert?

The Clune–Sedgwick wedding, arranged for mid-December, was to be the highlight of the year, its early advance fully understood since it then provided the Marquess with a proper partner for the coming coronation. The couple were seen together on several occasions in London, Isabelle sporting a very fine ruby ring with a circlet of diamonds. She had chosen that stone herself, bearing in mind the celebrated ruby *parure* worn by the Marquess's late mother on royal occasions.

Soon, with no call for a lady companion in her married life, Isabelle must free me, but I had misgivings that she might attempt to keep some hold on Lucy. She had been distinctly cool towards me since the deer-stalking episode and I sometimes caught her eyeing me in a calculating manner that boded ill. I declined all invitations to accompany her on shoots about the estate, on the excuse of alternative duties for her father. It would be too easy and too convenient for her if I became the victim of an accident with firearms.

Lucy, at almost nine months old, was a pretty child, now

mobile on all fours, strong and already able to pull herself to her feet against the legs of a heavy chair. Consulting with Nanny Tucker (who privately had thought me a poor thing that I could produce no milk of my own) I decided to supplement her Savory and Moore's Infant Food with Neave's Food, said to be rich in phosphates and potash.

On hearing this Lord Sedgwick declared I'd surely mistaken the child for a hothouse plant, for he was much in favour of the same chemicals for his prize blooms. He was attracted by her winning ways and would occasionally promenade her along the upper terrace in her cane dogcart with its tasselled canopy, the pair of them babbling happily and nonsensically together. While I found it essential to protect her from Isabelle's mercurial moods, I was sad to think I withheld from His Lordship the knowledge that he had a little grandchild. But there was the consolation that if Isabelle failed to provide more, her brother would surely one day marry and continue the family line.

This dynastic subject was apparently one to which the elderly Lord Clune had had the temerity to allude already to Isabelle, instructing her of his requirements. She was in high dudgeon when she admitted as much to me, for want of anyone else who shared her secret.

'For an *heir*, Eugenie! That is his entire reason for con-senting – yes, consenting; not wishing! – to take a wife. Not for my company, nor my beauty, nor intelligence, nor anything I might flatter myself over; but as if I were some prize cow, to breed from.

'And you know what that will get him. His just deserts; for when the years go by and we remain childless I shall have no compunction over accusing him of proving incapable.'

It was useless to tell her she was cruel and would build up a lifetime of bitterness and hostility. I even began

211

to feel some sympathy for the unlovable, elderly Marquess.

'Guess what?' Isabelle demanded one morning, almost dancing from the library where her father was reading his mail. 'Lolly is to be here with us for the wedding. Home from China, to report to the Foreign Office. And he is already on his way, due in at Liverpool by mid-November. Oh, what fun it'll be! How I wish I could stay on here at Stakerleys instead of in that disagreeable barn of Clune's.'

'At least you'll have the wedding here and a few weeks first of your brother's company.'

'If he isn't tied to his office in London.' She scowled. 'But of course he could entertain us in town, and take us shopping. Lolly's learned a lot about silk in the Far East. He can take us to Holborn to the Silk Market which is hard by Gamages. And I still haven't decided on the final design for the wedding cakes' decoration. Buszard's, in Oxford Street, are pestering me to let them know.'

'Then make up your mind now,' I said crisply. 'Don't leave any arrangements over to spoil your time with your brother.'

It surprised me that she included me in the projected London outings, and I suspected some ulterior motive.

Laurence proved good-humouredly amenable, although I sensed a firmness beind his indulging his little sister. Perhaps because she was so soon to leave Stakerleys for good, he wished to make her last days there ones to remember with pleasure. I also suspected he shared his father's misgivings about the match, but he made no open attempt to discourage her from it.

The gifts he brought back from China were exquisite: handmade carvings, porcelain and the finest of silk fabrics in rich colours. He had even remembered me – the sad companion of the musical concert – and presented me with a flat, inlaid box lined with quilted silk in which nestled an intricately worked ivory necklace and long ear-rings.

On our expeditions to London we were accompanied by Geoffrey Penrhydd whose adoration of Isabelle had withstood her engagement to an elderly rival, and I recognized his inclusion as a last-ditch effort by Viscount Crowthorne to offer his sister an alternative husband. With this in mind I was content to partner him and leave the other two as much together as was possible and proper.

Among the excitements of shopping and theatres in town, Isabelle was adamant that we must travel on the new underground train service from Waterloo to the City. We had already ventured on the clanging electric tramway which could carry up to fifty passengers and always seemed crammed with many more. Geoffrey was concerned that this great invention must eventually replace all the working horses because of its relative cheapness. The fifty thousand beasts stabled and maintained by London Transport were already being cut down in number.

On the so-called 'tube' platform I didn't care for the noise and crush in such a confined space, nor for the rough crowd jostling to find the way out after our trip. I was amazed at Isabelle's willingness to be so exposed to what she called the 'common herd'. But even her resilience seemed affected when with a moaning cry she seemed suddenly on the point of collapse and I ran forward to catch her.

On the track side Geoffrey was already supporting her on his arm, as Lord Crowthorne had offered me his arm on my right. But when I lunged forward for her, she seemed to convulse, throwing her weight backward and sideways so that for a moment I toppled off balance, caught in the mêlée. Her brother had momentarily released me to gather Isabelle up, but he whirled about and seized me violently as the harsh snort of the departing train sounded almost over my head. He swept me close as the first carriage slid past. I felt the wind of its passage across my exposed neck as my wide-brimmed hat was torn from my head, pins and all.

'Never again. Never, *ever* again!' Geoffrey threatened darkly. 'This is a fiendish place. We should not have contemplated bringing ladies here.'

'Because we are so maladroit?' I panted, attempting humour, with my heart still beating a tattoo under my ribs.

'Oh Genie, Genie! If you had fallen,' Lord Crowthorne muttered over my loosed hair. He continued holding me close and I was unsure then quite whose heart it was that pounded so.

There was all manner of fuss with railway officials and smelling salts, until at last Isabelle recovered sufficiently for us to take a cab to a nearby hotel where Lord Crowthorne was well known. We stayed there all afternoon resting, then returned by a hired motor car to Stakerleys for a late dinner.

For two days Isabelle avoided everyone, keeping to her room, and although it was obviously strange that she would not have me with her, no comment was forthcoming. It was Lord Sedgwick who took the initiative, finally knocked on her door and insisted on entering.

He came out frowning and held the door ajar for me to enter. 'My daughter would like to speak with you, Eugenie.'

The room was in semi-darkness, and before confronting her I dragged the curtains apart. It resembled too much her hiding away of her distended body when she skulked in Alexandria. But this time not for the same reason.

'Genie,' she started tearfully, 'they tell me I could have endangered your life.'

I stood a few paces off, arms folded and stared her out. 'Indeed you did, Isabelle.'

'How very terrible! You must know, Genie, that nothing more—'

'More *convenient* could have happened?'

She gasped. 'I don't know what you mean.'

'Oh, but you do. And even if your collapse had not been deliberate, you are still intelligent enough to know what I am implying: that you meant me to fall. Just as you meant the wretched Gabrieli to fall. He into a stinking canal, and I under a tube train.'

I moved closer. 'You are an evil woman, Isabelle. How can you imagine I would ever let an innocent child be delivered into your hands?'

She said nothing, her eyes enormous in a dead-white face.

'I know you well by now,' I warned her. 'And I have taken all necessary precautions. When I visited St Leonards, ostensibly to see my mother, I called on a lawyer in Hastings. In the event of my death, my daughter's future is secured.'

She stared at me aghast. Then hot anger rushed in. 'Never *your* daughter! Lucy is mine, and I'll have her despite you!'

When she saw that I remained resolute she was reduced to passionate tears. And I believed them genuine. I even thought then that she could feel some true motherly love for the child, as well as possessiveness and frustration at her will being blocked by another's.

'It's done, Isabelle; unchanging, as death is unchanging.

You may wish to harm me still if you see me as your enemy, but it will only lose you Lucy further if you act on it. Go to your promised husband at Clune, and I will make a life for myself elsewhere. But Lucy stays with me, because I love her and mind what becomes of her.'

'Your only claim is through false papers. I can ruin you, Eugenie. I will swear you made the alterations yourself. I will bear witness to what you did to Gabrieli, drowning him to be rid of a husband needed only on paper. Who will they believe? A lady like myself or such as you, a hired companion with an illegitimate baby?'

'If you accused me of that, then I should probably hang for the killing, but you'd have used documents that proved the child my bastard, mine to hand to whomsoever I chose. And you'd never let it be said that you adopted the illegitimate offspring of a murderess. You can't win, Isabelle.'

I advanced on her as she sat propped on one arm on her bed, defiant. Slowly I drew the chiffon scarf from my neck and held it out before me, tight between my two hands. I bent close over her.

'If I am to hang for Gabrieli,' I whispered, 'I'd as soon hang for one other. Remember, Isabelle, I am always one step behind you here.'

Her face was ashen as she cowered against her pillows. 'No! No, please, Eugenie! You know I would never really do you harm. It was a moment's madness. I have been lying here troubled ever since, cudgelling my brains to think what I could say to make you forgive me.'

'You want my forgiveness? You're changing your tune, Isabelle. Just now you were threatening me. And these "moments of madness" have occurred before. I must make sure, for everyone's safety, that they cannot happen again.'

I leaned over her, bringing the taut scarf close, ready to

216

whip it round the slender neck. As she screamed I stifled the sound with one hand; my practical hand, larger than her own. And she saw how strong I was, that she had no chance against me. Her eyes started from her head as though already the silk was cutting into her throat, and then suddenly she went limp, fainting away.

I was almost as sick a case myself, having pushed my dramatic talent to lengths I would once never have dreamed of.

Announcements appeared in the society pages and in all the London papers: the marriage arranged between the Most Honourable the Marquess of Clune and Lady Isabelle Delmayne, née Sedgwick, would not now take place.

Whispers had several explanations, most notably that the delicate lady had had an unfortunate breakdown in health, and that the Marquess had admitted his intention to continue his longtime alliance with his housekeeper just a few years his junior.

While arrangements went ahead for the grand coronation of Albert Edward as King Edward VII of England, Scotland, Wales and Ireland, Lady Isabelle Delmayne was thought to be again wintering abroad. She had in fact returned to the discreet nursing home in Marylebone, which as her dutiful companion I visited daily.

Nineteen

Isabelle had so cunningly disguised her secret weakness that I was slow in discovering how serious it was. Had I not been so taken up with Lucy's needs, perhaps I would have picked up the warning signs earlier. The truth was that recently I had given little consideration to my official post as Isabelle's companion, and now I blamed myself too late.

There had always been brandy available (and cachou tablets to sweeten the breath). Looking back I could pick out occasions when she had run to it after disappointments, or as an antidote to shock. Then we had drunk it together. I now learned that there were many other occasions when she consumed it alone, and not in moderation, to the point when she needed it increasingly to face each day's demands. Which might account for her more violent outbursts and quirkish behaviour.

The cure, it seemed, was long and uncertain, requiring all the loving support which her friends and family could give her. Lord Sedgwick was greatly distressed at the diagnosis, which Dr Millson passed to him through Mildred. Its discovery – and I never learned the circumstances of it – was made while I was called away to Hastings, where Mother, in falling awkwardly, had dislocated a knee and been sent to hospital.

I stayed there long enough to arrange adequate home nursing for after her discharge, and returned post haste on receiving a telegram that Isabelle too had fallen ill. I was alarmed that she had been admitted to the same nursing home where her earlier operation had been carried out, assuming that she had succumbed to some serious female disorder as a result of it.

In fact Dr Millson had recommended her being sent there, and I arrived to find Isabelle terrified that in conversation with consultants and colleagues he might learn of her earlier troubles.

'You must get me away, Genie,' she pleaded. 'I will go anywhere, do anything, if only I can be sure no inkling of my past misfortune can leak out. If old Millson gets to know of it, he'll surely tell the family I've secretly had a child, and I'll be utterly shamed.'

I thought it almost inevitable that he would be shown some record of her previous admission, but I had great confidence in the kindly old doctor's discretion. Yet Isabelle sounded desperate: deprived of her standby, she was prey to all manner of hideous fancies. I feared she might do something very rash unless I calmed her, but I could only urge her to cooperate.

'It doesn't rest with me, Isabelle. Your best plan is to do all you're told to do, accept the cure, however disagreeable, and then soon you will be free to leave. Dr Millson has worries enough of his own at present, since there's been an outbreak of scarlatina in the village.'

It seemed so simple to me at first: she had merely to give up drinking for a while and all would return to normal. I saw her incarceration more as the corrective for a social gaffe than as treatment for a real disease.

Then it came to light that what progress she had made had been reversed, when a maid at the nursing home tearfully confessed to regularly smuggling in 'a little some-thing' to ease the poor lady's distress.

Doubtless the girl had benefited financially, for Isabelle in her present state no longer troubled to win her way with charm alone. From then on she was allowed to handle no money, but all necessary reading matter, flowers and delicacies were funded by the Earl through Matron.

March of 1902 arrived with her still away, and now the Earl was saddened by his son's need to return to the Far East. There was a general gloom over Stakerleys at the prospect of his departure, and I was no stranger to it.

'But I'll be gone for a short while only,' Crowthorne assured his father. 'I am aware that this is a time for me to cease my globe-trotting and settle at Stakerleys permanently with you all. Besides,' he said, turning to me and taking my hand in his, 'I have good reason now to return, if there is any chance that all I hope for may be possible.'

So modest a declaration confused me. I stared at my hand in his and then at the Earl who was smiling and nodding. Lastly I dared look at Laurence, meeting the kindliness of eyes as blue as Isabelle's, but so vastly dif-ferent. Not round with affected innocence like hers, they were narrowed as if to filter strong sunlight, and at the sides radiated rather paler lines in the bronzed flesh to show where he constantly smiled: lines which, despite myself, I had often yearned to pass my fingertips along.

It seemed impossible that he could feel as I did, a fellow need, a warm longing. Something more than fondness for the brother of a friend.

Later I had time to think back to Gilbert, and feared I was betraying him. But the two men were so different, as was my love for them. In Laurence there was a solid strength which, however illogically, made me sure he would return safe and sound.

Perhaps my feelings for Gilbert had been more protective, because despite the glare of Egyptian sunshine, I had often sensed a shadow over him, in the intensity of his dark eyes, in the melancholy of his music, like a foretaste of failure.

I recalled promising that I would be most willing when at last I came to him. With Laurence I was something else: not just willing, but fervent. After these weeks of knowing him, watching and listening, disciplining myself to expect nothing, his declaration had opened the floodgates of a passion that would stay undimmed all my life.

After he had gone I continued visiting Isabelle in London and later when she was transferred to a secure place for treatment in Surrey. She fretted to be free of supervision, and her moods swung between raging anger and deep depression.

A doctor of mental health, called in to examine her, took me aside for questioning, and I admitted to him that I felt at fault over my recent disagreements with Isabelle.

'Indeed no,' he assured me. 'Your friend's illness has its seat in something much deeper and more personal than a mere disagreement between ladies.'

He couldn't know how ironically true his words were: no *dis*agreement certainly, but that one fateful Agreement between Ladies by which she had given away her only child, and I had become Lucy's mother.

I began to question whether it were better to have all brought out in the open now, not only for Isabelle's peace of mind, but for my own too. Already I wore Laurence's splendid diamond on my engagement finger, but how could I become his wife under the lie that I was the widowed mother of an infant? I who had taken two husbands' names on paper but had never slept with any man.

Laurence had even spoken, before leaving, of giving

Lucy his family name, by adoption. I could not bear to make him this further victim of my deceit.

Against the argument in favour of declaring the truth was the terrible conflict in Isabelle's mind, where the horror of discovery had grown to monstrous proportions. Either way she suffered. And as she suffered, her dependence on outside help increased. Since brandy was not to hand, she half killed herself by swallowing the stolen dregs of a bottle of cleaning fluid which she uncovered in a bathroom.

The outcome was horrible, and the accusation of intended suicide utterly unjust.

For weeks during her slow recovery we lived in dread of her being charged with that crime. When she learned of this, and that in a court hearing much of her history could become public knowledge, I feared she would truly resort to an attempt on her own life. It was mainly through her family's high standing and the persuasiveness of the Austrian psychiatrist attending her that the threat of prosecution was averted.

She was to rejoin the family in September, when Henley, Ascot and Cowes were safely past, and her dear Lolly due to return in a fortnight. We made great preparations to ensure her arrival should be all that she could wish for. Mildred gave instructions for her rooms to be redecorated and during the resultant upheaval I sorted through her wardrobe and cupboards to discard garments she no longer wore. It was while so occupied that I came on an Italian shoe-box containing correspondence.

There were about twenty letters, all opened but still in their envelopes, and suspecting some secret love of Isabelle's I began to pack them back, when I noticed the stamps. They had all been franked by the Army Post Office in Khartoum.

In a mental haze, I recognized my own name and the address of our hotel in Luxor.

I was too stunned to move and for a while the room about me seemed to ripple like a moving film when the camera has swung too fast.

Then I pulled myself together and unfastened the ribbon that bound them. The same shade of violet ribbon that had been round my dead kitten's neck, but the silk a little faded now. Every one of the letters was addressed to me, some in Upper Egypt, others at Alexandria. All written by Gilbert's hand. And the letters' contents were agonized, because I had failed to reply or to send any message as to where I had moved on.

In one he could not understand how I could have so deceived him about my feelings, and in the next he apologized, fearful that some terrible fate had overtaken me and so I was unable to get in touch. Then again he doubted his letters were reaching me – some wretched malfunction of the posts due to enemy sabotage or natural disaster. He endured every kind of torture, becoming ever more desperate, hopeless, until abruptly the correspondence ceased.

Because he had succumbed to typhus, and could not write from his deathbed to wish me goodbye.

I sat rigid, my fingers stiffened about that last letter, and the agony of it passed into me. I had not known until that moment that heartache could be actual pain. Something inside gnawed and tore at me so that for a moment I could scarcely breathe.

And then my mind began to stir. Gilbert had been faithful to me; it was I he thought had failed him. Because of Isabelle's treachery.

These letters were surely among those she had ordered the hotels to package on arrival and have sent up to her.

'Our mail' she would have called it, and there would have been no cause for anyone to hand me mine separately. I would be sent down to carry them to her. They had actually been in my hands and I had never known!

I understood now those final words of Mrs Trevelyan to me, rebuking me for hard-heartedness and indifference. She had known that Gilbert was writing, but receiving no reply. If only I had queried her meaning. If only she had been more specific in her criticism of me.

But Mrs Trevelyan was dead, as dear Gilbert was dead. Only Isabelle and I were left to make sense of the outcome. And then I saw plainly: there was no sense to be made. Our lives had moved on. I had found new love. Isabelle was at her lowest ebb and no one with any heart could tackle her with accusations now.

But it hurt so. And I had to struggle with the bitter after-taste of her greatest, cruellest deceit. On my next visit I did let her know.

'I have found Gilbert's letters, Isabelle. How *could* you do that to me?'

She went rigid with protest. 'Genie, I did it *for* you. It was quite unsuitable. He could never have made you happy.'

'For *me*? No. You never did anything for anyone but yourself.' I left her wailing and was half-way to the railway station before I relented and went back, to gather her into my arms.

Another blow was to fall on us that summer.

Some short while after Sedgwick's death, the new Earl had said whimsically, 'For me, the wisdom of years has come too late in life.'

We were sitting on the terrace, enjoying the sunshine but well wrapped against a keen wind. Mildred, watching her father, said nothing but waited for the rest.

When he spoke again his voice was vibrant with suppressed pain. 'I should like to have known earlier how to respond to my father in his last years. And now, when it is too late, I know – but cannot claim for myself – the sort of mercy I withheld from him.'

Then Mildred had smiled. 'Grandfather wasn't the easiest person to sympathize with.'

Now, some fifteen months later, my future father-in-law had his first seizure which left him paralysed on the right side and with his speech slightly affected. We all rallied to help the dear old man, but Mildred did more, dedicating her every waking hour to making his days as full and happy as they could be. And he did seem content, unalarmed by half-tasted death, and surrounded by the family he loved in the one place that meant more to him than any other.

For months I had put off telling Isabelle of my engagement to her brother, for fear of her uncertain reaction. Or, as I thought, her *certain* reaction. But Isabelle was changed, her confidence broken. When, back at Stakerleys, I showed her the ring, which previously I had removed or kept covered by a glove on my visits to her, she appeared confused. 'You will be Viscountess Crowthorne then? Some day wife to an earl.'

Mildred, seeking to ease matters said, 'So now Eugenie will be our dearest sister-in-law. And you will have her with you for as long as you care to stay here under our roof.'

Isabelle frowned back at her, barely understanding. 'Where else should I stay?'

'Perhaps, my dear, you will one day want a home of your own. When you marry again, as I hope you will, for certainly you will make someone a delightful wife and we all wish you the greatest happiness.'

'I was to marry Clune,' she said harshly. 'What's become of that disgusting old man?'

'Oh, forget him,' Mildred dismissed the Marquess, waving as if swatting away a fly.

'But I want to know.'

'He married the Paget-Harryson girl,' she said offhandedly. 'It was a June wedding and, as I remember, it poured all day.'

'December wedded to May,' Isabelle said sourly. 'She can be scarcely eighteen. And doubtless fecund. She has made her fortune by hope of it.'

She turned to look at me again after a moment of gazing into space. 'So, Genie, you are to marry Lolly and stay on at Stakerleys. So we shall remain forever bound together, you and I. Until death us do part.'

And this will be Lucy's rightful home, I thought, whatever may become of me. Laurence will adopt her and she will be safe. Isabelle will have had her way up to a point. It matters little to her that I've won her brother's love.

She had sounded more broken than menacing, but I would be constantly on my guard against her until she recovered her full senses, ready to pick up again the reins of her own life and leave me to mine.

And so, over six more years, she had continued half loving, half hating me – a spasmodic alcoholic, occasionally 'cured' – all through Lucy's brave fight against infantile paralysis and the birth of Edwin, and through her own final, exhausted agreement to marry the devoted Geoffrey, who bored her almost to distraction.

And never, to my knowledge, in all that time had she made any further attempt on my life – until now, when she would save herself at my expense. Recognizing the sinister, sideways flick of her eyes, I waited with dread for her ultimate manipulation, in having me hanged for the murder of the mysterious foreigner found battered in our river.

*　　*　　*

226

The third visit from the police came, like the first, as we sat at dinner; but just over a month later. Already the days were drawing in and it was quite dark when the pony trap with Inspector McGill pulled up at the entrance steps. This time Hadrill announced the arrival quietly to Laurence as he served cream with his *poires aux amandes*.

I had no special premonition, assuming the interruption concerned nothing more serious than a wine that was found *bouché* or some change on the cheeseboard.

It was when Laurence rose and came round to my chair that I felt the first alarm. 'Eugenie, my dear, there is something I think we should deal with at once, if everyone will excuse us.'

He took my hand and led me from the room. 'Inspector McGill has called again,' he said quietly. 'There is a senior man with him, a Superintendent Garstin from Aylesbury. They have asked specifically to speak to you.'

He must have felt the tremor that went through me, for he passed an arm round my waist and held me close. 'If you wish I will say you're indisposed and take it on myself.'

'This is something no one can take on for me,' I said, 'but I need a moment to prepare myself.'

'All the time you wish. Shall I go ahead and have a word with them?'

'No. I need you beside me.'

'Even when they speak to you?'

'Especially then.'

He looked so grave, his face suddenly quite drawn, that I would have given the world to be able to tell him that I'd done nothing wrong.

'You must help me,' I said. 'It's more than time that the truth became known. It's lain on my conscience for so long.'

He closed his eyes as if in pain then pressed me close again. 'Whatever you have to say, I will stand by you. You must know that. You know how much I love you: you're my very life's blood.'

And I must wound him.

'I want so very badly to hear you say that again, afterwards, when they've gone away and left us together. If indeed they do.'

His grip on my arm was painful now, his lean cheeks quite pale. 'Nothing,' he said, 'can change how I feel for you. I know in my heart you cannot have done anything evil.'

The two policemen were again waiting for us in the library, McGill very stern and no longer with any interest in the fleeing nymphs and pursuing satyrs above the panelling. The second man was bulky, neckless and square-headed, wearing a full beard and moustache. His small eyes, embedded in reddish flesh, fixed on me formidably. Only when Laurence addressed him did they switch away and he made some gesture towards civility.

'Milady,' he said directly, 'as a result of certain investigations carried out here and in Italy, I have some further questions for you.'

'I will certainly help if I can,' I said. 'Won't you sit down?'

He was uncertain, but conceded, perching insecurely on a chair which his bulk dwarfed. McGill seated himself to his left and a little to the rear, taking out a notebook which he balanced on one knee and pressed open with his pencil.

'Shall we begin, then?'

I nodded, having seated myself on the sofa opposite, with Laurence, standing behind me, laying a hand on my shoulder.

The superintendent used no notes, but spoke from memory, chin raised and eyes closed. 'I understand that before your marriage, milady, you were a Miss Fellowes.'

'That is correct.'

'Which was your father's family name, and your place of origin was St Leonards-on-Sea, Sussex.'

'Yes.'

'But this present marriage was not your first?'

'No. I was a widow.'

'Then why did you not use the surname of your first husband when the second marriage was registered?'

His eyes snapped suddenly open and challenged me to lie.

'Because I had reverted to my maiden name by deed poll. It was quite legally done, Superintendent.'

'As we discovered, ma'am. What I do not understand is your reason for this change.'

'I was such a short time married, Superintendent. I had not yet adjusted to the new name. It seemed more familiar to take on again the one I had always been known by in this country.'

'And that intervening name was—?'

'Gabriel,' I said shortly, using the English pronunciation.

He let a little silence build in which I could hear my own furious heartbeats. Then, 'More familiar', he quoted me, considering the words. 'More English, of course. Because the name was not spelt exactly the way you say it. The name, milady, was Gab-ree-elly. Am I not right, milady?'

'You are, Superintendent. The man I first married was Vincenzo Gabrieli, a doctor from Venice.'

'An *Italian* gentleman. Who was unfortunate enough to die very shortly after the marriage. By drowning, in a canal.' The little piggy eyes burned at me from inside their flushed wrinkles.

'We are here, milady, because we are investigating the death of a foreign visitor, in the river which runs through your estate. And this Italian person was here to find a kinsman who had come to this part of the world some years before.' He regarded me levelly. 'It seemed possible that you might yourself be that kinsman, by marriage.'

'May I ask if you have been able to trace the gentleman who shared the dead man's railway carriage to London from Dover?' Laurence put in with apparent calm.

'We have, sir. And he has furnished us with valuable information.'

'So the landlord of the inn where he stayed was incorrect in assuming that the visitor spoke no English?'

Now he was annoying the policeman. 'The Englishman had some Italian, my lord.' The superintendent glared, then turned back to me. He was that rare thing, a policeman unimpressed by social distinction: like a terrier on the scent of a rat. 'You must see that there appears to be a connection.'

'Or a coincidence,' Laurence suggested.

'An anomaly,' the superintendent produced stiffly, 'because during questioning here of family and staff you were asked for any known connection with the country of the dead man's origin. And none was forthcoming, apart from some useless story of a sometime valet's dead wife.'

'Now you have a useless story of a dead doctor's widow.'

'A little more than that, sir. We have two Italians found dead in water, for all that this second was murdered first; and both have a connection to Stakerleys estate.' He spoke to Laurence, but he was staring at me with eyes as hard as marbles.

'And both from the north-east region of Italy where your wife was previously married.'

I heard Laurence draw breath ready for some retort, but I put my hand over his to restrain him. He would only make the policeman further annoyed with us.

'Have you any other questions, Superintendent?' I asked quickly.

'One, madam. Will you tell me where you were on the day that your first husband fell into the canal?'

'Certainly. I was in Venice myself, having travelled there from Milan to see him and to pay off the servants where we had been lodging.'

'That agrees with the version given at the inquest by the cook-housekeeper Marina Vitelli. But she is sure that you left the house together. Immediately after being paid she looked from the front balcony and saw two figures together at the path edge, Dr Gabrieli and a woman beside him. That was approximately at the point where Gabrieli's body was later found floating in the water.'

'That would have happened after I left Venice,' I said huskily. 'I had come to say goodbye, and that was all I had to say to him. And all I did. We parted indoors.'

'And you were never questioned by the Italian police?'

'I returned to Milan and left for England two days later and I only had news of the drowning after I reached England. I understood Vincenzo had been drinking heavily and slipped. Did not the cook or the nurse Margherita mention his habit of heavy drinking?'

'I believe it was in their evidence.'

'And the coroner accepted that he was unsteady from drink?'

'That is so,' Garstin admitted.

'So perhaps after I had left him he went somewhere to drown his sorrows, and when he was on his way back—'

'—he drowned himself as well, by mistake,' Laurence suggested baldly. He moved towards the bell-pull and rang for a footman.

'Will that be all, Superintendent, because I have left my family at the table and they will be starting to get anxious about us.'

Reluctantly the two policemen lumbered to their feet, McGill tucking the notebook away inside his tunic. At the door Garstin halted and turned. He offered a square card to me. 'Perhaps you would care for a copy.'

It was a photograph of a corpse, Gabrieli as he had been drawn out of the water. I shuddered at sight of it. Dead, he stared back with the same defeated look in his open eyes that had disturbed me on our first meeting. But now I recognized what it meant. Vincenzo Gabrieli was a born victim, and had feared it all along.

Twenty

'It would be better if you told me now,' Laurence said heavily when they had left us alone.

'Believe me, I would be glad to, but I have given a solemn promise.'

Facing me, he ran his hands down my arms and took my hands in his. 'One should only give promises to those who themselves respect the sanctity of promises. It was to Isabelle, of course.'

He sighed. 'Since early childhood she has accorded herself the divine right to survive – at no matter whose expense. There are those who think blue blood excuses all manner of wrongdoing, but there cannot be two kinds of justice in the land, one for the weak and another for those of high standing.'

'I can't betray her, Laurence.'

'Then you've no need to. I'm not blind or stupid. If you share secrets with her, they are to her discredit. I believe completely that you are in no way implicated in either death.'

'It's true what I told the superintendent: I took my leave of Gabrieli indoors.' Yet I had stated I'd left Venice when Gabrieli went into the water. It was from desperation, when he reported the cook's evidence at the inquest.

They were Isabelle's skirts the cook had glimpsed, craning

from the balcony. Following behind, I would have been hidden by the arches below her. But of course she had assumed the woman to be me. At no time did I mention that 'la Contessa' had accompanied me to Venice when I paid the cook off, and Isabelle had not shown herself in the kitchen.

But Laurence was following another line of thought. 'It's all about Lucy, isn't it? She's Isabelle's natural child, and that is why she was hiding abroad, with you as her cover.'

I gasped. 'When did you guess?' I whispered.

'It wasn't guesswork. Simple observation. I had caught a glimpse of you when I visited my sister in Alexandria. You were making yourself scarce, slipping into the next room. But as you unlatched the door I had a vivid impression of a tall, erect young woman with dark hair and smooth features. And a tiny waist my two hands could almost have met around. An impression I carried with me forever after. So when the widowed *Signora* came to Stakerleys I knew her at once.'

'And that moment in Alexandria was a bare two months before Lucy was born.'

'That was a minor calculation I considered later, after I'd recognized Lucy's Sedgwick eyes. With an Italian father, it was more likely your child would have inherited eyes as dark as your own.'

I drew stiffly away. 'Am I to believe that you have known *all the time*? That you knew I was keeping this dark secret from you, and you said nothing? *Nothing*, Laurence? You have *let me go on* deceiving you for all these intimate years together?'

He said nothing in return, but watched me, head tilted as if waiting for me to accept the fact quietly and be reasonable.

But I was furious with him, furious that he had kept from me a secret equal to my secret. No, a worse one, a double deceit now: secrecy about a secret! It was as though this loving dialogue of ours over the years had always contained a hidden language which I alone couldn't understand.

'Eugenie, what's wrong? It's all over now; out in the open. We have *no* secrets from each other any more.'

'You speak as if it's all right. It's not all right!' I thrust my face so close that I felt his breath feather over my burning cheeks. I took him by the upper arms and would have shaken him but he stood firm. I hissed, 'You *patronized* me!'

In such a passion I could not control myself. My doubled fists hammered against his unresponsive chest. He let me beat away without any attempt to calm the storm.

There was only one way for it to end and he used it, tightening his arms around me so that mine were cramped between us, useless. And as he pressed hard against my rigid body a new fire instantly took over. We fought together as one then, not against each other.

Later, smoothing the damp hair from my forehead he smiled tenderly. 'Do you think I wouldn't finally have known: whether or not my bride was experienced in bed? I loved you the more for that, for your naïvety, your unshakeable loyalty and your discretion.'

'My deceits,' I whispered.

'Your performing art.'

'Oh, you may laugh, but I never at any time found it funny.'

'My poor sweet. But I understood almost at once. You see, as her brother, I understand Isabelle. Having lost our mother so young, and being continually flattered for her looks and rank, all helped to make her unstable. Grieving for Hugo Delmayne would have been a short formality, not the occasion for hiding herself away for almost a year.'

He shook his head, at the same time taking a strand of my hair and winding it about his finger. 'She has always devoured people who are drawn by her charm, nibbling at them gradually, bit by bit, leeching on to their good nature.' His voice was more sad than bitter.

I nodded. 'Forcing them farther and farther into deceit by every new appeal and her apparent helplessness,' I acknowledged, 'until at last they're as dishonest as she is.

'But Laurence, I'm so ashamed of not having been open with you. If only you knew how often I longed to confess . . .'

'But I did know. I watched you torn apart between promises previously made and the new loyalty owed to me.'

'I tried telling myself the old ones were for the past, and everything new with you was our future. And those promises to you I've never broken. I never could.'

'And you were careful never to lie to me about Lucy; simply left me to accept what others assumed. Just imagine,' he said humorously, gently squeezing my waist, 'I have that priceless gem, a wife who knows how to keep silent! I'm not likely to complain of that.'

We lay close-locked in each other's arms, until I reminded him of the others waiting for our return.

'What shall we tell them? Must it all come out now, before the superintendent comes again?' I asked tremulously.

'There's a chance that the police won't trouble us again. They have no material evidence about this present crime, whatever they may imagine happened seven years ago in Italy. And you have answered them on that.'

This couldn't calm all my fears, because here at dear

Stakerleys one of us was guilty of vicious murder, not just pushing the victim into the river, but beating him senseless first. Such violence must have taken considerable strength. Even in a fury, could Isabelle have managed that? Surely it would have taken a man to do it?

And since Laurence had guessed so much all along, without letting it be known, must I believe that he was responsible, intent on protecting both his sister's reputation and mine? Laurence, the upright, just man, forced in his turn into wrongdoing by the wretched girl's impetuosity?

He left me no time to worry over such possibilities, having an excuse ready for our sudden absence during dinner.

The others had moved on to the drawing-room for coffee. When we arrived back to face their curious glances we stood together before the empty gilt and marble fireplace while Laurence made our official announcement that, please God, in some five months' time little Edwin and Lucy would have a baby brother or sister.

There were exclamations of delight and surprise, although to Mildred and Dr Millson it must have been evident already. The old medico's eyes were sharp enough to pick up my symptoms, and I knew he shared confidences with my older sister-in-law.

They had a most tender and long-standing relationship, which I had furthered as soon as I became mistress of the house, by rearranging rooms so that theirs were connected, with a sitting-room between. At that time he was a frequent guest from Saturday to Monday. And when the good doctor's cottage had been damaged by fire, the thatch catching sparks from Guy Fawkes Night celebrations in the village, on my suggestion he had quietly moved into Stakerleys for good.

Smiling round at them now, I had to admit that he, as a man, was as likely as Laurence to fill the role of Facci's killer, for he would have done all in his power to protect our family. As indeed might Geoffrey, if he believed Isabelle's name was in any way to be dragged into disrepute.

I realized then that any of them might have been accosted by the Italian on the river bank, have quarrelled over his demands and, in fighting him off, could have cracked his skull open. It would have been an accident, but then surely whoever was involved would have hastened to get medical aid and ensure that Facci was taken care of?

Whether our announcement fully accounted for our absence or not, it certainly diverted attention from alternative speculations. The general joy in the coming child served to bolster my confidence. I retired that night reassured that the Buckinghamshire police had no evidence against me over Facci's death, and had learned nothing from the *carabinieri* that I could not answer to with apparent innocence. They would press the investigation no further out of deference to the Sedgwick name.

Before becoming Viscountess Crowthorne I had lived in fear of Isabelle publicly accusing me of Gabrieli's murder. When she had asked who would be believed – a lady such as herself, or a paid companion – I had myself threatened violence to silence her. But now, with superior rank – even revealed as the dead man's widow – my word would surely stand against that of a woman sometimes confused by drink.

But in the matter of young Facci's death – grandson to the dying peasant whom I'd married in that wretched mountain village – there could still be danger, for in the shock of encountering him by the river, and as we walked there discussing the demands he made to ensure his silence, I had heard movements among the trees and glimpsed a woman's form indistinctly moving away.

In that brief instant I had no clear impression of who had observed us: Isabelle, Mildred or one of the maids who had come there off-duty. The outline was vague, and among the rich summer foliage the woman's clothing was smudged to a neutral grey.

When next I saw them, Isabelle had been in pale blue, Mildred in heliotrope. All the female staff at Stakerleys wore a uniform of two shades of *café au lait*. It could have been any of them overhearing our conversation. Not knowing was unnerving, since I couldn't tell from which side to expect sudden revelation.

That night I went again to check that my marriage lines and Lucy's birth certificate were still securely locked away. With the passage of years their ink had faded uniformly from black to sepia, and the alterations to names and dates were impossible to detect. I was Signora Gabrieli, and the name Facci did not appear anywhere. Unless Isabelle were to betray me and demand comparison between these papers and the original documents lodged in Italy, I should be safe.

The following day I knew I was not, for I caught Evie, a new cleaning woman, scrabbling through my wardrobes. At first I imagined she was acting from envious curiosity or a desire to steal, and I took her with me to Laurence for his decision on how we should deal with her.

She appeared more annoyed than frightened by the prospect of dismissal. When Laurence mentioned advising the police – though it was mere pretence – she gave a sardonic smile, and instantly I knew what she was about.

'Evie,' I said, 'you know the Bible says a man cannot serve two masters? Isn't it the same for a woman? I want you to tell us who asked you to search through my things.'

She said nothing, merely tightening her lips and standing with her hands loosely clasped behind her. Perhaps it was her stance that made Laurence enquire, 'Was it Superintendent Garstin?'

From her stubborn silence, it was clear his suspicion was correct. It appalled me that the police should have introduced a spy into my house. I wanted her paid off and removed instantly, but Laurence held me back.

'Perhaps,' he suggested, 'you should tell us what it is you were searching for. We might then help you to find it.'

The woman bit at her underlip, turning the idea slowly in her mind.

'I promise you,' Laurence said, 'the search shall be fair. We have nothing to hide. Simply tell me what you are expecting to find and we will all three go and look together.'

She had nothing to lose, and since we knew who had sent her we would surely be letting her go free afterwards.

I was not unduly alarmed, assuming it was my papers she was after and these I had already checked on. We would let her read them through and then she could report back that they were in order.

But I was wrong. She put a hand in the pocket of her skirt to draw out an envelope, from which she carefully extracted a small object and held it out on her right palm.

It was a silk-covered button, olive green, and I recognized it at once. It seemed to have been torn from fabric, for it still had threads of matched sewing yarn attached.

'You're looking for the frock or costume this came from?' Laurence demanded – faintly, as I thought. He must have known the dress well, for it had been a favourite of mine for three seasons.

The woman agreed.

'And what is its significance?'

Again she seemed reluctant, but after a moment's consideration she explained.

It seems that in a violent death sometimes the cadaver suffers a spasm that makes him clench his hands about whatever comes in reach. Despite the later immersion in water, young Facci, killed instantaneously by a single blow to the skull, had been found with this button tightly clenched in his fingers.

The implication was that the button came from his killer's clothing.

'A woman?' I gasped. Who else would have worn such a pretty thing?

'Exactly. So I am interested in women's clothing, especially some garment of this particular green, with one button missing.'

Perhaps she had not been long enough in our household to know that my personal maid would have overhauled my clothes as they were taken off, and mended any defects found. This Evie would certainly, *almost* certainly, not find any dress, of whatever colour, that had a missing button.

'Let us go and look then,' I said, rising and leading them both out.

I sat on the bed while she made her examination, bringing out each outfit separately on its hanger to spread alongside me, until all the wardrobes were as bare as Mother Hubbard's cupboard. No olive green garment came to light, but the woman was not to be defeated so easily. 'The laundry,' she demanded brusquely, 'and then the sewing-room.'

My heart sank at this. She was capable and determined. I had heard that in great cities there were occasions when constables' wives were employed to circulate unknown and gain information from other women, but I had not dreamed that it happened in the county police forces of Thames Valley.

I had to suspect Isabelle's hand in this business for even when I first spoke with the young Italian I had not been wearing green. I remembered now: it was a simple dress of printed cotton voile. Over a white background was strewn a pattern of periwinkles and pink roses. Had my sister-in-law gone to my wardrobe and torn off the button herself from some dress there, to implicate me?

My unease increased, because the green dress was not to be found in either room. Was this some further refinement of Isabelle's, to let me think I was escaping discovery and then triumphantly produce the required dress as evidence when I was feeling safe from accusation?

But no, because how could Isabelle have placed the button in the dead man's hand? My mind was in turmoil. Knowing there was an explanation, I could not reach it.

The woman who called herself Evie was at last compelled to admit defeat. 'Do you wish to search any other lady's room?' Laurence enquired coldly.

She did not. I was, after all, the only suspect: the one with Italian connections. Laurence had her escorted to the courtyard where a pony and trap were prepared to return her to Aylesbury. Surely, even for the dogged Garstin this must signal the end of his harassing me.

The incident had not gone unnoticed. Mildred and John Millson sat in the morning-room waiting for our explanation. Tired of concealment, I came out with this most recent worry. Then, 'Tell me,' I demanded of the good doctor, 'is this spasm she spoke of a recognized medical fact?'

'Indeed it is. But certainly rare. You may depend on it

242

that their assumption is correct and the man grasped the button at the very moment of death.'

'And he was killed by a single blow to the head?' Mildred wondered. 'Yet the button appears to have come from a woman's costume.'

'If his skull was particularly thin it could have shattered easily. It wouldn't have taken great strength in that case.'

I was still convinced that the button was planted to incriminate me, since it came from a dress of mine. 'Wouldn't it be possible,' I pleaded, 'for someone to prise his fingers open and fold them round again after the button was placed in his hand?'

Dr Millson shook his head. 'The fingers could be broken in the opening, and they wouldn't stiffen again until rigor had set in. Meanwhile, in swiftly flowing water, the button would have been washed away.'

But I had not worn the missing dress. So either someone else had done so, pretending to be me, or there was another dress of similar style and colour worn by the woman who killed Facci. If Evie had accepted Laurence's offer to have the other ladies' wardrobes searched, we might have known her identity for sure. Green was a favoured colour for country living. Almost everyone had something of the kind.

I couldn't remember what Isabelle or Mildred had first worn on that morning over a month ago; only my own cotton voile which I muddied at the hem as I struggled to plunge the dead weight of Facci's body into the stream.

It all surged back on me: the steamy heat of midday, when I had arranged to bring him the money, at the hour when I was supposedly resting in my room; my annoyance that he failed to answer when I called to him; then clambering down the bank to the little red Japanese bridge and finding him lying there dead, his head split

243

open; my horror, and the feverish attempt to be rid of the body, floating it out and seeing it wedge below the surface, an unrecognizable spread of dark hair, like seaweed, marking the position of his down-turned face.

The heat of that remembered day was again building in me towards storm climax. I relived my fear that our afternoon picnic would be marred by the body's reappearance; my insistence that we punted safely upriver of the boathouse. And all the time a growing horror at the way the past could rise like an avenging phantom.

'Is there anything we can do, Eugenie?' Dr Millson asked, taking my hand and feeling its fever.

'Not for the present. If you will all excuse me from luncheon I think I'd like to lie down for a while.'

As Laurence gave me an arm to go upstairs, we passed Isabelle standing motionless at the first landing, watching me with fathomless eyes. I tried to walk tall, but stumbled over my long skirt. Looking back, I thought she seemed to be smiling.

I did sleep eventually, leaning against my husband's shoulder, and when I awoke I had decided what I must do, but had no idea how it could help.

'You'll find nothing, all this time later,' Laurence tried to dissuade me. 'The police have searched along the whole bank there.'

'Nevertheless, indulge me.'

So we cancelled my hour with the children and walked together down to where the little Japanese bridge had once been.

Under the trees and close to the water the grass was still long and green, but progressively up the bank it was flatter and bleached.

We sat a while in brooding silence. There was no sound but the stutter of a blackbird and the occasional *plop, plop* of the pebbles which Laurence desultorily picked up to toss into the stream.

'That's curious,' he said after a while. 'What do you suppose this could be?'

He put in my hand a piece of twisted metal. 'It's silver,' I said. 'Look, there's the maker's hallmark.'

He took it back and tried to open out the crumpled shape. 'A sort of small cup,' he said. 'The kind to match a brandy flask. But it's been trodden on and ground into the earth, so that it's hardly recognizable.'

Brandy, I thought. Which could mean Isabelle. So this was a secret place where she came to sink her sorrows.

Then I looked at the piece of silver again, only partly straightened in Laurence's hand. And I knew everything.

'Darling.' I stood up and held out my hand. 'Let's go back indoors now. I have something to tell the others which can't wait.'

'Won't you tell me first?'

'Why not? It was you who solved it for me. Oh, Laurence, we're all safe! Nothing terrible is going to happen after all.'

'Tell me then, tell me.'

So I did, and we clung together for a timeless moment, then scrambled up the bank to run back hand in hand like children.

I let Laurence explain about finding the piece of flattened silver, and then I told them what it had once been.

'And I remember that last day, as she got into the carriage, she was using the late Earl's walking stick, not her own with the silver handle like a pug's head. It didn't mean anything to me then; but also there was this habit she had of always going through my wardrobe and taking away anything she could make use of.

'I'd given up wearing the olive green silk because of my growing waistline, but it was in good condition and only needed turning up at the hem to allow for our difference in height. Which she must have done earlier that morning, and put it on for me to admire.'

'She would have followed you down to the river,' Laurence said, 'where you were first accosted by Facci. And she overheard how he threatened you with exposure as his grandfather's wife if you didn't pay him off.'

'I was to go back at midday with a hundred pounds and a promise to send more to him in Italy every half-year. I shouldn't have agreed, but I had money by me to cover household expenses, and it seemed to save all the grief of the whole story coming out.'

'To save my name as well as yours,' Isabelle said thickly. 'But I think everyone here had guessed the truth about Lucy already. And had forgiven me.'

'I thought you might have done it. Killed Facci, I mean.'

'I know, Genie. But it doesn't seem to matter any more what people think of me, and I never even knew the man had come here.'

'Then at one time I was afraid that Laurence or Geoffrey or John Millson might have fought with him and accidentally killed him. I even suspected that Mildred had taken a hand to protect the family name.'

'But instead it was your mother.'

'For whatever reason. Perhaps from sheer anger at the man's effrontery in demanding money from me. She overheard our conversation, and kept my rendezvous with him a little early. They quarrelled. She wasn't used to being crossed. Then a single angry whack with her stick, and the handle mount tore off. She'd killed him, but – more likely I think – intended just to keep him quiet. Her life has always been ruled, you see, by the need for respectability.'

'A fine motive for murder,' Dr Millson said ruefully.

'What constantly astounds me,' Laurence marvelled after a moment's silence, 'is the capacity for calm deception in women. You all have your secret lives and your own private solutions. Not least that admirable little woman who set off to return home alone, having done what she saw as her duty, and saying nothing of it to anyone. And everyone forgot that she had even been here!'

'But that is what women are about,' said Mildred drily. 'Like tigresses. A family thing: the protection of their young.'

She stood looking at me, her long sheep-face gentle, almost maternal. Then her gaze swung on her half-sister, and the familiar sardonic expression had come back.

'And who else but the women can know who actually is family or not?'